PENGUIN CRIME FICTION

MURDER ON CUE

Jane Dentinger started her acting career at
the age of fifteen, though some members
of her family believe it began earlier,
along with her bent for all things criminal.
Fortunately her work as an actor, director,
teacher, and writer have kept her busy and
on the right side of the law—so far.

MURDER ON CUE

JANE DENTINGER

PENGUIN BOOKS

PENGUIN BOOKS
Published by the Penguin Group
Viking Penguin, a division of Penguin Books USA Inc.,
375 Hudson Street, New York, New York 10014, U.S.A.
Penguin Books Ltd, 27 Wrights Lane,
London W8 5TZ, England
Penguin Books Australia Ltd, Ringwood,
Victoria, Australia
Penguin Books Canada Ltd, 10 Alcorn Avenue, Suite 300,
Toronto, Ontario, Canada M4V 3B2
Penguin Books (N.Z.) Ltd, 182–190 Wairau Road,
Auckland 10, New Zealand

Penguin Books Ltd, Registered Offices:
Harmondsworth, Middlesex, England

First published in the United States of America by
Doubleday & Company, Inc., 1983
Published in Penguin Books 1992

1 3 5 7 9 10 8 6 4 2

PUBLISHER'S NOTE
This is a work of fiction. Names, characters, places, and incidents either
are the product of the author's imagination or are used fictitiously, and any
resemblance to actual persons, living or dead, events, or locales is entirely
coincidental.

THE LIBRARY OF CONGRESS HAS CATALOGUED THE HARDCOVER AS FOLLOWS:
Dentinger, Jane.
Murder on cue.
I. Title
PS3554.E587M8 1983
813'.54 82–45595
ISBN 0-385-18411-5 (hc.)
ISBN 0 14 01.5841 3 (pbk.)

Printed in the United States of America

For my parents and Meri and Arthur.

With sincere thanks to Dr. Mark Dentinger, Dr. Jay Cherner, Dr. Jean Balderston, Robert Bradshaw, Lee Adams and James Chubinsky for their help and support.

MURDER ON CUE

CHAPTER 1

Jocelyn woke up in her least favorite way: she was hung over and, somewhere in her REM cycle, pissed off about some damn man when the phone rang.

The ringing of a phone before noon can be a very ugly sound to most people in the theatre—except for those exhausting overachievers who are out hustling diaper commercials while you're perusing the morning paper and nursing a cup of coffee.

Jocelyn dragged herself across the loft bed toward the offending phone. A dazed hand flopped over the edge of the bed and eventually the receiver reached her ear.

"Hello." It was a credit to Jocelyn's years of study that her voice came across rich and low at such an unspeakable hour.

"Hi, Jocelyn. It's Albert. How soon can you be at Studio 48 for an audition?"

A thought sharply cut through Jocelyn's REM cycle: "My twerp agent calls me three times a year and he has to do this to me at 9 A.M.?"

Jocelyn's voice, however, said, "Probably within the hour—sooner, if they're into necrophilia." (She had to get some of her irritation in.)

"It's Hatchell and Greenfeld and it's for their new show *Term of Trial*."

"*Term of Trial?* Albert, there's only one woman's role in that and it's the snappy lady lawyer who comes in in the last act and zaps it to the Supreme Court judge!"

"Yes, my dear, I know that."

"But, Albert, I'm twenty-nine. I'm too young."

"Of course you are. This is an understudy audition."

"Oh. And who am I—hypothetically—understudying?"

"Josh . . . do me a favor, just go to the audition. Okay?" (The use of the nickname "Josh," used only by her intimates, told her that he was stonewalling in a big way.)

"Who is it, Albert?" (She never called him Al.)

There was a long pause. "It's Harriet Weldon."

"Albert, that dull, lowing cow?"

"I know she's not one of your favorite people . . ."

"Is Wayne Newton one of your favorite singers?"

"It's too early for sarcasm, Jocelyn. Do you want to read for the understudy or not?"

Loathing him, she said, "Yes, you know I will. Eve Harrington always wins in the end, doesn't she . . . ? But how did Harriet Weldon get a hot role like that? Did her illustrious publishing family come up with another prestigious opus on the New York theatre by one of our great theatrical families?"

"Jocelyn, you are a fine talent with a vulgar and suspicious nature. Can you make it or not?"

"I'll be there."

What perturbed Jocelyn most was the fact that she was excited. She climbed out of bed and revived herself with a bath and breakfast. Then she applied a makeup that was subtle and sparing to take all the "ingenue" contours from her face.

Harriet Weldon— God! Jocelyn couldn't remember exactly which Players' Club Ladies' Dinner it was when she had turned to a fellow actress, while pointing somewhat drunkenly to Harriet, and said, "In faith, is that not the most tedious of artsy-fartsy actors in this great metropolis?"

"Josh, control yourself. She'll see you pointing. You just hate the fact that she's forever kneeling at the feet of the great and near great . . . and she's obsequious as hell."

"No, that's *not* true." (No one can be as dignified as the near-drunk.) "I hate the fact that she makes the most boring choices possible onstage and gets away with it with the critics because she comes from a publishing family that they'd all give their left ball to have a contract with."

"Jocelyn, how well you mince words!"

"I'm cruel but fair, Annie. She's a theatrical Uriah Heep and you know it."

At this point Annie finally gave way.

"No, dear. She'd only be a Heep in a supporting role. In a major role, I'd bet she'd be a veritable Captain Queeg."

As if on cue, the sole progeny of Cyrus Weldon, co-founder of Weldon and Banning Press, wafted toward the two younger women and passed by them with a gracious smile and nod. Annie stifled a laugh in her gin and tonic while Jocelyn gazed happily after the retreating figure and said, "Harriet taught Nancy Reagan how to smile, you know."

Annie howled with delight and spilled half of her drink on Jocelyn's best silk blouse. Jocelyn, a survivor of twelve years of parochial schooling, saw this as what the nuns might call Instant Retribution.

CHAPTER 2

Fifty minutes after Albert's call, Jocelyn emerged from a cab at Broadway and Forty-eighth Street into the sweltering heat of Indian summer and wished that September would start behaving properly. Three aspirin had not yet banished the hangover and her clothes felt sticky. She took an elevator to the fourth floor and signed in; an earnest young man in aviator glasses gave her a copy of the scene that she would be reading.

Five minutes later, she came up for air. The scene was stupendous; especially to Jocelyn, who was a true sucker for courtroom drama. And this was real *Inherit the Wind* material; it reeked with integrity (but not the smarmy kind) and was packed with the right dynamics. Of course the scene took place in a judge's chambers, not a courtroom, but it was all the better for the intimacy of the confrontation between the aging judge and the impassioned lady lawyer.

She was just envisioning what the character would be doing right before she comes into the chambers when they called her in to read.

The room was large and square and quite empty, except for a long table around which the director, author and several producer types were seated. During the formal introductions, she started mentally decorating the barren space with heavy drapes, a mahogany desk and various other "judicial" appointments. She'd just finished shaking hands with Charlie Martin, the director, a man in his early thirties with shaggy black hair and an abundance of facial hair that lent his schoolboy looks a wolfish air, when she came upon the playwright and froze in the middle of, "It's so nice to meet . . ."

The name on the script had read Austin Frost, but sitting in front of Jocelyn, wearing a dark, shapeless suit, was none other than Austin Bracknell from college. Austin had been in the Drama Department a year ahead of her and they'd worked on countless shows together, even done the obligatory courting scene from *The Taming of the Shrew* for acting class which, given Austin's stork-like physique and Jocelyn's former pudginess, had lent a new dimension to the word "miscast."

A slow grin spread across her face. "Well, teeny-tiny world, ain't it, 'Mr. Frost'?"

"Getting itsier all the time, Miss O'Roarke."

Austin was smiling his particular Eeyore-smile that touched off a hundred memories for Jocelyn; one in particular had been the beginning of their friendship. Jocelyn had been a freshman doing yeoman work as prop mistress on a student production of *Two for the Seesaw* in which Austin had had the lead opposite an especially hellish leading lady of erratic Italian temperament. One of Jocelyn's jobs had been to supply the "letters" that Austin's character got from his wife and, to bolster him during his scenes with the diva, Jocelyn had taken to writing reams of graphic pornography involving the leading lady and enclosing them in the envelopes. This small act of kindness got Austin through the run and cemented their friendship.

"It's a pleasure to meet you in your new incarnation, Mr. Frost. What happened? Got tired of all the handbag jokes?"

"Oh, that too, yes. So many people *can't* do Edith Evans. But mostly it was the unreal expectation people had that someone named Bracknell *had* to write drawing-room comedies. Well, Josh, you've made my week. Do you like the scene?"

"Very much indeed," she said simply.

"Thought you might."

It fleetingly crossed Jocelyn's "vulgar and suspicious" mind that Albert Carnelli might have had less to do with arranging this reading than he'd led her to believe. Her train of murderous thought was broken by Charlie Martin's voice.

"You have a very nice resumé here, Jocelyn. Tell me, how old are you?"

"I'm twenty-nine."

"Ah, yes . . . as you know, the character, Lindsay Harding, is a woman of about thirty-five . . . but since this is an understudy audition . . ."

She suppressed a wince. In her delight in seeing Austin, she'd forgotten that Harriet Weldon (who was farther away from thirty-five than she was) already *was* Lindsay. Martin stumbled on. ". . . and there is the small role of the law clerk in the first act . . ."

Which is how it will be billed in the program, thought Jocelyn, "Lady Law Clerk." Charlie Martin was winding down.

". . . so now that you know what the job entails, let's get down to the scene."

Setting up the scene with the actor who would be reading the judge, Jocelyn found her feelings to be at war with each other. Part of her thought, "Who wants this lousy job? Who wants to stand day after day in the wings and watch Harriet massacre this lovely role!"

And the part of her that didn't "think," that was pure actor, kept saying, "Lovely, lovely scene. Wonderful language. I bet I know just how Austin would like to see her first entrance—totally thrown away and unassuming. The audience should barely notice her until she begins to speak . . ."

Jocelyn began the reading very low-key. Then, in the middle of the reading, something came over her—an unforeseen emotional imperative. This is not an uncommon experience for an actor; and what the smarter ones do is just keep breathing and let it take over.

Somewhere halfway through her speech to the judge, she knew she wasn't merely appealing for the rights of man; she was pleading for the life of a character, Lindsay Harding, who shouldn't be delivered into the hands of a mundane actress.

When she finished the scene, an uncomfortable but encouraging silence hung in the air. Austin just smirked and nodded as Jocelyn attempted to collect herself. Again Charlie Martin broke the silence.

"Uh . . . very nice, Jocelyn." (This man was big on "nice.") "Casting should be decided by the end of this week."

Jocelyn had yet to fulfill her dream of the ideal audition, when, as soon as you finish your reading, they all throw down their scripts and say, "She's the only one in the world for this part!" But life is earnest, life is real. Instead they all said their goodbyes very nicely, especially Austin; Jocelyn made a mental note to meet him for drinks and pump him for dirt about the production.

But the most interesting feature of the whole situation didn't occur to Jocelyn until she was back in her apartment, smoking a joint to wind down from performance pressures. It was then, as she gazed at a Maxfield Parrish print, that an ancient shard of remembrance pierced her consciousness: Austin Frost, née Bracknell, abhorred Harriet Weldon.

CHAPTER 3

Jocelyn recalled the incident vividly: it was during spring break in her senior year—Austin had moved to New York the previous year. She'd come into town and they'd made a date to meet at a matinee performance of an Off Broadway remounting of *The Merchant of Venice* that featured an old college acquaintance as Bassanio and a brittle Harriet Weldon as Portia and had very little else to recommend it.

Jocelyn and Austin consoled each other in the lobby during intermission. What Jocelyn always liked about Austin was that he reminded her of that needlepoint pillow that Alice Roosevelt had, which said: "If you haven't got anything nice to say . . . come sit by me."

"By my troth, Jocelyn, my little body is aweary of this great Portia."

"Good sentences, and well pronounced."

"She has no imagination. Her life must be 'one long yawn.' God forbid that any play of mine be burdened by so plodding a performance."

Jocelyn, kinder in those days, said, "Now, Austin, calm down. Portia just may not be the right role for her. She might be splendid in other things."

Austin arched a scathingly eloquent eyebrow at her and Jocelyn felt herself begin to blush . . . with good reason, as it turned out. Time and tide and Weldon and Banning Press proved Austin right.

But then, what in blazes was Harriet Weldon doing in Austin's *first* Broadway play? She had to get hold of him and find out. Jocelyn leapt to her feet and began ransacking her apartment for old address books. She started chronologically backward from 1979 and was just observing what a high-fatality year she'd had in '77, judging from a list of men whose phone numbers had *not* been carried over into the '78 book, when the phone rang.

"Jocelyn, we have business to discuss." It was **Albert Carnelli.**

"They want me to come back and read again."

"No."

"Oh." (Ouch!)

"They've offered you the job. The terms are quite good and . . ."

"Albert, that's impossible—it's unheard of!"

". . . and I don't think that you should let any small, personal aversion dissuade you from a fine opportun—"

Jocelyn never could deal with Albert when he was doing his self-righteous, Mother Superior spiel. "Alright. I'll do it, Albert."

"Wonderful! Come in tomorrow to sign the contract. You start rehearsal on Monday."

"Fine. See you around noon."

Not bothering to put the phone down, Jocelyn cleared the line and immediately began dialing Austin Frost's number.

CHAPTER 4

September decided to become autumnal just in time for the eleven o'clock reading *Term of Trial* on Monday morning—for this Jocelyn was profoundly grateful. Even with the delicious breeze blowing into the rehearsal studio from four huge windows that looked out on West Forty-ninth Street, Jocelyn still felt somewhat hot under the collar. For one thing, she hadn't succeeded in getting hold of Austin over the weekend, and no Austin meant no inside dirt on the production; this made Jocelyn uncomfortable. Though she was hardly machiavellian, she had enough sense to know that it is always best to know which players hold what cards before the betting gets heavy.'

And here it was eleven twenty-five and Austin still hadn't shown—the beast. This seemed most unlike him. Unless things had changed greatly from college days, when Austin always arrived at least twenty minutes early for every reading and you'd walk in and find him placing tiny pretzels in bowls around the room.

So there they all sat, in a more or less amiable silence, waiting for their absent playwright and—of course—Harriet Weldon to appear. Charlie Martin sat slumped in a chair, chewing on a pencil eraser. Martin had directed a highly successful nostalgia musical, *Twinks*, about two years ago, which was still, as they say, packing 'em in. But his last musical hadn't gone so smoothly and *Term of Trial* was to be his first "straight" play on Broadway.

As a matter of fact, thought Jocelyn, Charlie Martin is certainly *not* the obvious choice for director of this particular script. Though she herself had never worked with him before, she'd heard from colleagues that he was an imaginative, if sometimes erratic director. Still it seemed odd that he would take on *Term of Trial* as his first nonmusical; rather like jumping from limericks to Sandburg.

Jocelyn's train of thought was broken by the imminent approach of the stage manager. Peter Morrance crossed the bare room in easy strides, the September breeze ruffling his jet-black curls and Hawaiian print shirt. Jocelyn had never worked with Peter before, but they were old acquaintances. Peter lived with a girlfriend of Jocelyn's, a stage manager named Carrie Ross whom Jocelyn had worked with Off Broadway, and Jocelyn couldn't have been more pleased to discover that Peter was running the show. From all reports, Peter Morrance could do for artistic temperaments what Adlai Stevenson did for the UN, and some premonition told her that such tact might well be a godsend in days to come. The Irish, even the half-Irish, tend to be psychic.

Peter plopped down in a chair beside Jocelyn and said, with an elfin smile, "I *hate* this part of rehearsals!"

"What, Peter, the waiting?"

"No, just the early days before things really get rolling. It usually takes a while into rehearsal before you get that 'pulling together' feeling, the precision, the excitement . . ."

"The poker games."

Peter's smile broadened. "Ah, Josh, ever my psychic twin!"

"Have you found out who plays yet?"

"Max Bramling—the judge—he doesn't."

"Then he'll have trouble with the character. Every lawyer's a gambler in some respect."

"Josh, sometimes I just wish to God you'd shut up and become a director. Charlie Martin *does* play."

"You don't say? You and he old poker buddies?"

"Lord, no. It just came up during our interview. Hatchell and Greenfeld really wanted me for this show, but Charlie had final approval. It was the craziest interview, Josh. I went into his office and there were these two nearly life-size 'Twinks' dolls in the corner of the room, in those fluffy blond wigs, you know? And lying on the office rug are these two pure-bred Irish wolfhounds. Well, I sit down in a nice leather armchair and we start to talk semi-turkey. But about halfway through the interview, one of these wolfhounds gets up and trots across the office and tears the head off one of the 'Twinks' dolls with his teeth. Then he comes to me and drops the doll's head in my lap!"

"Peter, I love it . . . What did Charlie do? What did *you* do?"

"Charlie didn't bat an eyelash, so what could I do? I threw the doll's head across the office."

"And?"

"The goddam wolfhound fetched it back again. This went on through the whole damn interview! Josh, it was a circus."

"But you still managed to bring up poker!"

Their banter was interrupted by the simultaneous arrival of both Austin and Harriet. They came through the door into the rehearsal room almost side by side, though there was very little to suggest that any camaraderie had brought them into the room together. As soon as they entered their paths took divergent courses: Austin's toward Jocelyn, and Harriet's, fulsomely, toward Charlie Martin.

Just as Austin reached Jocelyn, she saw Harriet's head bend over Martin's outstretched hands; she averted her eyes just in time to avoid the spectacle of another Weldonian swan dive at the feet of her "maestro." Jocelyn had a very real respect for the theatrical profession, except for these contrived moments of effusiveness, which she found sick-making. As Austin warmly kissed her on the forehead, he gazed into her hazel eyes and saw the unformed question.

"Her doctors tell Harriet that she *must* do twenty deep knee-bends a day, whether there's someone famous around or not."

"Ah! . . . A very martyr to health, in fact?"

A slightly uncomfortable expression flitted across Austin's face. "You might say that."

Things finally got rolling after Harriet finished a protracted apology to Charlie for her tardiness (which was, of course, unavoidable). Then Martin called the cast and crew around him and started to explain the set. On the table in front of him was a miniature of John Baron's design for *Term of Trial*. Baron himself, a slight, dark-haired man in his mid-thirties, stood a little behind Martin, wearing tan shirt and slacks, a black vest and his perpetual Cheshire cat grin, and watched the director construe his creation.

Jocelyn had done a show with Baron about two years ago and enjoyed his gentle Southern manners, which were the perfect foil for a merciless wit. Obviously nothing had changed in two years, because she had glanced at John sometime during Harriet's entrance scene and his face had been a study in sheer devilment.

Jocelyn drew nearer to the table to get a better look at the model. *Term of Trial* was to be his debut as a Broadway designer after what some might call an overly long apprenticeship Off Broadway and in regional theatres. Jocelyn wasn't disappointed: John's model was a gem of theatrical ingenuity, with one huge revolve accommodating four separate, intricate settings; the judge's chambers, a courtroom, the ruthless young lawyer's office, and the judge's home. It was all done in an elegant but spare style, for Baron was a master at creating mood through suggestion. She raised her eyes above Charlie Martin's shoulder and gave Baron an approving nod to which he replied with a slight, almost indiscernible, mock bow.

Charlie Martin was finishing up his initial pep talk with all the standard bromides, including: . . . a handpicked group of the finest professionals . . . a fresh, important new script . . . a chance to do something really different . . . knock this town on its ass . . . make Barnes sit up and take notice—or at least stay awake through the first act . . . (this last accompanied by knowing chuckles all around, Harriet's being the heartiest and most knowing).

During the director's closing remarks, Peter Morrance had managed to distribute scripts to those still lacking them and set up the chairs in a wide circle. So by the time Charlie Martin was pulling it all together with, ". . . and I think, if we can just keep those words of Chekhov's firmly in mind, we're gonna have a damn fine show on our hands," they were ready to begin the reading. Jocelyn was relieved. Obligatory speeches such as Martin's—even when well done—tended to make her uncomfortable.

The reading was going well. Austin was hunched forward in his chair, listening with a rapt, absorbed countenance that Jocelyn well remembered. She was having a fine time watching Max Bramling as the steely old judge and Kevin Kern as the calculating lawyer hack their way through their first scene together. They seemed to have a good chemistry going already. The contrast between the two men was instantly effective: Max Bramling was what you got when you crossed Orson Welles with Heidi's grandfather, and Kevin Kern was what you got when you crossed insanely handsome with smart and sexy.

With a Tony nomination under his belt, Kern was definitely in the up-and-coming category, and Jocelyn had recognized him as soon as she'd come into the studio. There was something about his dark auburn hair, sea-green eyes and indolent mouth that registered an instant nine on her This-Man-Could-Mean-Trouble meter and propelled her swiftly in the direction of Peter Morrance's safe and friendly presence. For despite the fact that Jocelyn was a great afficionado of the male person—especially in its more glorious forms —she had a policy about entanglements with fellow cast members. On the whole it was inadvisable and unwise and, from what she'd heard via certain other actresses, Kevin Kern was a living, breathing Gordian knot— But, by Jesus, the man was gorgeous and he could *act!* Talent can cover up a multitude of sins.

With no small effort, Jocelyn returned her gaze to the script in her lap. It was almost time for her scene and, in spite of the meagerness of the role, she was looking forward to playing with the character of the as yet unnamed lady law clerk. She wanted to play the woman as an eager beaver of seamless though slightly manic efficiency; Jocelyn saw her as a hybrid of Rosalind Russell in *His Gal Friday,* bright, tough and wise-cracking, and Radar O'Reilly, one of those people who hand you a memo two seconds before you ask for it. If she pulled it off, it would add some needed levity to the first act.

Kevin Kern gave Jocelyn her cue and she plunged in. At first Charlie Martin stared at her as if she were from Mars, but Austin caught her drift immediately and started silently bobbing his head up and down. John Baron's smile got a little broader and Kevin Kern had an interested glint in his emerald eyes. Harriet Weldon's strong-boned face wore an expression of clinical seriousness, but Jocelyn saw that she was filing her nails under the table.

When they had finished reading the first act Peter Morrance called a ten-minute break. Hands shoved deep into the pockets of his Levi's, Charlie Martin ambled over to the corner where Austin and Jocelyn were having coffee and cigarettes.

"Hey, Austin, don't you think Jocelyn's character should have a name?"

"Terrific . . . Josh, you can do the christening. Be my guest."

"Well, I think it should be a kind of androgynous name like . . . uh . . . Jackie Tibbit! That's it!"

"And just once she'll be referred to as Ms. Tibbit," said Austin.

John Baron, who had been hanging on the periphery of their little group, piped up, in a deceptively bland and innocent drawl, "And don't y'all think it would be fun if Tibbit had a secret passion for the lawyer, Ferris?"

"What, you mean *Kevin's* character? That could be a lot of fun, eh, Charlie? And Josh is a whiz at playing that kind of subtext, aren't ya, Josh?"

Both Austin and Baron were grinning at her. It was a bit discomfiting to Jocelyn to have friends who knew so well where one's weaknesses lay.

Peter began assembling all the actors for the reading of the second act. Sometime during the break a tall, portly man in his fifties came into the studio and stood talking to Harriet and Martin. His hair was dark but heavily streaked with gray; he wore an impeccably tailored pin-striped suit and the countenance of the saddest basset hound Jocelyn had ever seen. She had no idea who he was, but she saw that Austin did.

The second act began smoothly. Jocelyn's part was over, leaving her free to watch Harriet Weldon arrange and re-arrange with delicate precision the folds of the silk scarf around her throat. The well-dressed basset hound sat in a folding chair, slightly behind her. They were just about to start the scene between Lindsay Harding and the judge. Jocelyn held her breath and waited for Harriet to do to Austin's dialogue what Lizzie Borden did to her parents. But the ax never fell.

Quickly looking up at the other actress, Jocelyn saw that her skin was almost paper-white against her dark hair; there was incredible tension in her lower jaw and tiny beads of sweat stood out on her upper lip. Harriet Weldon had the bearing of a woman enduring a good deal of pain.

CHAPTER 5

Austin, ruminating over his last morsel of New York sirloin, raised a beer mug in salutation. As soon as the reading was finished, Jocelyn had charmingly, in her best Celeste Holm manner, kidnapped Austin and whisked him over to Gallagher's for steaks and ale. Three hours of sitting and listening had left them both famished . . . and Jocelyn had some serious "pumping" to do. Austin finished the dregs of his ale and progressed to coffee.

Itching for details about the show, Jocelyn racked her brains for a casual but effective opening gambit. Austin supplied it for her.

"So, what did you think of the reading, Josh?"

"Well, you know I think the script is dandy; it moves beautifully and there's not an ounce of fat on it."

"My butcher will be so pleased."

"Don't be facetious—you know exactly what I mean. Max Bramling has the perfect look for the judge and can probably come up with the goods. Kevin Kern is already shaping up to be fairly stupendous . . ."

"Noticed that, did you?"

"Shut up. Peter Morrance is supposed to be the Svengali of stage managers and Charlie Martin is a smart, successful director . . ."

"And?"

"Oh, Austin . . . Why Harriet Weldon?"

"Ah, there's the rub! I didn't think Harriet would be your ideal choice for Lindsay Harding."

"Uh, well . . . no."

"Mine either," he said briskly.

"Well then? I know it's your first major production, so you may not have full cast approval, but still . . . Is it Cyrus Weldon's . . ."

Jocelyn was momentarily distracted; the gray-haired, pin-striped man from the rehearsal studio had entered the restaurant and was approaching the bar. Austin finished her question for her.

"Cyrus Weldon's money? No, not really. He has some money in the show, but it's not significant."

"Then whose money is 'significant'?"

"Harriet's husband, Harold Tewes,' a banker who's very well thought of on Wall Street."

"Harold Tewes? I've heard that name but I don't think I've ever seen the man."

"Of course you have! He was at the . . ."

At this moment Jocelyn saw the basset-faced gentleman coming across the room toward their table.

"Well, speak of the devil, here he is . . . Jocelyn O'Roarke, I'd like you to meet . . . my cousin, Harold Tewes."

Harold Tewes shook hands, sat down and proceeded to order brandies all around while Jocelyn sat there in a dazed and stupefied silence, wondering if she were in the last act of a Molière farce. Austin's cousin married to Harriet Weldon? He'd never said a word!

"I'm so glad you're with the company, Miss O'Roarke," Tewes said.

"Oh, please—Jocelyn."

"Thank you. I enjoyed you very much in *Veneers*. So did my wife."

Austin's face told Jocelyn clearly, "Like the plague, she enjoyed you!" But Tewes seemed sincere enough; his comments on her performance were intelligent and enthusiastic, but not fawning. His large hands cradled the brandy snifter with a curious gentleness.

"Austin tells me that you two went to college together."

"That's right. We had a perfect friendship: Austin nagged me about my—and I use the term loosely—'boyfriends' and I nagged him about his . . . ties."

The double entendre was not lost on Austin, who leapt into the breach.

"Do you know, Josh, that I'd been in New York for over two years without ever coming across Harold, or he me?"

"That's right. And it might have taken a lot longer if it hadn't been for my secretary, Sybil Stearns. Sybil saw Austin's name on a flyer for one of his plays that they did at St. Clement's and asked me if he might be related to my aunt."

"Which play was that, Austin—*The Fourth Genie?*"

"That was it—the one Carolyn Grazio found to be 'both moribund and overly whimsical.'"

"She must not have liked her date that night; it sounds like a review of her sex life. Personally, I think she's been bitter ever since *Godspell* closed."

"Excuse me, Mr. Tewes, I'm sorry to interrupt, but I have the car out front. You did say that you wanted to get to the Exchange by four."

The lilting voice belonged to a slender, middle-aged woman with ash-blond hair who now stood beside their table. Jocelyn admired the classic lines of her linen suit and the look of quiet authority in her eyes. Harold Tewes smiled up at her.

"So I did, Sybil. You've met Austin, haven't you . . . ? Jocelyn, this is my secretary and general custodian, Mrs. Sybil Stearns."

A delicately boned and exquisitely manicured hand extended itself to Jocelyn. When she grasped it, the skin felt warm and dry. Jocelyn, who was the queen of the split-second first impression, inferred a lot from handshakes, and she decided that Sybil Stearns's went with her eyes.

"I'm sorry to have to tear Mr. Tewes away. I know he's been looking forward to meeting you."

"Ah well, I expect that has to do with Austin telling lurid tales about me—he likes to picture me as Moll Flanders on the Upper West Side. I'm sure I've disillusioned him by now."

Tewes rose slowly from the table, leaving a bill large enough to cover the three brandies and most of Austin and Jocelyn's lunch.

"As a matter of fact— Austin, why don't you come to dinner Friday night and bring Jocelyn? If you're not tied up, that is."

"Uh . . . no, I don't think so. How about you, Jocelyn?"

Jocelyn, who had a tentative date that night, found it impossible to ignore the silent pleading in Austin's eyes.

"Oh . . . yes! That would be lovely."

"Fine. Then it's settled. We'll see you around eight, say? I know Harriet will be dying to talk to you. Give you two a chance to get acquainted; maybe swap a few ideas about that Lindsay character, eh?"

People outside of the theatre, even those related by marriage, cannot help seeming hopelessly naive at times. To Jocelyn, the idea of Harriet and she exchanging tips about a role was about as likely as the United States and Russia having a candid talk about Afghanistan.

"That sounds delightful. We'll see you Friday, then."

Harold Tewes and Sybil Stearns weaved their way between the

crowded tables and out of the restaurant. Jocelyn could barely contain herself as she watched them make their final rotation out of the revolving doors.

"Jesus H. Christ—*Cousin* Harold!?! Still playwrights run deep, I must say. Tell me, how is Thanksgiving dinner with Harold and Harriet? I'll bet she just bursts out of the kitchen à la Loretta Young and genuflects the damn turkey onto the dinner table, huh?"

Austin was meandering somewhere amid anger, embarrassment and laughter.

"The sad thing about your nasty yet trenchant imagination, Jocelyn, is how often it comes near the mark. Nevertheless! I owe a lot to Harriet and Harold . . ."

Smiling, she said, "I bet you do."

"Damn it, Josh! Don't be so frigging flippant. Do you realize that I've come close to a legitimate Broadway production *twice* before only to have everything come apart at the last minute because a producer screwed up or a backer backed down? And it's not as though I went begging either. Harold found *me,* not vice versa."

"Did he offer to back the other two shows?"

"Oh, he was 'supportive' but not a 'moving force' if you know what I mean . . . But then the other two scripts didn't have as juicy a role for a woman. Oh hell, Josh, I know Harriet doesn't have the right fire and steel for the part, but she won't *hurt* the show—and frankly, I'd sell my soul to see this play mounted."

Breathing like a man who's been running hard, Austin swigged down the last of his brandy and lit a cigarette while Jocelyn searched for the right words in the ensuing silence.

"My dear, I'd feel exactly the same way if I were you. So if it makes you feel any better, I don't care if Harold got the money by selling his grandmother's gold fillings. And if Harriet wants to play her whole scene on point in a sequined tutu, that's fine with me, too."

" 'You overpower me with good breeding,' Miss O'Roarke."

" 'The very pineapple of politeness,' aren't I? . . . Now listen, guess who got married last month—and they said it couldn't be done . . ."

CHAPTER 6

"My dears, you're here at *last!* I was about to send runners out into the streets to look for you. But I won't scold. If I know you two, you were probably off in a cozy bar reminiscing over your salad days at school."

"Harriet, you're positively sibylline, you know that?" said Austin.

The shadow of a frown crossed Harriet Weldon's face as she ushered her late arrivals into a large living room with high molded ceilings and two tall windows which looked out onto Park Avenue. Jocelyn made all the appropriate noises of charmed delight with the apartment while mentally applauding Austin's diplomacy. What they had been "reminiscing" over was a bowl of excellent black hash which Jocelyn had persuaded Austin to smoke with her back at her apartment, arguing that they would both need fortification for the evening ahead of them.

Standing in the center of the Tewes's Persian rug with a glass of Chablis in her hand, Jocelyn saw Kevin Kern sauntering across the room toward her. Few men outside the world of dance moved with his kind of lithe, animal grace. Brown pleated slacks and a green corduroy jacket did nothing to disguise his admirable physique as he stood towering above Jocelyn. He arched an eyebrow at her and she took a sip of her wine while the room righted itself again.

"Good evening, Miss Tidbit." (Kevin had tagged her with this sobriquet the second day of rehearsal and Jocelyn knew she would be stuck with it for the duration.) "God, I'm glad we've finished blocking the damn thing, aren't you? I hate standing around feeling like a chess piece."

"Ah well, maybe that's all we are. At least *you* get to be a knight, not just another pawn."

Kevin grinned down at her and replied in the clipped tones of George Sanders, "'You're maudlin and full of self-pity. You're magnificent.'"

Jocelyn laughed happily and suppressed a strong desire to push back a lock of auburn hair that had fallen over his forehead.

"How much of Act Two did you get through after I left?"

"The whole damn thing. Charlie tore through it like a madman . . . though he and Harriet had to stop a few times during her scene with Max to uh . . . straighten a few things out. But we finally got that last scene blocked."

"The one between your character and Lindsay after the judge dies? How did it go?"

He was noncommittal. "Okay . . . I must say, it's a little disconcerting to play opposite Harriet, though."

"Why's that?"

"Don't you know? My dear Jocelyn, you and Austin are not the only ones to share old school ties. Harriet was one of my teachers when I was at MST."

Jocelyn knew of course that Kevin, along with several other prominent New York actors, was an alumnus of the highly touted Manhattan School of Theatre, but she had forgotten that Harriet had once been on the faculty.

"You don't say? And this is the first time you've trod the boards on an equal footing, eh? . . . That must feel a little strange. Tell me, what was Harriet like as a teacher?"

"She could be overpowering at times, especially with the more timid first-year students. But she was okay if she liked you and she seemed to . . . uh . . . take an interest in me."

Instantly wondering if it were the same kind of "interest" that Mrs. Robinson had taken in Benjamin Braddock, Jocelyn could not refrain from asking, "Is that how you came to read for *Term of Trial?* Through Harriet?"

"Oh, no! Charlie's the one who got me in," he said quickly. "We did *She Loves Me* about two years ago in Cincinnati. Ever since then he's been dying to cast me in a straight play so he could break me of what he refers to as my 'music hall mannerisms.' Harriet had nothing to do with it."

Kevin Kern was beginning to look a little uncomfortable and Jocelyn, who didn't like to discomfit gorgeous men for no good reason, was about to change the subject. She was spared the task by the approach of Paul Radner, Harriet's son from a previous marriage, whose gaze was fixed somewhat worshipfully on Kevin's arresting profile. Paul, a strawberry-blond nineteen-year-old with azure eyes, was no slouch when it came to male comeliness. Studying him in his cream-colored suit and blue silk tie, Jocelyn decided that, although he would without a doubt grow into a handsome man, he had the kind of refined features and high cheekbones that any Wilhelmina model would kill for.

"I don't mean to interrupt, but Mother would like everyone to start wafting toward the dining room. Angelique has made a stuffed sole, which is one of her specialties, and she doesn't like to keep it sitting in the oven too long. Mother, who in most cases is rather fearless, would prefer a slow death on an anthill to offending Angelique. She's scared shitless of her, you see."

Having delivered his little speech without so much as cracking a smile, Paul dutifully disappeared in the direction of the dining room, leaving Kevin and Jocelyn to quell their mirth as best they could. In unison, they put out their cigarettes as Harriet sailed past them with a subdued John Baron in tow. Though still a little pale, Harriet looked much better than she had on Monday in a cream-colored satin blouse and floor-length velvet hostess skirt. But as Kevin and Jocelyn dutifully followed in her wake, Jocelyn seemed to detect a slight unevenness in her gait. "The woman can't be drunk," she thought, "she hasn't had a glass in her hand all evening." When they reached the dining table, John Baron pulled out a chair for Harriet at the head of the table and, as she seated herself, Jocelyn could have sworn that she caught a glimpse of an Ace bandage wrapped around Harriet's left ankle.

The excellence of Angelique's stuffed sole was no idle boast, and the white asparagus and crisp Cabernet Sauvignon which accompanied it were as good. Theatre folk, with their perennial worry over where the next job and/or meal is coming from, make gratifying dinner guests, and so it was at this gathering, with the sole exception of Charlie Martin, who joined in the flow of conversation only sporadically and merely tinkered with his food. Observing Martin, Jocelyn wondered if it weren't a little early in the day for "director's doldrums" to have set in. But as soon as the dessert was served she forgot all about it.

As the group retired to the living room, Tewes said to Austin and Jocelyn, "I thought you both might like some Courvoisier with your coffee."

Jocelyn thanked him and suggested that they sit down as Austin seemed a bit tipsy. "I see Mrs. Stearns isn't with us tonight, Harold."

"No. Holding down the fort, I'm afraid. She's entertaining some clients of ours from San Francisco; taking them to dinner and a show —*West Side Story,* I believe."

Austin began humming "A Boy Like That" under his breath and Jocelyn piped in quickly, hoping to cut him off before he launched into his flawless Rita Moreno impersonation.

"Tell me, did Harriet do something to her ankle? I thought I saw a bandage on her leg."

"Oh, that." Tewes frowned and gave his massive head a quick shake, much like a basset hound just after an unwelcome bath.

"I don't know why she still wears the damn thing, the doctor told her it wouldn't help."

Austin shot his cousin an apprehensive glance. "Help what? Harold . . . is something wrong with Harriet?"

"Oh no, not really. Damnation, Harriet will be furious if this gets out. Believe me, it's nothing serious but perhaps you should know about it, Austin . . . and perhaps you too, Jocelyn . . . Harriet's been having some trouble with blood clots in her left leg. She was having a good deal of pain for a while there but she's much better now. Really."

Jocelyn had a sudden flash of Harriet's face during last Monday's reading and felt a pang of remorse. Blood clots could be very nasty things; Jocelyn's father had suffered from them at one point and she had not forgotten his distress. Austin, sitting on the very edge of the sofa, asked, "Has she been to see a doctor?"

"Yes, naturally—one of the best, Dr. Harvey Samuels. He's a friend, actually; we were at Harvard together. Got me through advanced chemistry, bless him. Anyway . . . Harvey's got Harriet fixed up just fine, don't you worry."

"What's he prescribing for it? Coumadin?"

Harold regarded Jocelyn with mild astonishment. "As a matter of fact, yes But how did you know?"

"Jocelyn is one of the last of the Renaissance women, Harold. Also, her brother is a doctor. Isn't that so, Josh?"

"Yes. Plus my father had some trouble with leg clots and they had him on Coumadin. It's one of the more common anticoagulants."

"Well, it seems to have done the trick. But I'd appreciate it if neither one of you said anything about this, especially to Martin . . . or to Harriet herself, for that matter. She likes to think of herself as nigh on invincible. It took me forever to get her to see Harvey."

Even as Austin assured his cousin that they would both be as silent as the ocean depths, Jocelyn considered the unlikelihood of Harriet's malady remaining a secret during three weeks of intensive rehearsal. Max Bramling and Kevin Kern were sure to notice something if Jocelyn had. And, from the curious glances Charlie Martin was directing their way, it looked as if he already smelled something potentially rotten in Denmark.

Jocelyn looked over at Austin, whose face was a study in perplexity, but to Jocelyn the underlying question was plain: if Harriet's leg gave out, would Harold Tewes's financing follow suit?

CHAPTER 7

Ginger-haired Max Bramling, who sometimes came to morning rehearsals looking like an ancient bear just roused from hibernation, was in fine fettle for the Thursday morning run-through that was to be their last in New York before leaving for the preview run in Boston. Jocelyn, despite the onslaught of a vicious head cold, was enjoying herself immensely. Harriet was late getting back from a final costume fitting and Charlie Martin had asked Jocelyn to walk through the scene with Max.

"Surely, Miss Harding, you realize that the body of jurisprudence must not be distorted by emotional biases."

"Nor should it be dictated to by any sort of intellectual monomania, don't you agree?"

There was excitement in the room as Max and Jocelyn wound up to the end of the scene. Over Max Bramling's right shoulder Jocelyn spied Harriet getting off the elevator and pausing by the doorway.

As soon as the scene ended she said, "My dears, I apologize for the inconvenience. The fitting took forever but it was worth it: Thea Allen's worked her usual magic. And Jocelyn, it was sweet of you to fill in the gaps. Charles, where do you want Kevin and me for the beginning of the last scene?"

For no good reason Jocelyn was livid as she picked up her script and walked off the floor. In an effort to pull herself together, she reminded herself that the nature of an understudy's job was to always be the bridesmaid; the thought did not console her greatly . . . but Kevin Kern did. As he walked to the center of the room to begin his scene with Harriet, he whispered sotto voce to Jocelyn, "A Daniel come to judgment! Yea, a Daniel! O wise young judge, how I do . . . honor thee!"

The confounding thing about actors is their ability to say the right thing at the right time.

Kevin and Harriet took their places and began the final scene:

Lindsay and Ferris' last reckoning of idealism versus pragmatism, which tied the various strands of Austin's themes together so superbly. It was a scene that required great simplicity and restraint and anything you could steal from Gregory Peck in *To Kill a Mockingbird*. Kevin Kern had obviously seen *To Kill a Mockingbird*, whereas Harriet's performance gave every indication that she had just come from a screening of *The Nun's Story*. It was this near-religious quality in her work that annoyed Jocelyn; not to mention the fact that Harriet had an unfortunate tendency to "editorialize" when acting, as if her job was not merely to play the role, but also to *explain* the story to any members of emerging Third World nations present. If "talking is painting to the ear," Harriet came very close to painting by numbers.

"You don't feel *any* sense of . . . LOSS, do you, Ferris?" Then, in elaborately measured tones, "I . . . pity . . . you."

"Uh, people, can we take this back a bit?"

Charlie Martin, who looked as if he would be happier directing a Kabuki play in summer stock, approached them with hands shoved deep in the pockets of what looked like an old school sweater. So far Martin had been a gem of tact and patience in rehearsals, but Jocelyn thought she could detect the sound of the camel's back beginning to break.

"Harriet, dear, you've been upstaging Kevin through half of the scene. And you keep making this same gesture of pressing your hand over your heart. It's a little too reminiscent of Reverend Dimmesdale and *The Scarlet Letter*, I'm afraid."

There was a brief silence in the studio, accentuated by a collective holding of breath among the cast who waited for the proverbial shit to hit the Weldonian fan. Harriet, however, who apparently made it a point of honor never to do anything that Deborah Kerr wouldn't do, merely regarded Charlie with a look of sad disappointment, as if he were a little boy who had the bad taste to break wind at the dinner table. The voice of sweet reason spoke.

"But Charles, you know the effect I'm going for . . . I'm trying to externalize Lindsay's enormous sincerity and caring. She *is* speaking *from* the heart here, don't you agree?"

Martin stood his ground admirably.

"I agree in principle but not in performance, Harriet. This scene's pretty straightforward and we don't want to beat them over the head with it. No point in carrying coals to Newcastle, is there?"

Harriet's arched brow clearly indicated that she felt there was no possible correlation between coal transport and "great art," but good manners and Deborah Kerr restrained her.

Reasonably, she said, "You know I'm one hundred percent behind what you're . . . trying to get at in this scene, Charles. I'm just trying to create a little emotional ballast to Kevin's cynicism and . . . aridity. I think the scene requires it, don't you?"

John Baron paused behind Jocelyn's chair to whisper, "Well, well . . . I see our Harriet isn't above a little theatrical buck-passing. Tarnishes the halo a bit, don't it?"

"Uh-huh—most gratifying. Though I think Kern is a poor choice for scapegoat. It looks as though she may be courting a cynical and arid shot in the ole kisser."

Kern's flushed face and grim mouth bore out Jocelyn's observation; on an if-looks-could-kill meter, it appeared as if he already had Harriet well ensconced at Forest Lawn. Between clenched teeth he muttered, "I think the scene requires that we just say the goddam lines and play the goddam intentions and very little else."

Charlie Martin's eyes flew desperately around the room in search of a deus ex machina, which he found in the person of Peter Morrance. Peter rose calmly from his chair with a meaningful look at his wristwatch and announced, "We've been at it for three hours, Charlie. It's about time we broke for lunch. So, could we have Harriet and Kevin back at one-thirty to finish up this scene and the rest of you back at two. That okay with you, Charlie?"

"Super! A good morning's work, everybody. Now go have a good meal, we've got a lot of work ahead of us."

The tension in the room dissipated amid the general hubbub of chairs being scraped back and scripts snapped shut. Jocelyn, stuffing the latest Rona Jaffe novel back into her bag, watched Kevin Kern stride angrily out of the studio. Fearing that she would be the last person left alone in the room with Harriet, she beat a hasty retreat to the ladies' room, where she viewed the ravages of a sleepless night and stuffy sinuses on a face that men had once been pleased to call "fair." The merciless fluorescent light above the bathroom mirror did nothing to ease her wounded vanity.

Deciding that makeup would only help her look more embalmed, Jocelyn splashed cold water on her face and drew a brush through her tangle of black curls. She came out into the hallway just in time to see Harriet Weldon approach Kevin Kern, who stood waiting for the elevator, seemingly lost in thought. To get his attention, Harriet placed a tentative hand on his arm. Kevin spun around as if he'd been touched by a hot brand. Jocelyn couldn't hear what they were saying to each other: Harriet's voice was low and conciliatory but it didn't look as if Kern was having any. He made a curt reply and Jocelyn saw something that she had never seen before: what looked to be a genuine, spontaneous emotion flashed across Harriet's face . . . and that emotion was rage. The elevator arrived just then. Kern pulled open the heavy metal door and let Harriet get in, which she did with alacrity; he then let the door swing closed without getting on the elevator himself. Wishing to remain unnoticed, Jocelyn quietly made her way toward the back stairs, but just as she was about to descend a hand fell on her shoulder—Kevin Kern's hand.

"Hey, Josh, what are you doing for lunch?"

Caution struggled with curiosity . . . caution didn't stand a chance.

"Why, uh, nothing."

"Then be a sport and come have lunch with me, alright? God, could I use a drink."

Without further ado, Kevin neatly tucked Jocelyn's arm through his own and led her down the stairs.

CHAPTER 8

"I know it's a cliché, Jocelyn, but couldn't you put ground glass in her makeup? If I were Harriet's understudy I'd sure want to, and you'd be upholding a time-honored theatrical tradition, not to mention doing us all—and the play—a big favor."

"She's not all *that* dreadful, Kevin."

"*You* try playing opposite her, then. It's like trying to get blood from a stone, I swear. Harriet Weldon—computer programming's gift to acting!" Kevin raised his wine glass in a bitter toast.

"Eat your teriyaki, it's getting cold."

Knowing that most of the cast, including Harriet, would be lunching at Joe Allen's, Kevin had suggested a small Japanese restaurant on West Forty-sixth Street.

"Honestly, Josh, doesn't it just kill you to watch her hack away at that part? I don't see how you bear it with such equanimity."

"I don't, actually. My apartment is littered with little wax figures that look just like pincushions. But—don't you think Charlie can do something with Harriet?"

"Do what? You saw what happened this morning. Charlie's a good director, but his hands are tied. I mean he's just basically a hired hand, like the rest of us. Between Harriet and Harold, they've got this show sewn up tighter than . . . than those sexy jeans you're wearing."

Despite an uncomfortable stirring in the aforementioned jeans, Jocelyn stuck to the point at hand. "So you know that Harold Tewes is our sugar daddy, eh?"

"Yeah, Charlie let it slip one night when we were out for drinks. I would've found out sooner or later, anyway. Listen, you're tight with Austin, can't you talk him into throwing his weight around a bit?"

"What? You mean against his cousin and his cousin's wife? What do you expect him to do? Punch the gift horse in the mouth?"

"No. You're right. It's just that *Term of Trial* is such a good script and Ferris is such a great part, I hate to see a monkey wrench like Harriet thrown in the works, that's all."

"Come on, Kevin! No matter what Harriet does with the role, you're still going to come out smelling like a rose with the critics—so what's your worry?"

"Oh, I don't know. Maybe you're right . . . I'd just feel much better if you were doing Lindsay. Harriet makes me so uncomfortable."

"That's probably because she used to be your teacher, that's all."

"No, it's not just that, it's . . . oh, I don't know. This part is very important to me, Josh."

"Of course it is—Ferris is a great role. But nobody can take that away from you."

"You don't think so, eh? Well, maybe you're right . . . Maybe I'll survive rehearsals and maybe if we're lucky Harriet's leg will act up."

"So you know about that, too, do you?"

"Oh sure, Harriet ever so subtly let it slip in rehearsal one day with just me and Charlie and Peter. Charlie was riding her about her rigid body movements and she blamed it all on her 'excruciating' blood clots. And I'll tell ya, it did the trick with Charlie; he doesn't want to see his golden goose laying a bum egg."

"Of course not. Theatre, even more so than politics, makes strange bedfellows."

For the first time since they had left rehearsal, a cloud seemed to lift itself from Kern as he smiled roguishly at Jocelyn.

"Speaking of bedfellows, sweet Jocelyn . . ."

"Finish your teriyaki, Kevin."

CHAPTER 9

The 9 A.M. shuttle to Boston was circling over Logan Airport. Jocelyn sat slumped by a window, dabbing a crumpled Kleenex to her red eyes and runny nose with a bottle of erythromycin capsules clasped in a weak hand; she gazed speculatively out the window, contemplating whether a quick leap out might not be preferable to attending the scheduled eleven o'clock run-through at the Wilbur Theatre. Austin sat beside her with a slightly wild-eyed look about him, his long hands gripping the arm rests. The state he was in was a natural one for any writer whose brainchild is about to be delivered into the hands of the implacable Boston theatre public, and this trepidation was heightened by his antipathy for air travel. That was why he had arranged to leave in the early morning hours with Jocelyn rather than fly up later with cousin Harold in a chartered plane; he could depend upon Jocelyn's charity and restraint should he feel the need, which he often did, to stick his head between his legs during takeoff and landing.

"Is it true that if they hate you in Boston they don't throw rotten tomatoes but dead cod at the stage?"

"No, Austin. They just sit out there *looking* like dead cod, that's all."

"How reassuring."

"Buck up. *Term of Trial* is sure to become a cult hit with the Harvard Law School."

"So I can count on a rave in the *Law Review,* eh? Swell."

Functioning better than she felt, Jocelyn managed to deposit Austin and her luggage at Copley Square and get herself over to the Wilbur by eleven on the dot. As it was she was still among the very first to arrive. When she entered the theatre she was greeted by a study in chaos: a herd of techies swarmed all over the stage, trying to accomplish twenty different tasks at the same time. Conducting this symphony of manic effort was the ever serene Peter Morrance, who stood in the center of the stage directing traffic like Patience on a monument, smiling at Grief. Despite all this he spied Jocelyn as soon as she came in.

"Good day, Miss O'Roarke. Your virgin record of punctuality remains unblemished, I see. Sister Mary Ignatius will be presenting you with the Best Attendance medal at this Friday's assembly."

"Don't toy with a dying woman. Where's everybody?"

"Everyone's timetables got all screwed up, as usual. Charlie's on his way here from Logan. God, you look like hell."

"Push your luck and I won't leave you my automatic card-shuffler."

"Ah! Speaking of cards . . ."

"When?"

"Saturday between shows in the Green Room."

"Who's playing?"

"You, me, Charlie, Kevin, Nan the dresser—and, get this!—none other than our—how should I say it?—'founding father' himself, Harry Tewes."

"Well, bust my designer britches! How did this come to pass?"

"He overheard Charlie and I setting up the game and asked if he could come in on it. We were both too flabbergasted to do anything besides say, 'Of course, by all means, etcetera, etcetera.'"

"So Harold plays poker, bless his heart. I wonder if Harriet approves. I read somewhere that her father, Cyrus Weldon, abhors it."

"I don't know. I get the feeling that if she doesn't approve, she's still not about to interfere. Well, as long as you're here, why don't you go upstairs and check out your dressing room; it's on the second floor at the back. Sorry, babe, it was the best I could do."

"That's alright, Peter—just kiss the card-shuffler goodbye. See ya later."

Peter gave her a playful whack as she pranced backstage and headed for the stairway. By the time she reached the first landing she was done prancing and back to heaving as she made her way down the long corridor to the next flight of stairs. As she passed the second dressing room on her right, she was halted by a familiar and overly mellifluous voice.

"Jocelyn! My faithful standby. Do be an angel and come stand by this ladder so I don't break my neck."

Jocelyn entered Harriet Weldon's dressing room marveling at the endless human capacity for trust. Harriet was, indeed, standing on

the second rung from the top of a tall ladder, unscrewing a light bulb
in one of the overhead fixtures and replacing it with another.

"Harriet, couldn't you get one of the crew to do that for you?"

"They're all so busy now, poor men, I'd hate to trouble them. Besides I'd feel a little embarrassed. You see, it's just that I hate overhead lights, so whenever I come into a new dressing room I always
put in these wonderful soft pink bulbs."

Jocelyn, who was not above employing a little strategic lighting
herself, was disconcerted to find herself experiencing a moment of
empathy. Perched up on that ladder, wearing impractical high-heeled
shoes and replacing a light bulb to spare her vanity, Harriet looked
too human not to identify with. It's the small things that bind women
together. Jocelyn steadied the ladder with both hands.

"There, that's in," Harriet said, climbing down the steps. "Now, if
we can just slide the ladder down this way a bit, I think I can get to
that last fixture up there."

Jocelyn silently helped her move the ladder. If her head hadn't felt
so stuffed with cotton, she might possibly have offered to do the job
for Harriet. As it was, she merely suggested that Harriet remove her
heels before making her final ascent, which she did. Harriet's faithful
standby was stoically supporting the ladder, feeling a bit like Alice
watching the Red Queen play croquet, when John Baron came into
the dressing room.

"Peter said you wanted to see me . . . Oh, hello, Jocelyn! Darlin',
you look like Camille on one of her real bad days . . . I see you've
taken to hanging your own lights now, Harriet—such zeal. You'll be
after my job one of these days."

Baron, whom Jocelyn had known to utter the most devastating
comments and still come off looking like St. Francis of Assisi,
seemed to have a definite and uneasy edge behind his pleasantries
this morning.

Heavily, Harriet said, "Oh, hello . . . John," making an awkward
descent down the ladder.

As she carefully slipped on her shoes, Jocelyn observed traces of
one of Harriet's favorite poses, which Jocelyn had mentally labeled
"wounded nun": she was the spitting image of Sister Immaculata ad-
monishing an uppity religion class.

"I'm glad you're here before all the others, John. I did want to
have a word with you."

Jocelyn decided that it was time to "skip class" and made for the hallway.

"If you'll both excuse me, I want to go up and check out my dressing room before we start the run-through. See you on stage."

John and Harriet seemed barely aware of her exit. Like the good student she never was, Jocelyn closed the door softly behind her and made her way down the corridor. Sniffling her way up the second flight of stairs, feeling very sorry for herself, she made a mental note to buy some Vitamin C and a few soft pink bulbs.

CHAPTER 10

"I'll bump it another five dollars."

Jocelyn spoke in a level voice which masked her inward hysteria. After two days of grueling rehearsals and previews, she found herself dopey from medicine and embroiled in a rapidly escalating game of seven-card stud with Harold Tewes. A Bostonian branch of the Weldon clan had whisked Harriet away to a family dinner immediately after the matinee and Harold, who had begged off muttering something about transatlantic cables, was relishing his bit of backstage gambling as much as a young boy playing truant from Sunday school.

After what had been a long session of lively bidding, the only two people left in the game were Harold, with two pair showing (kings over fives), and Jocelyn, with a modest pair of tens. Jocelyn, who was not accustomed to playing for a pot that was over a hundred dollars, felt fairly certain that Tewes had another king or five in the hole. She forcibly restrained herself from glancing at her covered cards while Harold made his final ante.

Peter Morrance, with the formality of a Wimbledon official, said, "Let's see what you've got—Harold?"

Flipping over the anticipated five of clubs, he said gleefully, "A boat."

"And Jocelyn?"

Exhaling deeply, she said, "Four tens."

A reverential gasp went up from the entire table at the sight of four natural tens and Jocelyn grinned, knowing that they all had thought she was pulling an infamous O'Roarke bluff. As she raked in her winnings, Tewes gave a courtly nod.

"Nice playing, Josh."

"Decent of you to say so, Harry."

It was impossible to call a man Harold after you'd been playing poker with him for three hours; Tewes was in an expansive mood despite the trouncing he had just taken, and seemed inclined to chatter.

"There's a lot to be said for the luck of the Irish. With that dreadful cold, you still manage to win at cards and play a flawless Ms. Tidbit, to boot."

Jocelyn smiled at his use of her character's nickname. Even if it was a conditioned response after years of living with Harriet, Tewes was no slouch at handing out compliments. He was also a miracle of diplomacy, which is remarkable in someone who has the power of life or death over a show. He took people aside individually to praise them for their efforts on the show's behalf, without implying at the same time that they must reciprocate with wild paeans to his wife's stage charisma. On the whole Jocelyn thought that Harold Tewes was equipped with a pretty good "theatrical barometer." If her guess was right, Harold probably already knew where the high pressure center was hovering—directly over Harriet's performance.

Even last night's house, which had been a good Friday night audience, had grown restive during Lindsay's scene with the judge, and Charlie Martin looked like he was at the end of his rope. Austin had spent the morning in bed with a migraine and Peter Morrance was definitely off his poker game. There were storm warnings everywhere, but Harriet and Harold seemed to function calmly within the eye of the hurricane.

Jocelyn thoughtfully wiped the tip of her now red and raw nose, artfully concealed by a nearly geological layer of Ultima II, as Tewes asked solicitously, "What are you taking for that cold, Jocelyn?"

"Nothing much . . . just erythromycin. But I think . . ."

All conversation ceased as John Baron entered the Green Room with a copy of the Boston *Globe* under his arm and an indecipherable smile on his face. At the back of their minds, this is what they had been waiting for all during the card game: the first notices. Charlie Martin, oblivious to the fact that he had just been dealt two aces, was the first to speak.

"Is it in there, John?"

"Uh-huh."

"Have you read it?"

"Just glanced at it, really," Baron drawled. Jocelyn was the first to break.

"Well, John, dear heart, why don't you just 'glance' at it again . . . out loud . . . NOW."

"If you insist—'unaccustomed as I am to public speaking' . . ."

A chorus of voices said, "JOHN!"

With a satisfied smile and a mock clearing of the throat, Baron began to read.

"Headline: TERM OF TRIAL ACQUITS ITSELF WELL."

Charlie Martin threw his head back and groaned.

The *Globe* review was more than favorable and less than a rave. The first act fared very well, garnering praise for its "victory of dynamics over didactics" and its "biting wit and clarity"; Austin Frost was touted as a contemporary Robert Sherwood. Kevin Kern grinned helplessly and had the good taste to blush, upon hearing his performance proclaimed "breathtaking and hypnotic," and Jocelyn's short scene with Kern was singled out thanks to "Miss O'Roarke's hint of passion beneath her patter." Jocelyn immediately envisioned her tombstone engraved with "There Was Passion Beneath Her Patter."

It was with the second act that the reviewer began to have reservations. Despite Martin's "smooth and sure direction" and John Baron's "scenic legerdemain" there was an absence of "the previous act's hair-trigger tension and air of immediacy in the scene between Judge Castle and the woman lawyer." Unfortunately at this point the reviewer was suddenly afflicted with a case of "compost mentis" and meandered on for a full paragraph with no certainty as to whether the blame lay with the players, the director or the script. The review ended with the lukewarm assertion that *"Term of Trial* deserves its day in court. Go down to the Wilbur Theatre and *judge* for yourself."

Charlie Martin winced slightly, then cast an encouraging glance around the room. "Well, happy habeas corpus! We're still in business."

"Except for Kevin—who's in clover," Jocelyn laughed.

Kevin gave Jocelyn's shoulders a squeeze and leaned down to whisper, "And just when do I get to see the 'passion behind the patter,' eh, fair cruelty?"

Unheard over the general din, Jocelyn hissed, "This is neither the time nor the place to discuss 'country matters,' Mr. Kern."

"You're absolutely right. Let's schedule a seminar later tonight at Copley Square, shall we? I've prepared a long discourse on animal husbandry."

"Which I'm sure I would find 'breathtaking and hypnotic.'"

"Owl!"

"Really, Kevin, thanks for the invitation but I just can't tonight. I haven't felt this lousy since I played Masha in *The Sea Gull.*"

Actually Jocelyn was over the worst of her cold and already felt better than she looked or sounded. However, while her libido still wrestled with her reason, she thought it best not to inform Kevin of that fact, in the hopes that some other likely lass would take his fancy and spare Jocelyn from temptation. Kern caught something in her expression which caused him to smile and remark, "It's not just delaying tactics, is it, Josh? Maybe you figure I won't last as long as your sniffles. Well, you'd be wrong. I can be a very patient man when I want to. Patience can be very—rewarding."

Like a heroine in a Gothic novel, Jocelyn was snatched from the brink of a dangerous precipice by the sound of Harry Tewes's voice.

"Well, we don't want to get carried away but I want you all to know I feel very optimistic . . . and I think I've made a good investment."

He was interrupted by a spate of whistles and cheers.

"And I think if we all just . . . screw our courage to the sticking place, we'll not fail."

There was an instantaneous cessation of sound in the Green Room as all eyes stared at Harold Tewes in dismay. They were all astounded that, in his ten years of marriage to Harriet Weldon, he had apparently never come across that most solemnly regarded and upheld of all backstage taboos: one must never, never speak of, allude to or—heaven forfend—quote from that darkest of the dark plays, *Macbeth*.

Harold's puzzled eyes searched their faces for an explanation. Kevin Kern's hand gripped Jocelyn's shoulder tightly and, for some awful reason, she could hear an inner voice chanting, "The charm's wound up!"

CHAPTER 11

It was nine o'clock Sunday morning and the phone was ringing in Jocelyn's room at Copley Square. Though she was not an overly su-perstitious person, Jocelyn could not help but recall the last phone call she'd gotten at this hour and picked up the receiver with a sear-ing sense of dread. A worried stage manager spoke, "Josh . . . ? It's Peter."

"Holy shit!"

"Now get a grip on yourself. Harriet's leg kicked up on her last night and Harold took her over to Boston General."

"Holy shit!"

"She's much better now but . . . ah, I think you better meet me at the theatre by eleven."

"Hell and damnation! Why did that idiot man have to go and quote *Macbeth?*"

"Be reasonable. You know the lines cold and we'll just make sure everybody moves *around* you, that's all."

"Peter, don't try to lull me into a false sense of calm."

"Come on, Jocelyn, where's your sense of adventure?!"

"Adventure, my ass! I'll meet you at the Wilbur by ten-thirty."

Jocelyn leapt into the bathroom, turned the taps on vigorously and plunged herself into a steamy shower in the hopes of clearing her congested nasal passages. As she shampooed her hair, she began singing a few bars of "One More Bell to Answer" to open up her voice.

Luckily she'd run lines with Kevin often enough to feel fairly confident about their final scene, but she hadn't been onstage with Max Bramling since that run-through in New York. A new face might throw the aging character actor: she would have to go very slowly with him and hope he would trust her.

Against the background of a gray and foggy morning, Jocelyn cata-pulted herself out of a cab into the depths of the Wilbur Theatre. It was just ten-fifteen, but Peter Morrance was already inside waiting for her with two cups of coffee and a bag of sandwiches. They were just walking through the first of Lindsay's scene when the back doors of the house burst open and Kevin Kern strode in with a groggy Max Bramling in tow.

"Why if it isn't Ruby Keeler upon the boards! Good morning, Miss O'Roarke—Mr. Morrance. I want you both to know that I got drunk as a skunk last night, but I am absolutely at my best in eleventh-hour situations such as these, so have no fear."

Max Bramling simply rubbed his unshaven jowls and asked, "Where do you want to take it from, Jocelyn?"

Experiencing one of those rare moments in life that are right out of a Frank Capra movie, Jocelyn swallowed a lump in her throat and said, "How about from where you come in and find Lindsay at the window?"

Before anyone could believe it, it was four-fifteen, the matinee was on and Peter was calling places for Act Two. It was a good house and the first act had gone without a hitch. Harriet was out of pain but still out of commission. Jocelyn, knowing that Austin and Harold Tewes and a few second-string Boston critics would be out front, numbly applied the finishing touches to her makeup as Peter knocked softly on her door.

"Your call is ten minutes, Miss O'Roarke . . . And allow me to say, 'knock 'em on their ass, boobala.' "

"Byron couldn't have said it better. Thank you, Peter."

After five minutes of staring at her hands, Jocelyn got up and moved down the corridor in a trancelike state, all the while stroking Lindsay Harding's leather briefcase. As she stood in the wings, all she could remember was something James Cagney had once said, "You plant your feet, you look the other guy in the eyes and you tell the truth." Hearing her cue, she took a slow breath, walked out on stage and placed all her chips on Cagney.

Knowing her lines but not being absolutely certain of what was happening next forced her to stay within the moment at all times. Max Bramling played against her with a fine balance of gruffness and delicacy that imparted a father-daughter poignancy to the scene. Jocelyn would have gladly walked on her knees through the Sahara for him at that moment. The scene passed in a flash and, before she knew it, Jocelyn was onstage with Kevin Kern for the final denouement.

Kevin had made no idle boast about his eleventh-hour virtuosity; he was positively electric, not to say uncanny. He didn't try to overwhelm Jocelyn's quiet conviction but baited her character with a fiery, cynical bravado. They clicked.

Jocelyn made her exit into the wings and collapsed gratefully against Peter Morrance's broad shoulder. When the waves of applause came, Peter shoved Jocelyn back out onto the stage for the curtain call. She managed her bows without toppling over, thanks to the support of Kevin and Max. As soon as the final curtain was rung down, Kevin Kern took an uncomprehending Jocelyn into his arms and gave her a long and lingering kiss.

The next instant Austin was whirling her about the stage, while Charlie Martin pressed her hand warmly and Harold Tewes muttered something about a "brilliant stopgap effort." That evening Jocelyn and Kevin dined sumptuously and necked like teenagers in the cab on their way back to the hotel, though Kevin's early morning radio interview demanded that they part, semi-platonically, in the lobby.

By Tuesday Harriet and her left leg were in working order again and the rest of the Boston run passed uneventfully.

CHAPTER 12

Jocelyn awoke to the seductive strains of Loggins and Messina coming from her clock radio. Kenny and Jim were joined by a third male voice, that of Kevin Kern. Kevin began kissing her slowly while still accompanying the band.

"Kevin!—What do you want for breakfast?"

"I'm having breakfast."

"My earlobe may be tasty but it's hardly nourishing."

"You underestimate your lobe. This is all the sustenance I need."

"Kevin, we have rehearsal at noon and you said that you had to stop by your agent's office this morning—it's nearly ten now! And I promised Max I'd come a little early and run lines with him."

"Max knows his lines. He's just worried because he doesn't know what to do about that scene in Act Two. Personally, I think he should hide Harriet's little anticoagulant pills."

"Kevin, that's terrible."

"Oh come off it, Josh! It's been an open secret ever since that Sunday in Boston that a lot of people—including the director and the playwright, I'd imagine—would be happier if you were playing Lindsay and Harriet were off somewhere polishing Harold's golf shoes. Now, where were we? Oh, yes . . ."

Eleven-thirty found a tardy but triumphantly unrepentant Jocelyn racing down Eighth Avenue toward the Ambassador Theatre with the scent of Kevin's cologne still on her fingertips. She was filled with a heady and slightly breathless sense of well-being. After two weeks on the road, Jocelyn had expected Kevin's ardor to wane once they got back to New York but such was not the case, and Jocelyn was beginning to wonder how long they could keep the affair clandestine: the last four days in Philadelphia Austin had given her nothing but meaningful glances.

Jocelyn's reverie was disturbed by the sight of Sybil Stearns and Harold Tewes coming out of the Ambassador Theatre. This sur-

prised Jocelyn somewhat, as Harold's presence behind the scenes had
been noticeably lacking for the past week or so. Apparently the sudden flare-up of Harriet's leg in Boston had badly shaken him. Peter
Morrance had told Jocelyn that Tewes had driven Harriet back to
New York that Sunday to be examined by their friend and physician,
Dr. Harvey Samuels, who had pronounced her sufficiently recovered
to resume her role. Harriet had gone back onstage Tuesday night
with barely a reference to the incident, other than to say that she felt
"perfectly rested and marvelous" and, as she and Harold both
seemed disinclined to talk about it, the rest of the company had followed their lead.

As Harriet seemed fit and had the encouragement of the Philadelphia reviews, which had been more glowing than the Boston notices, Jocelyn thought that Harold would have regained his equanimity by now. However, as he stood by the curb trying to hail a cab,
he looked agitated and distracted. Indeed, Jocelyn would have
passed unnoticed into the lobby if Sybil Stearns had not glanced up.

"Why, Miss O'Roarke, how nice to see you again. Let me congrat-
ulate you on your eleventh-hour rescue in Boston the other week. I
understand you saved us from a fine mess."

"I think the only thing I saved was my own face—barely. But
thank you all the same."

Jocelyn was once again struck by Sybil Stearns's grace and quiet
confidence. Standing beneath the theatre marquee in a simple, dove-
gray angora dress which did marvelous things for her wheat-colored
hair and blue eyes, it struck Jocelyn that Sybil herself was almost a
prototype of Lindsay Harding: grace and intelligence matched by
unshakable resolution. For some reason that image made Jocelyn uneasy. Harold, however, was back to his old courtly self.

"Nonsense! You saved the show that day. Don't know what we
would've done without you. Though I feel quite responsible for the
whole unfortunate affair. I was so busy attending to business that I
completely forgot to oversee Harriet's medications. She's quite hope-
less about these things and I'm sure—what with the pressures of
opening out of town—she just forgot to take her Coumadin for a few
days."

"Well, that would do it, certainly. But you mustn't blame yourself.
Anyway, Harriet certainly seems in the pink now," Jocelyn said.
"And I'm sure Dr. Samuels has things well under control."

"That he has," said Tewes with a dry chuckle. "Old Harvey put the fear of God into Harriet about taking her Coumadin faithfully. I don't think she'll forget in the near future. As a matter of fact, I'm taking her over to his office during your dinner break so he can do another Protime reading on her."

"That's a good idea," Jocelyn said, nodding. "They used to do those on my father once every three weeks or so."

Noticing Sybil Stearns's look of puzzlement, Jocelyn explained, "A Protime reading is something they do for people with clotting disorders to determine exactly how swiftly or slowly the blood is coagulating per second. Then the patient's maintenance dosage of Coumadin is decided accordingly . . . What have they got Harriet on, Harold, about five milligrams a day?"

"Yes, that's about right. Jocelyn, you must realize how aggravating tension and stress can be for someone with this condition. Harriet has promised me that she'll be religious about taking her medication and looking after herself, but I'd appreciate it if you could keep an eye on her. She respects you and I'm sure she'd take your concern to heart."

Struck dumb by such an unexpected request, Jocelyn wondered just exactly what sort of a guardianship Tewes was soliciting. His naiveté concerning the delicate nature of the relationship between star and understudy seemed endless.

A checkered taxi pulled up to the curb before Jocelyn had time to mutter more than a feeble, "I . . . uh, I'll do what I can, Harry, but I don't . . ."

Handing Sybil Stearns into the cab with infinite care, Harold Tewes turned back to Jocelyn and said, "Thank you, Jocelyn. I know I can depend on you. I always said you'd be a big asset to the show and you are, in more ways than you know."

With that cryptic adieu, Tewes snapped the door shut and the taxi sped off down Forty-seventh Street leaving a stupefied Jocelyn in its wake. She turned and entered the foyer of the Ambassador. Ordinarily she would have entered through the backstage door via the side alley, but her agent had requested that she reserve him two seats for opening night. Despite her certain knowledge that Albert would be more interested in who was in the audience than in her performance, Jocelyn dutifully approached the box office window and set aside the last house seats available.

She pushed open the lobby doors and plunged into the darkness of the inner house. Two figures standing by the deserted lobby bar sprang apart at her approach. As they stepped from the shadows into the shaft of an exit light, Jocelyn discerned a mildly disconcerted John Baron and Paul Radner. Even in the dim light she recognized Harriet Weldon's angelic offspring, despite the fact that his outfit— tight jeans and an even tighter T-shirt—was a good deal more provoc- ative than the one she had last seen him in. John Baron gave Jocelyn a look that was both ironic and pleading. Turning toward the boy, he said, "The trademark of the true professional is a nicely timed en- trance. Miss O'Roarke is a true professional . . . aren't you, Josh?"

"Well . . . I do have a somewhat shabby reputation to uphold, don't I?" Moving on briskly in hopes of remaining ignorant of things she did not wish to know, Jocelyn asked, "Do either of you know where Max is? I'm supposed to run lines with him."

"I think he must still be onstage. Mother was cloistered up there with him a few minutes ago. I hope she hasn't left the man totally de- pressed."

It wasn't the clothes alone that had changed since the last time Jocelyn had seen Paul Radner; there was a new arch to his brow and curve to his upper lip. Despite his sarcasm and precocious sophis- tication, he still exuded a potent charm judging from John Baron's enraptured gaze. "Poor John," thought Jocelyn, "he's really fallen down the well this time."

Jocelyn, with her back to the stage, saw both their expressions si- multaneously assume a masklike quality as soft footsteps came up the center aisle. Filled with sudden apprehension, she turned to ob- serve the approach of a bilious-looking Harriet Weldon. For the past week Jocelyn had noticed a mounting tension in her, but that was nothing compared to this present state; her whole body was a study in rigid self-control. Yet, as she drew near the trio, she managed to summon up her characteristic smile of noblesse oblige.

"Paul dear, I thought you had a lecture to attend at Fordham this afternoon. Aren't you going to be late?"

"No, Mother, it's not until two. I just wanted to see how they were coming along with the set."

"That's sweet of you, dear . . . but hardly necessary. I think we can trust Mr. Baron to keep things well under control, can't we, John?"

The subtext of Harriet's question was lost on no one, least of all John Baron, who flushed uncomfortably as he lit a cigarette.

"So, Paul, if you have time to kill before your lecture, perhaps you could stop by a hardware store and get me some pink light bulbs for my dressing room?"

Paul mumbled his acquiescence and sullenly departed, but not without shooting his mother a spiteful look as he passed through the lobby doors. An awkward silence ensued until Jocelyn made her excuses and left in search of Max Bramling, leaving John and Harriet frozen in stances of silent confrontation.

"Ready to run lines, Max?"

A thoroughly dejected Max Bramling looked up from his open script.

"Oh, Josh, hi . . . I sure am. Thanks for coming in early."

"No problem. Let's get started, okay?"

Jocelyn pulled up a chair opposite Bramling and they ran crisply through the scene. Bramling was letter-perfect and never once glanced at his script. When they had finished, Jocelyn looked up at the veteran actor and said, "You're fine, Max. You got nothing to worry about."

"You think so, Tidbit? I hope you're right. You know, this is the best script and the best part I've come across in the past ten years. I don't mind telling you, it's been a godsend, but I can't help feeling that it could all go up in smoke if we don't pull off this scene—the whole second act hinges on it! And frankly, Josh, I'm at the end of my rope."

Jocelyn leaned toward Max and gave one of his large freckled hands an encouraging squeeze. He met her gaze, his eyes filled with a silent beseeching, as she searched for the right words of reassurance.

"Max, you've got to go easy on yourself! You can't take responsibility for the scene, or the act, or the whole damn production. You're only responsible for finding your characterization and making sure it serves the script. And I can tell you, your Judge Castle is so solid it could give the Rock of Gibraltar a complex."

The lines around Bramling's bloodshot blue eyes crinkled as he smiled at Jocelyn. "O'Roarke, you make me understand how the Irish survived all those potato famines."

"Well, you know the old saying, Max: 'God invented whiskey so the Irish wouldn't rule the world.'"

A new voice chimed in, "Then He must have invented champagne so the French wouldn't tell us how to pronounce everything."

Jocelyn grinned at Austin Frost as he entered through the wings with a script under his arm. He acknowledged her with a perfunctory smile, but his Eeyore-like face wore a dolorous expression. It appeared to Jocelyn as if she and Kevin Kern were the only two who'd had an even remotely cheerful morning. Strength was lent to her supposition by the clamoring tones of Charlie Martin reverberating from the back of the house.

"Damn it, John! Don't they have those Fresnels hung *yet?*"

He was answered by Baron's calm but plaintive drawl. "The crew's been working since eight this morning, Charles. They're on a break . . . The Fresnels will be in by tonight's run-through, don't worry."

"Well, I hope to God you're right. There'll be no point in teching the damn show if those Fresnels aren't in . . . I want to get through all of Act Two before we break for dinner."

Kevin Kern burst through the lobby doors just then, looking like the cock of the walk. Oblivious to his co-workers' moods, he greeted them expansively.

"Top of the morning. What a gorgeous day, eh? Awful to be stuck inside on a day like this, isn't it?"

"Yeah, dreadful—unfortunately that's what we're being paid for," snapped Charlie Martin. "You're late, Kevin. We're setting up for Act Two, in case you've forgotten. Can we have everyone in place, please?"

Kevin gave Martin a surprised but not particularly offended glance and sauntered nonchalantly onto the stage. Passing by Jocelyn he whispered, "Tell me, am I being paranoid or is everyone a bit uptight today?"

"You're not paranoid. Take a look at Charlie; he looks downright dyspeptic. I'm afraid he may start quoting Chekhov any second now."

"Charlie's got problems."

"What do you mean?" she asked, suddenly alert.

"Nothing." Kevin avoided Jocelyn's inquisitive gaze as Peter Morrance called places for the second act. "Well, I guess there's nothing for it but to 'strut and fret our time upon the stage' . . ."

Jocelyn gasped, "Kevin!"

"What? Oh, hell, I did it, didn't I? I'm as bad as Harold. I quoted that damn play! *Merde!* Don't tell anybody, Josh. Okay?"

"Course I won't, Kevin. But somehow I can't help feeling that I'd like this day to be over."

Soon enough she would wish that it had never begun.

CHAPTER 13

Several hours later Jocelyn sat crouched in the wings, like an ostrich fervently wishing for a pail of sand. Charlie Martin was working like a demon in what was obviously a last-ditch effort to reshape the floundering scene between Max and Harriet; he adjusted blocking, changed line-readings and harped relentlessly on pace and timing but still there were moments that would not coalesce, connections that were not being made. Austin, who had spent the first forty minutes of rehearsal wretchedly pacing the aisles, had finally stepped outside to chain-smoke, and Max Bramling's face was beginning to resemble that of an aging samurai resolved on hara-kiri as his only honorable solution. Harriet was being very serious and subdued, though her air of martyred politeness seemed to suggest that "certain people" were making things unnecessarily difficult.

"Harriet, I asked you to stay upstage of Max for this speech. You keep trying to come downstage by inches every other line."

"I'm sorry, Charles. But it's very hard to confront a man's *back!* I feel very disconnected to the moment the way it is now."

"Well, I'm sorry too, dear. But for this particular speech it's more important for the *audience* to confront Max than for you to. Unless you'd like to play the whole thing downstage of Max with your back to the house—if that would help you feel more 'connected'?"

A dubious note came into Harriet's voice, which lent her next remark an ominous edge. "I'll do it the original way. After all, you're the director."

They finished the rest of the scene without further interruption from Martin, who stood, white-faced and tight-lipped, in front of the proscenium. After a ten-minute break they began the final scene between Harriet and Kevin, during which matters progressed from bad to worse. Kevin, whose initial bonhomie had been gradually eroded by the oppressive atmosphere, was less than his usually brilliant self. Harriet, barely able to conceal her fit of pique, started the scene with a vengeance and proceeded to chew up the scenery for the first ten minutes until Martin was forced to stop her. He strove to keep his voice low and deferential.

"Uh . . . Harriet, don't you think you're rushing it a little? We've got a good six pages till the actual climax and you're leaving yourself no place to go. Also you've got your face . . . uh . . . sort of screwed up. It makes you look . . . ah . . . a little pained and tense, dear."

Jocelyn watched, fascinated against her will, as a kaleidoscope of expressions passed across Harriet's face before she settled on dignified indignation.

"For heaven's sake, Charles, I don't know how else you expect me to look with these god-awful lights glaring in my eyes! I don't think there's a gel on a damned one of them. It really makes things quite impossible!"

There was nothing Charlie Martin could do but call over his shoulder to John Baron.

"John, aren't there gels on all these lights?"

Reluctantly, John sauntered out from the darkness of the lobby into the house. "About half of them are and half of them aren't yet. It'll all be done by tonight, Charles."

"Well, please make sure that it is. Meanwhile—Peter! Can we have the lights lowered a bit, please?"

While they paused to adjust the lights, after Harriet's handy piece of "divert-and-conquer," the stage door man walked out from the wings and announced, "Phone call for Miss Weldon. Shall I take a message?"

"No, I'll take it—if that's alright with you, Charles. I assume it will take them a few minutes to get the lights right."

"Go right ahead, Harriet," he said dully. "Peter can fetch you when we're all set up again."

After Harriet had exited up the back stairs to the pay phone on the second-floor landing there was an immediate sense of relief among the remaining company members. Everyone brightened a bit except for Charlie Martin, who seemed to be sinking into a morass of misery, and Kevin Kern, who simply rocketed back to his earlier high spirits.

"Listen, Charlie old boy," he said, "I've got this great idea for a bit of business when Lindsay and I are at the desk together going over the judge's papers. What if I start out standing behind her chair handing her the papers over her shoulder, so neither one of us can gauge the other's reaction? Might make a nice, say, pictorial inverse of that moment in the last scene when Max is downstage of Harriet, don't you think?"

Instantly seeing the potential of his idea, Jocelyn nonetheless waited for Charlie to snap the audacious actor's head off. But Kevin's enthusiasm was so infectious and his idea so intriguing that a flicker of interest was kindled in the weary director's eyes. However, he replied with reserve, "It's not a bad idea, Kevin. I just don't know if it would be wise to spring anything new on Harriet just now. She might get a little . . . thrown by it."

With a mischievous twinkle in his eye, Kevin, who was not about to be dissuaded, pressed on, "Well . . . why not seize this opportunity to give it a whirl? Jocelyn can mark it with me, can't you, Josh? If you like it, maybe we can try it with Harriet—a bit later on." Kevin was, after all, no fool.

Charlie turned his questioning gaze to Jocelyn.

"What do you say, Josh—want to give it a try?"

"Why . . . sure, Charlie. Kevin, where do you want to take it from?"

Jocelyn was vaguely reluctant to take her place onstage, so great was her sense of courting disaster. Despite her apprehension, the scene took off almost as soon as Kevin gave her the cue. The effect of Kevin's presence behind her, flicking pages into her hands with a razorlike precision, lent a taut and kinetic drive to their exchange.

Charlie Martin paced back and forth in front of the stage with more animation than he had exhibited all afternoon as the scene crackled along, but suddenly a deep, hoarse voice broke in, which was terrible in its controlled calm and fury.

"Just *what* is going on?"

A dozen pairs of eyes flew to the back of the stage where Harriet Weldon stood, framed in the backstage doorway with one arm dramatically pressed against the doorjamb, though this time Jocelyn felt sure it wasn't just for effect. Judging from the other woman's stormy brown eyes, and lips which were compressed into a single thin line, it was apparent to Jocelyn that Harriet had finally stepped over some boundary that Deborah Kerr had never crossed.

"Is it your policy, Charles, to only let understudies in on major scene changes? Or were you going to have Peter notify me of the adjustments sometime during dinner break?!"

With the palms of his hands extended full-front Charles approached his star appeasingly. "Harriet, we were only trying something out. Kevin had an idea . . ."

"I'm well aware that Mr. Kern is chock *full* of 'ideas' for this production, but whether they're aimed at enriching the script or his love life is another matter, don't you think?"

Barely able to believe what she was hearing, Jocelyn gripped the edge of the table as a wave of nausea passed over her; at the same time she was comforted by a strange sense of release as she thought, "This is it—this is the sound of the other shoe falling. It's ugly, but this is the worst that it can get . . . and then it will be over." Charlie and Kevin began to speak at the same time.

"That's hardly fair."

"Harriet, don't . . ."

With uncaring scorn, she said, "Don't *what*, Kevin?! Don't take the spotlight off your Sunday matinee savior? It's a shame, Kevin, that you can't act comfortably across from anyone who isn't a close intimate."

Charlie Martin's pallor stood out in sharp contrast to his shock of black hair as his mouth worked soundlessly. Kevin took two dangerous steps toward Harriet before Jocelyn's tight grip on his wrist halted him. As she rose from the table with an unreal feeling of cold calm and resolution, she began to speak.

"Kevin had an idea for a piece of business, Harriet. Charlie asked me to help while you were on the phone and I obliged. That's all there is to it. And if you make one more derogatory remark, I'll bring you up on charges before Actors' Equity. That's a promise. Charlie, if you need me, I'll be in my dressing room."

There was shocked silence on the stage as Jocelyn made her way past a gray-faced Kevin Kern toward the stairs; she managed her exit nicely considering that her kneecaps had turned to ice water and her limbs to mush. Her only regret was for her previously unblemished employment record; Jocelyn had never been fired from a show and she knew that within the next twenty-four hours, despite any pressures that Austin might exert, she most certainly would be. But all in all it had been worth it. When she reached her dressing room, which was adjacent to Harriet's, she lay down on her lounge and did what she always did in times of crisis; she took a nap. Sixty minutes later Peter Morrance knocked on her door and entered quietly.

"Josh, dear heart, we're breaking for dinner soon."

Groggily, she said, "Thanks, Peter . . . What time is it?"

"About four. You've been up here about an hour . . . Did you sleep well?"

"All things considered, yes I did. Except for some noise from Harriet's dressing room."

"That must have been Paul. He came in a while ago with Harriet's lighting equipment. Listen, Josh, I can't tell you how bad I feel about what happened . . ."

"I know, Peter, it's alright. How did the rest of rehearsal go?"

"About as well as Custer's Last Stand, I'd say. Charlie pulled Harriet aside for a tête-à-tête and I took Kevin into a corner and convinced him that mayhem was not the answer."

"Did things settle down then?"

"No. They lay down and died. Harriet and Kevin gave two of the most embalmed performances I've ever seen and Charlie was totally at a loss. Then at the very end of the scene—out of nowhere—Harriet starts playing Joan of Arc! I swear, she even had her hands clenched behind her back like they were tied to a burning stake, so Charlie had to stop her. When he suggested that she might possibly be overplaying, Harriet charmingly suggested that the speech demanded just such a delivery and if Charles thought it was wrong, Austin would simply have to rewrite it to fit."

"Oh hell!—she didn't?! Was Austin there?"

"Yup—and you know, I've never actually seen anyone turn green before."

"Oh no, a sort of pea soup color?"

"Almost exactly, I'd say."

"That's bad—that's bile. Austin's gorge only rises once every nine years, but when it does it's awful. And it's such a lovely monologue besides—it must have killed him! What did he do?"

With infinite simplicity, Peter laid a hand on Jocelyn's shoulder and looked her in the eyes, saying, "My dear, if you were going to have a baby and the doctors told you it would have to be born missing two fingers or be stillborn, what would you say?"

"Sorry—dumb question. Where's Austin now?"

"Onstage, working on the monologue. He heard about what happened, of course, and I think he'd like to see you."

"Oh, Peter, I just can't right now . . . when we're both feeling so awful. I don't want to make him feel worse than he must already. Let me just slip out the alleyway and get a quiet bite to eat, okay?"

"Whatever you say, Josh. Try to take it easy, old girl . . . Try to think of it as a poker hand, if you can."

Jocelyn chuckled ruefully. "That's easy enough—it's that same sensation that you get when you don't draw to an inside straight on your last card."

"But it's how you play the hand, too . . . and you played yours just fine, Josh. You did what you had to."

"Peter, you're a treasure. Now go and get yourself some dinner, and give my love to Carrie."

"I will. Take care."

No sooner had Peter left the dressing room than there was another tap on the door. Before Jocelyn could answer, Kevin Kern slipped into the room, looking as ghastly as it is possible for someone with flawless features to look. He took two tentative steps toward Jocelyn before something in her demeanor stopped him short; perhaps he intuited her mood. He spoke in a low voice, damped down with misery.

"God, Josh, you must hate me—I feel like a friggin' Judas!"

With a gentle laugh, she said, "Oh, Kevin, it's not all *that* bad. I have no intention of being crucified!"

"I don't know how you can joke about it. It was all my fault, and you took the brunt of it while I stood there like a jerk and let that bitch humiliate both of us! I could strangle that woman. Christ—to think I once—"

"Once what?"

"Nothing. It doesn't matter now. What matters is that I square things with you, Josh. I'm going to quit the show."

"You'll do no such thing! Forgive me, my sweet, but you're being a bit melodramatic. Every show like this has one big blowup at some point. Harriet just happened to hit on me and I dealt with it the only way I could—and, believe me, I'm old enough to accept the consequences. What's important now is that the incident end and the show, as they say, go on. If you quit it would leave Austin in the lurch and I just won't have that!"

"You're a formidable woman sometimes, O'Roarke. You know that? I bow to your wishes—now come have dinner with me."

Deft an actor as he was, Jocelyn still detected a tinge of relief in Kevin's beguiling smile. Despite her recent nap, she suddenly felt tired all over.

"Thanks, Kevin. But I'll pass if you don't mind . . . I just need to be alone for a bit to sort things out."

"Alright, Josh. Whatever you say. It's just that . . . I'd hate to see things spoiled between us because of one woman's stupidity and pettiness. I'll never forgive her if that happens—never!"

Jocelyn thought it highly unlikely that Harriet would ever deign to ask for Kevin's forgiveness but forebore mentioning it.

"Don't worry, love. That won't happen. Now go and get yourself something to eat. You've still got a long night's work ahead of you."

"I hope so, Josh . . . I do hope so."

After Kevin's departure, Jocelyn gathered up her book and her purse and made her way stealthily down the corridor so as not to attract attention, most especially Harriet's, whom Jocelyn could hear moving about in her dressing room. She was just about to head down the stairs to the backstage exit when she spied something out of the corner of her eye. She crossed toward the pay phone in the corner of the second-floor landing and stooped to pick up a small plastic vial lying on the floor between the phone and a water fountain. There was a label on the side bearing the legend "Alpert Pharmacy"; neatly typed below was the inscription, "H. Weldon—Coumadin—5 mg. One tablet each day." Absently shaking the bottle, which was nearly empty, Jocelyn wondered what she should do. If Harriet hadn't yet taken her pill for the day, she would certainly need it by that night's rehearsal but, despite Harold's earlier exhortations, Jocelyn felt that she would just as soon walk into a den of theatre critics as knock on Harriet's door at that particular moment. Slipping the vial into her bag, she resolved to hand it over to Peter Morrance when he returned from dinner.

Six o'clock found Jocelyn sitting on the end of the Forty-third Street pier feeding the last of her dinner, a fat and greasy pastrami sandwich, to some scruffy-looking sea gulls, as she debated, for the fiftieth time, whether it would be better to wait for them to hand her a pink slip or simply to go back to the theatre and tell Peter that she was quitting the show. The "fighting Irish" in her objected strenuously to a meek acceptance of defeat, but her Gallic sense of tact wished to spare her old friend Austin any further pain and embarrassment. After all, she probably wouldn't have gotten the part in the first place if it hadn't been for Austin's intervention. Still, it rankled that Harriet was to be allowed to get away with such atrocious and unprofessional behavior.

The French and Irish factions were still waging war as Jocelyn made her way back to the theatre. She was on the verge of resorting to the old flip-of-the-coin solution when she reached the corner of Eighth Avenue and Forty-eighth Street and stopped dead. Looking up the block toward the Ambassador, she saw an ambulance and half a dozen patrol cars parked in front of the theatre. Fighting a paralytic sense of foreboding, Jocelyn broke into a full run. The ambulance was just pulling away from the curb as she reached the theatre. Yanking open one of the swinging doors, she stepped into the foyer and saw Harold Tewes and Austin standing side by side; both men looked totally drained of color and Austin seemed barely to recognize her as she crossed to him and put a hand on his shoulder.

"Austin, what's wrong? What's happened?"

Gradually becoming aware of her presence, Austin turned his stricken gaze toward Jocelyn.

"Josh? Oh, thank God, it's you . . . I didn't know . . . I . . ."

"Austin! What is it?"

"We went up together . . . knocked on the door . . . but she didn't answer . . . you . . . she didn't . . ."

Austin started shaking his head slowly back and forth. Jocelyn shot a questioning glance at Harold Tewes, who looked at her gravely and with infinite sadness, and said, "She's dead, Jocelyn. I'm sorry . . . I . . . Harriet's dead, you see."

CHAPTER 14

"So you spent your dinner break sitting on the Forty-third Street pier, Miss O'Roarke. Was anyone with you?"

"Just a few derelict sea gulls as far as I know, Sergeant."

Detective-Sergeant Phillip Gerrard sat opposite Jocelyn in the small office which occupied one end of the theatre's foyer and was usually reserved for the business manager. Jocelyn, among the last to be questioned, found herself giddy with fatigue, which she recognized as the aftermath of shock, and fought back an inappropriate and nearly hysterical need to be flippant by concentrating on the man sitting across from her.

Gerrard, with hands searching the pockets of an immaculately tailored overcoat, sat chewing furiously on a toothpick while regarding Jocelyn's lit cigarette with the unconcealed longing of a recently reformed two-pack-a-day man. A short, broad-shouldered man with short-cropped, jet-black hair and a hawklike nose, he seemed to be the perfect amalgamation of Tyrone Power and Charles Aznavour, save for his penetrating gray eyes, which were as incisive as those of a brain surgeon.

"Do you usually walk to that pier on your dinner break?"

"Not usually, no."

"Did you meet anyone as you were going out of the theatre?"

"Not a soul. I left through the back alley."

"About what time was it when you left?"

"I'm not exactly sure . . . I didn't wear a watch today. But Peter Morrance came up to my dressing room around four and we spoke for a moment. Then Kevin Kern stopped by on his way out, so I'd guess that it was close to four-thirty by the time I finally gathered up my things and went out."

Gerrard glanced down at a notebook lying on the table in front of him as he rummaged through his pockets for a fresh toothpick.

"Mr. Kern said that he invited you to have dinner with him but you declined. Any particular reason why you opted for the sea gulls?"

She studied Gerrard's face intently, searching for some clue as to how much he had heard about her run-in with Harriet during rehearsal, but Phillip Gerrard possessed the perfect poker face and Jocelyn, realizing that she could not even guess the man's age much less his thoughts, took a deep breath and prepared to lay her cards on the table.

"I just needed to be alone for a bit—I had some decisions to make."

"About what, if you don't mind my asking?"

"About the show. I was debating whether or not to quit the play or wait to be given my walking papers."

Surprised by this unexpected candor, Gerrard shot her an appraising glance, and she felt some measure of perverse satisfaction at having momentarily disrupted his stoicism.

"What made you so sure that you were about to be fired, Miss O'Roarke?"

"I hope you'll forgive my presumption, Sergeant, but I think you already have a pretty fair idea why." She took his silence to indicate assent and pressed on. "If you want me to recap everything that happened at this afternoon's rehearsal, I will . . . but before I tell you a lot of things I think you already know, I wonder if you'd mind telling me something I *don't* know?"

"What's that, Miss O'Roarke?"

"Well, everybody in the company's pretty shaken up right now and no one's been able to tell me exactly how Harriet . . . how Miss Weldon came to . . . Christ! I'm lousy at euphemisms—how did she die, Sergeant?"

For the first time in the course of their interview a recognizably human expression crossed Detective-Sergeant Gerrard's face and it was one of quiet amusement. Nonetheless he took a full minute of silent self-consultation before replying in a dry and colorless voice.

"Very well, Miss O'Roarke, these are the facts as we know them: Mr. Tewes arrived at the theatre at approximately five forty-five to take his wife to her doctor's appointment. He stopped briefly at the box office to see how the advance sales were doing; when he entered the house he found Mr. Frost sitting in the first row of the orchestra —working on rewrites I believe. Mr. Frost told him something about the . . . incidents that had taken place during rehearsal and Mr.

Tewes suggested that they should both go upstairs to see Miss Weldon. They knocked on her dressing room door several times and, receiving no answer, they entered the room. Miss Weldon was lying on her back on the floor by an overturned chair.

"There was a broken light bulb on the floor about a foot from the deceased's right hand. We won't know the exact cause of death until we get the coroner's report, of course, but on the face of things, I'd say that she died of a brain hemorrhage resulting from a blow to the back of the skull."

"But that means . . . it was an accident, wasn't it?"

"So it seems, but even accidents have to be inquired into, you know."

"Yes, I know . . . I also know a few things about subtext, Sergeant. You just placed a particular accent on the word 'seems.' Any particular reason for it?"

There was a partial thawing of Detective Gerrard's features as a slow smile spread across his face; his voice, however, maintained its edge.

"Do you know what the floors of those dressing rooms are made of, Miss O'Roarke?"

"Cement. Why?"

"Cement is very hard stuff; it tends to crack things that fall against it. But there was no fracture to the skull."

"Is that so odd? It's just a short fall from the chair to the floor. She might have put an arm out to break the fall, too, and that would have lessened the impact."

"That's possible, yes."

"But obviously not probable in your eyes. What else?"

"What's located on that corridor besides dressing rooms?"

"Well . . . there's the pay phone at the top of the landing. And a shower and toilet between my dressing room and . . . oh, and there's a utility closet between Max Bramling's dressing room and Harriet's."

"What's in the closet?"

"I haven't the foggiest."

"Allow me, then."

So saying, Phillip Gerrard opened a drawer in front of him and removed a small sack-like object, which he placed on top of the desk. The Ambassador was one of the few older Broadway theatres which had not converted to the counterweight method of flying flats and scrims and still used sandbags as counter-ballast. On the desk lay a five-pound sandbag, commonly used to prop behind standing flats. Jocelyn noticed a small tear on the side of the sack and looked inquisitively at Gerrard.

"That closet is filled with buckets and brooms and a small pile of these bags."

"So?"

"Well, it's a small thing, I'll grant you, Miss O'Roarke, but we did find traces of sand on the floor of Harriet Weldon's dressing room."

CHAPTER 15

It was nearly eleven o'clock when Jocelyn took her leave of Detective Gerrard, who remained in the business manager's office, making tiny pyramids out of the contents of the sandbag. She had found his last question most unsettling.

"Tell me, Miss O'Roarke, with Miss Weldon . . . gone, will you be playing her part in the show?"

She had replied, quite honestly, that she had no idea what the future status of the production, let alone the casting of the Lindsay Harding role, would be. But Jocelyn had read enough detective fiction to realize that, if Harriet's death was not purely accidental, her own name was bound to be high on the police list of those who had sufficient motive and ample opportunity. She entered the foyer with a troubled mind and heavy heart.

Most of the company, including Kevin Kern, had been dismissed by the time they had gotten around to Jocelyn, but as she was about to make her way out onto Forty-eighth Street, she heard a murmur of voices from the inner lobby and went to see who the last hangers-on were. Aside from a few policemen, the only people present were Austin, his gaunt frame pressed against a wall, a cup of coffee clutched in his hands and a cigarette that was one-third ash dangling from his lips; a middle-aged man with thinning blond hair in a rumpled raincoat, whom she did not recognize; and Harold Tewes and Sybil Stearns sitting side by side on a settee at the far end of the lobby. Sybil, who had arrived at the theatre shortly after Jocelyn, was a perfect study in silent compassion and understanding as she sat next to Harold Tewes with one consoling hand on his shoulder. For the first time it became obvious to Jocelyn that her relationship to Tewes was more than that of employee and employer; it appeared that she took his griefs and tribulations to be her own. Austin was the first to speak.

"You look dead tired, Josh . . . How'd it go in there?"

"The usual, I guess—though I have no idea what the usual is in a situation like this. You look like you could do with a twenty-four-hour nap yourself, my dear."

"An excellent idea, Jocelyn. I think we could all do with some rest." This from Sybil Stearns, who rose from the sofa, summoning the last reserves of her formidable self-command to take control of a shaky situation.

"I don't think you've met Harvey . . . Dr. Samuels, that is . . . Harriet's physician. Harvey, this is Jocelyn O'Roarke."

Jocelyn turned to shake hands with the blond-haired man in the wrinkled raincoat, and encountered the saddest pair of watery blue eyes that she had ever seen. His hand was as cold as ice and sweaty at the same time, yet there was something in his wan and tentative smile that kindled an instant liking on Jocelyn's part.

"It's good to meet you, Miss O'Roarke . . . Harold has spoken so highly of you . . . I just wish it could've been under happier circumstances."

"Yes, of course, so do I . . . Well, I think I'd better be going . . . Austin, would you like to share a cab?"

"Thanks, Josh, but I'm spending the night at Harold's."

"Jocelyn, perhaps Dr. Samuels and I could go uptown with you, as we all live on the West Side . . . but let's get Austin and Mr. Tewes off first, shall we?"

As Harold Tewes seemed quite beyond simple speech, let alone decision making, the rest of the party was content to let Sybil Stearns marshal it out onto the street, away from the oppressive atmosphere of the theatre. Remembering her earlier conversation with Harold and Sybil at this same spot, Jocelyn could hardly credit that it had taken place a mere eleven hours ago. She went to embrace Austin before he got into the cab but it was like trying to hug a rod of iron and, as he would not meet her gaze, she simply whispered, "Take care, my dear. I'm here if you need me."

"Oh, Josh!" He squeezed her shoulders, then stepped into the cab, which sped away.

With the departure of Austin and Harold, the awkward trio of semi-strangers made its way over to Eighth Avenue and quickly found a taxi of its own. The ride uptown, which could have been an agony of discomfort, was expertly glossed over by Sybil's gracious thanks to Harvey Samuels and to Jocelyn for "being there for Austin."

This last remark Jocelyn found slightly specious, seeing as she had had no other choice, given the circumstances. Still, she would have accepted the other woman's avowal in good faith had she not caught the look of subtle wariness that Sybil shot her before getting out of the cab on the corner of Fifty-ninth and Eighth Avenue; it was a look not dissimilar to the one Detective Gerrard had given her before he produced the incriminating sandbag. She had already cast herself in the Susan Hayward role in *I Want to Live* when Harvey Samuels' voice broke in on her morbid fantasies.

"You know, I can't help feeling at fault, somehow."

Dumbfounded, she said, "Why on earth should you feel that?"

"I shouldn't have waited so long to do another Protime reading on her. You see, a Protime reading determines . . ."

"I know. My father had blood clots, too. But what does that have to do with Harriet falling off a chair and hitting her head?"

Despite her feeling of camaraderie with the doctor, she still was hesitant to share Detective Gerrard's speculations with him.

"It was so fast, you see."

"What was?"

"The hemorrhaging. She died so quickly—somewhere between four-thirty and five-thirty from what I overheard the police saying. And it was such a short fall—the impact to the skull couldn't have been that great."

Jocelyn, disturbed by how closely Harvey Samuels' thoughts were mirroring those of Detective Gerrard, replied more harshly than she meant to, "But what does that have to do with you?"

"Well, the Coumadin, you see . . . If you know about blood clots you know . . ."

"I know, it allows the blood to flow more freely—but you only had her on five milligrams a day. That's the minimum dosage." In reply to Harvy Samuels' questioning gaze, she added, "Harold told me."

"But you know there are rare cases when a patient can develop a severe reaction to the drug. Though I must say, Harriet showed no signs of it. When Harold brought her to me after that trouble in Boston I considered increasing her dosage, but when I took a Protime reading on her she seemed fairly stable. I thought the leg clots had only kicked up again because she'd been remiss about taking her medication. Harriet was forever doing that, you know; she hated to admit to any kind of physical liability, so Harold's always had to supervise her. Even when she told me that she'd been religious about taking her prescription, I had my doubts . . . She could be like a child sometimes. I should've watched over her more carefully."

Gently, Jocelyn said, "I'm sure you did everything you could. You mustn't torture yourself about it."

"No, I suppose you're right. Well, thank you for letting me unburden myself, Miss O'Roarke. It does help to talk about it to someone . . . I just didn't want to trouble Sybil or Harold, poor fellow. I'm a bit worried about him, you know. He's never been one to show emotion easily; he keeps himself to himself—always did, even when we were at school together. But this is a bit more than one man should have to bear alone—still, he's got Sybil, and I expect she'll get him through this ordeal if anyone can. I just hope I . . . oh, never mind. I'm babbling again. Well, good night, Miss O'Roarke—and thank you once again."

The cab was drawing up to Jocelyn's stop on Central Park West and, by the light of a streetlamp, Jocelyn could see that the doctor's eyes were growing moist and his lower lip was beginning to quiver. Feeling a surprisingly strong wave of sympathy for the older man's distress, she laid a hand upon his sleeve and said, "There's no need to thank me . . . and please, do call me Jocelyn. If you want to talk some more feel free to give me a call. Good night, now."

Slightly embarrassed by her own effusiveness, Jocelyn quickly left the cab and made her way down Eighty-fifth Street. Halfway down the block toward her apartment, she was hit with a sudden flash of intuition: Harvey Samuels had been in love with Harriet Weldon. So certain was she of this hunch and so absorbed did she become in pondering its possible ramifications that she heard no sound behind her as she fitted her key into the downstairs door. She nearly screamed with terror as a hand pressed her shoulder.

"Josh, I had to see you."

"Christ, Kevin! You . . . you nearly frightened me to death! How long have you been here?"

"Not long. When I left the theatre I went to Gallagher's and had a double Scotch—I needed one after talking to that android Gerrard— God, what a creepy character he is! Then I walked all the way up here . . . I need to talk to you, Josh."

"Right now? Kevin, I'm all in. I don't think I can . . ."

"Please, Jocelyn."

Gradually recovering from her shock, Jocelyn was able to discern that Kern was in a bad way indeed; despite the chill of the evening he was bathed in sweat and his eyes seemed twice their normal size. Making a superhuman effort to surmount her desire for rest and solitude, she unlocked the door and told him to come on up.

Once inside, all conversation ceased as Jocelyn, zombie-like, went through the motions of lighting a log in the fireplace and fixing him another tall Scotch. For herself, she poured a glass of beer. An uncomfortable air of restraint caused them to choose opposite ends of her long blue sofa.

"Josh, do you think it was an accident?"

"Oh, Kevin! How on earth do you expect me to know? . . . It *looks* like an accident."

"Well . . . do you think that Gerrard thinks it's an accident?"

"I wouldn't even venture to guess what Gerrard thinks about the weather. He's way too deep for me. But what does it have to do with you?"

"During the dinner break I was still upset about what happened at rehearsal, so I just walked in the park and grabbed a hot dog."

"Did you tell Gerrard that?"

"Of course I did. What choice did I have?"

"Well, you were right to. He's not someone to toy with. But I still don't see what the problem is. Harriet wasn't about to have *you* canned."

"No, of course she wasn't. But, you see, that's part of the trouble."

"Let me freshen your drink. It could only make you more lucid at this point— *What* trouble?!"

Inhaling deeply, he said, "You know I went to the Manhattan School of Theatre? Harriet was on the faculty at that time."

Jocelyn said, "And you were very young and she took an interest and helped you make a few contacts and . . ."

"And we had an affair."

"You what?"

"I should've told you before but I just couldn't, Josh. I didn't know what you'd think."

"But, my God, that was nine years ago . . . you could only have been . . ."

"Twenty . . . and she was thirty-four. God, I was a moron and I thought she was the sophisticated older woman offering new vistas of experience—but it was a pretty hollow passion from the start. I think we both liked the idea of it more than we ever liked each other. I was so damned relieved when it was over, you can't imagine."

"How did you end it?"

"I didn't have to, luckily. After about eight months, Harriet met Harold, whose intentions were far more serious and honorable than mine. She had the good sense to realize it and, because she was most anxious that Harold not get wind of our little liaison, we simply stopped seeing each other. Hell, our paths had only crossed maybe five times over the past nine years and it was always very cordial and politely distant on both our parts . . . at least, until we started rehearsals for this show."

"Then what happened?"

"At first, nothing. But after the first week or so of rehearsals I started noticing the occasional 'meaningful glance'—but it was nothing that I couldn't handle. I just kept playing at being the admiring ex-student. Things got a little stickier at that dinner party. Before you and Austin got there she had me in a corner and started suggesting what a good idea it would be if the two of us got together for lunch to discuss the 'inner workings of our mutual subtext.' I'd sooner sit through an Equity committee meeting. When you and Austin showed I felt literally saved by the bell. I guess it was then that I first started to think of you as my good luck charm, Josh."

"Charmed, I'm sure. What happened after that?"

"Not much until that rehearsal when Charlie started riding Harriet's ass and she tried to pass the buck to me—that was the first time we had lunch together, remember?"

"Oh, I remember all right. Go on."

"Well, the whole stupid scene made me pretty testy and I guess I didn't trouble to hide it much. When I went out to the hall to catch the elevator, Harriet followed me and tried to make some back-assward apology—not really admitting that any of it had been her fault, you understand. She just kept saying that she couldn't bear for there to be a breach between us after 'all we had been to each other.' God, this is embarrassing—it's like a bad forties movie! Anyway, I simply told her that I was just there to do a job and would she please let me get on with it, as there hadn't been all that much 'between us' in the first place and what had happened was best forgotten as far as I was concerned."

"Boy, she must've loved that."

"Well, it was the truth."

"Remind me to explain to you about women someday, Kevin. How'd she take it?"

"She went sort of an ashy gray color and just muttured something between clenched teeth about how important 'cast harmony' was and made her exit. I didn't know whether or not she'd let on to Harold about it but the whole next week I was waiting to see if I'd get the ax."

"But you didn't, so she must've gotten over it."

"Yeah, that's what I thought. She became polite and distant again, which was fine with me except I still had this eerie feeling that she was keeping an eye on me. I'd just about written it off to pre-Broadway paranoia until we got to Philadelphia."

"Why? What happened in Philly?"

"*You* happened, my dear. Remember you spent the night with me after our Philly opening and the next morning when you were getting dressed you accidentally spilled some of my cologne on your blouse?"

"I remember. The spot never came out."

"Good . . . anyway that morning at rehearsal I was standing in the wings with Harriet going over some script changes and you passed by us."

"So?"

"Well, you fairly reeked of Paco Rabanne. Harriet got one whiff of you and her face became the mask of Medusa. I knew then that, despite all your mad stratagems for discretion, our cover had been blown but good."

"God almighty! She must have hated my guts. Why didn't you tell me?"

"I didn't want to upset you. Look, Josh, she *already* hated your guts—ever since you filled in for her in Boston. It was no secret that you gave a better performance on a moment's notice than she'd been able to come up with in three weeks of rehearsal. But I thought your position was fairly unassailable; you had Austin in your corner and, whether you know it or not, Harry Tewes is quite a fan of yours. She couldn't very well go to her husband and tell him that she wanted you dropped from the show because you were sleeping with one of her ex-boyfriends, could she?"

"No, guess not. How much do you think Harry Tewes knows . . . about you and Harriet, I mean?"

"Not a thing as far as I can tell—at least he's never let on to me that he knew about it. No, I think Harriet did an A1 job of sweeping the whole regrettable incident under the carpet. Anyway, Tewes isn't the one I'm worried about; it's Gerrard that's got me scared. If he got wind of my affair with Harriet, he'd have me in the hot seat for sure."

"Kevin, you're dramatizing again. I admit that Gerrard has all the soothing charm of a cobra but the man's not clairvoyant! We're talking about something that happened nearly a decade ago—who's to remember?"

"John Baron."

"What?"

"John used to design sets for some of the major productions at MST. He was there doing a set for *Godot* when Harriet and I were having our little fling."

"Are you sure John knew about it?"

"No, not positive. We were pretty covert about the whole thing. Harriet didn't want to damage her image as Our Lady of Art—hell, she could barely stand to climb down from her pedestal in private. And Harriet made the CIA look like the Hardy Boys. Still, you know what a hotbed of gossip a drama school is—it's like living in a fishbowl. So it's quite possible that John got wind of it."

Lamely, she said, "Well, even if John knew at the time, he might've forgotten all about it by now, you know. It's old dirt."

"Yeah, but I've got an awful feeling that Gerrard's going to help him remember . . . Oh Josh, what am I going to do?"

"Have another Scotch, Kevin."

It was close to 2 A.M. before she got a slightly sodden Kevin Kern out the door and semi-convinced that he was not a major candidate for immediate indictment. Unfortunately, she was unable to perform this neat trick for herself; Jocelyn couldn't suppress the awful fact that, if she were in Detective Gerrard's shoes, she would be the most likely suspect. Those three ugly words, Motive, Means and Opportunity, kept swimming in her brain and, even after she had dragged herself up the ladder to her loft bed and closed her eyes, the saturnine gaze of Phillip Gerrard hovered before her as she unwillingly replayed their entire interview in her mind. Just as the sleep she devoutly desired was almost upon her, one of Gerrard's questions flashed through her head.

"Did you meet anyone as you were going out of the theatre?"

"Not a soul . . ."

No! That wasn't right! She'd been concentrating on people that she knew in the company, people that knew her—but she *had* passed someone in that doorway to the alley. Who was it? Nobody in the cast, certainly, or the tech crew; she knew most of them by sight. Someone else—a man—that was it. A maintenance man in baggy green overalls and with a painter's cap on his head that totally obscured his face. But why totally? Oh yes, he was carrying something —a cardboard box. And he was looking down at it as if it contained something fragile that he didn't want to drop or break; that was why she hadn't seen his face. But if he worked for the theatre or was making a delivery, he could be traced and, once found, he could verify her story for Gerrard. An overwhelming sense of relief swept her almost immediately into slumber but her dreams were troubled by visions of Susan Hayward strapped to her chair in a gas chamber wearing Jocelyn's best Calvin Klein dress.

CHAPTER 16

The morning of Harriet Weldon's funeral was a fittingly gray and gloomy one, accompanied by driving rain and gusty winds that held the first hint of winter's approach. It was four days since the accident; the family (i.e., Cyrus Weldon) had angrily petitioned for the release of the body, to which request the police (i.e., Detective Gerrard) had finally and reluctantly consented. The service was being held in a small and exclusive funeral parlor off Park Avenue. The family had opted for a closed casket—for which Jocelyn was extremely relieved, as she had spent her Catholic childhood standing next to more open coffins than she cared to remember.

The mourners began to take their seats, taking their signal from the approach to the front of the room of Rev. Thurmond Harris.

Between Reverend Harris' singsong tones, the stifling air and the cloying smell of lilies, Jocelyn was in danger of nodding off, so she roused herself to alertness by examining the faces of those around her. In the front row sat a stonelike Harold Tewes beside his father-in-law, Cyrus Weldon, a small, compact man whose deportment was perfectly in keeping with one's image of the scion of a major New York publishing firm. His magnificently full head of silver-white hair was bent upon his chest with what seemed to Jocelyn the weight of grief but not despair, and she remembered the cool and appraising glance he had given her when she'd first entered. In the row behind them sat Austin and Sybil Stearns. Across the aisle sat a distraught Kevin Kern, whose gaze she'd been avoiding for the past hour, and beside him a subdued John Baron and an exceedingly restless Charlie Martin, who kept glancing at his wristwatch. Surprisingly, Paul Radner sat in the last row next to a pale Max Brambling.

"... a fine actress, a devoted daughter and a loving wife and mother, Harriet Weldon played many roles in life, as well as on the stage, and played them all very well—indeed, with grace and caring . . ."

Jocelyn was mentally composing an amendment to the Constitution calling for the separation of Church and Stage when Detective Phillip Gerrard made his silent entry into the parlor and took his place, unobtrusively, in the last row. Gerrard's laserlike gaze swept the congregation and eventually came to rest on Jocelyn's face. Gerrard's brow furrowed slightly as their eyes locked, and Jocelyn recalled their conversation of two days earlier.

"So now you're saying that you *did* see someone as you left the theatre that afternoon. Why didn't you recall this before, Miss O'Roarke?"

"I *told* you! When you first asked me, I was thinking of people I *knew*, within the company or crew, or house staff, even. This was a total stranger—some anonymous delivery man in green overalls and a cap. But he was carrying a box. He must've been making some sort of delivery to the theatre and *somebody* must've taken it from him or signed for it or something. Somebody else had to have seen him. Surely you can find out?"

"We'll certainly try to, Miss O'Roarke."

Now Jocelyn cursed the fact that she was an easy blusher as she suffered under Gerrard's relentless scrutiny. She barely heard Reverend Harris' doleful summation.

The mourners began to disperse. Jocelyn, having previously expressed her condolences to Harold and Paul and feeling badly in need of respite from extended spiritual metaphors, made her way swiftly to the front hallway. Upon reaching the foyer, she found her path blocked by Harvey Samuels in consultation with Detective Gerrard. Gerrard was the first to notice her approach.

"Hello, Miss O'Roarke. Are you going out to the cemetery?"

"No, I can't, I'm afraid. I have an audition at two o'clock."

"For another play?"

"No, for another toilet bowl cleanser."

Gerrard allowed the smallest of smiles to crease his face.

"Perhaps I could give you a lift to wherever your audition is?"

"Thank you but it's hardly necessary, Mr. Gerrard. It's not very far from here."

"But it's still raining and my car's right out front. You don't want to arrive dripping wet. I can see you didn't bring an umbrella."

Deeply mistrustful of Gerrard's gallantry but sensing that any further gainsaying would be useless, Jocelyn allowed herself to be escorted down the steps and into the waiting squad car. As the car pulled away, her last glimpse was of Kevin and Austin standing on the steps looking after her, their faces mirroring a mutual apprehension.

They drove in silence for the first few minutes, though Gerrard's first remark bore out her forebodings.

"We've been making inquiries about your mysterious delivery man, Miss O'Roarke."

"Yes . . . and?"

"We haven't been able to get any confirmation on it. Most of the company had already left for dinner. The crew was busy hanging lights for the evening rehearsal. Mr. Frost doesn't remember seeing anyone, though he went to great lengths to point out that he was so engrossed in his rewrites that, in his words, he wouldn't have noticed if 'Hannibal and all his elephants had trooped across the stage.' And nobody on the house staff signed for any deliveries or recalls seeing anyone of that description. We even questioned Mr. Tewes, in case the man left through the front of the house. We drew a blank there, too."

As Gerrard's last words hung in the air, she stared miserably at the windshield wipers as they ineffectually slapped away at rivulets of water.

Gerrard spoke again in marginally gentler tones. "It might help if you could come up with a more detailed description of the man. Have you remembered anything more since we last spoke?"

Fighting to suppress an overwhelming sense of futility, Jocelyn concentrated hard, but when she finally spoke her voice sounded hollow and thin in her own ears.

"He was a large man—fairly tall and broad, I think. But I didn't get a good look at his face . . . He was wearing that cap that hid his face and he was looking down at the box when I passed him. I think he might have been wearing glasses—the aviator kind—because I couldn't even see his eyes . . . I don't think he was a very young man; the way he moved gave me the impression of someone middle-aged."

She shook her head, trying to jog her memory.

"That's all I can think of. I know it sounds pretty lame—but I *did* see him."

"Well, it's better than nothing, though it doesn't give us much to go on. If you remember anything else, let me know."

They drove on again in silence until Jocelyn was unable to refrain from asking, "Why did you agree to release the body?"

"There was no reason not to. I got the lab report and it told me what I needed to know."

"Which was?"

"Something very small—something that they might've missed if I hadn't specifically asked them to look for it."

Knowing that she was being baited but unable to resist the hook, she took her cue. "And what were you looking for?"

"Sand, Miss O'Roarke. There were a few grains of sand in Miss Weldon's hair and some of it had trickled down between the collar of her blouse and the back of her neck. And it's the same kind of sand that's in those sandbags in the utility closet. It's a minute point but crucial, all the same. Just think, if the murderer had picked up another bag, one with stronger seams, I wouldn't have a case; we'd have called it an accident. But, as it is, I do have a case. Someone killed Harriet Weldon."

Now that it was out in the open, the actual words having finally been said, Jocelyn could still barely grasp the enormity of it. Someone had murdered Harriet and, very likely, someone she knew. All her years of experience in putting herself into imaginary situations and dealing with all the possible ramifications of human behavior still did not prepare her for this icy cold shock. She hardly noticed that the car had drawn to a halt and Gerrard was waiting for her to get out. She fumbled for the door handle but, before she could open it, his voice arrested her movements.

"By the way, Miss O'Roarke, there's something else you might like to know—though I don't know if it's my place to tell you. When we were questioning Mr. Tewes about your delivery man, I asked him what, if any, his plans for the show were. According to him, *Term of Trial* will go on and you're slated to take over Miss Weldon's role. Good day, Miss O'Roarke."

Jocelyn made her way up to the offices of Hanson and Fennell like a person moving underwater. Her hand shook as she initialed the sign-in sheet but the receptionist seemed not to notice as she handed Jocelyn her copy.

After dropping Jocelyn off, Phillip Gerrard started heading uptown. He stared with grim concentration at the wet and glistening road ahead and tried to order his jumbled thoughts as he made his way through the sluggish noonday traffic. His ideas on a case like this usually clicked into place with the well-ordered precision of a computer filing system, and it dismayed him that they refused to do so now. He kept thinking back to his conversation with Sergeant Tommy Zito, his chief aide, during their ride to the funeral parlor.

"I tell ya, Phil, nobody saw a guy with a cardboard box come into that theatre! For my money, there was no guy in green overalls there that afternoon or any other time."

"Why would she lie about it?"

" 'Cause she's rattled and she's tryin' to cover her tracks. Aren't ya always tellin' me that in a case like this, nine times outa ten, the obvious choice is usually the right choice? Well, the O'Roarke dame's got 'obvious' written all over her. Christ! We got her practically handed to us on a goddam silver platter. What more do ya want?"

"Not much. Just a little hard evidence and some logic."

"Logic? Okay, I'll give ya logic. The Weldon broad chews her ass off at rehearsal in front of the whole damn company and she has to stand there and take it. *Plus* she knows that Weldon has enough clout to get her fired and probably will. She's upstairs by herself for at least an hour while the rest of them go on rehearsing and she hears or sees the Radner kid drop off those light bulbs—she already knew that he was going to get them, we got two witnesses to that—the kid and Baron. So she decides to stage a little 'accident.' She picks up one of the sandbags, then she waits around till everybody's gone out for dinner and the deceased is in the next dressing room waiting for her husband. She goes in, maybe on the pretext of patching things up, and when Weldon's got her back turned, she clouts her one from behind. In one move, she not only saves her job and gets her revenge but she also cinches a juicy part for herself into the bargain."

"I still don't like it, Tommy. She's a smart lady. If she wanted to throw us off the track with a fictitious delivery man, she would've mentioned him during her initial questioning—she had enough time to get her story straight before we got to her. Coming back to us with that information later on—it would be a stupid move if she was the murderer. But it rings true to me. An innocent person's initial recollection is usually a little vague but becomes more specific when they make the effort to recall things more exactly. Secondly, as you say, she had a good hour upstairs by herself; even if she had decided to commit the crime at that moment, I think that she's bright enough to have taken the time to choose her weapon well—she would've noticed a weak seam. I think our killer had very little time and picked up the first sandbag that he found. Then there's the time element—Harriet Weldon received a dull blow to the back of her head. O'Roarke knew that Tewes was coming to get his wife. How could she be sure that the woman would hemorrhage so quickly as to be unconscious by the time her husband arrived and unable to give out a final clue as to the identity of her assailant? It's all too iffy and I don't think Jocelyn O'Roarke's an iffy woman. I'm not saying that she's incapable of killing but I think that if she staged an accidental death, she'd do it right."

"But what about her phony delivery man?"

"We don't know for certain that he is phony. There was at least one other person at the theatre besides Miss O'Roarke who might've seen him and wouldn't be able to tell us about it—Harriet Weldon.

"Now think, Tommy! It's a very short distance from that back-stage entrance to those stairs to the dressing rooms. Everybody on stage was busy—it was a madhouse! It's not inconceivable that some-one could come in backstage and go up those stairs unnoticed . . . and, if he got in without being seen, chances are he could've left without being noticed, too."

Tommy Zito ran one stubby hand through his dirty-blond hair and shook his head in disbelief.

"But what about that cardboard box? We didn't find no box in Weldon's dressing room . . . 'cept the box with the light bulbs."

"Exactly. That's another reason why I think Jocelyn O'Roarke's telling the truth. If she were trying to fake an alibi, why not just say that she saw a man—period. Why endow him with an imaginary box that can't be accounted for?"

"But I still say, where's the box?"

"It could be anywhere. We didn't even start looking for it until nearly two days after the murder, and there's garbage pickups every day at the theatre."

"But who would throw it out?"

"The murderer, perhaps . . . especially if he or she had happened to see the man in the green overalls come in."

"Why the hell would he bother?"

With a deep sigh Gerrard said, "To throw suspicion on someone else . . . Look, Tommy, I know I preach a lot about following the obvious leads but there's something about this case against O'Roarke that's just a little too pat—I think she's being set up."

"Phil, listen to yourself. First we're talking about a murder that's been rigged to look like an accident. Now you're sayin' it's all been arranged for the O'Roarke broad to take the rap! Which is it?"

Rankled because he felt forced into a position which gave intuition priority over his jesuitical sense of logic, Gerrard snapped at his friend. "It's *both!* A crime reflects the personality of the criminal. This murder was planned and planned carefully. Hell, if it weren't for a few crummy grains of sand, we wouldn't have jack-shit to hang a case on. It *was* intended to look like an accident but this is a cautious killer, someone who had the foresight to allow for contingencies and was prepared to make them work in his favor. I think Jocelyn O'Roarke is part of his 'Plan B'—that's what I think."

As the two men drove on in uneasy silence, Phillip Gerrard's thoughts were troubled by the vision of a pair of clear hazel eyes staring into his.

CHAPTER 17

By the time Gerrard found an illegal parking place on Madison Avenue, the rain had stopped. A few sickly shafts of sunlight were attempting to dry the puddles on the gray pavement as he made his way to 485 Madison, an impressive office building with a black marble lobby and a full complement of security guards. An elevator soundlessly whisked him to the eighteenth floor, the home of Tewes and Randolph Financiers, where, after a brief word with the receptionist, he found himself in a spacious and well-appointed ante-office and in the presence of Sybil Stearns.

Phillip Gerrard found himself admiring her fine aquiline features and regal bearing. At the same time he noticed that the dark circles under her eyes were even more pronounced then they had been on the night of the murder and that there was a slight hesitancy in her smile. Gerrard shook her hand and tried to suppress the sense of schoolboy awe which she evoked in him.

"Thank you for seeing me this afternoon, Mrs. Stearns. I know this must be a difficult day for you."

"Not so bad, Mr. Gerrard. I wasn't planning on going to the cemetery, in any case. There are several matters which need attending to that I don't want Mr. Tewes to be troubled with when he returns to the office."

"And when do you think that will be?"

"Oh, probably tomorrow or the next day. Immersing himself in his work will give him both a sort of solace and diversion from his grief."

"You seem to understand your boss very well. Tell me, how long have you worked for Harold Tewes?"

"Nearly seven years now. I came to work for him shortly after I came out of retirement . . . after my husband's death. My husband was in the service with Mr. Tewes—in the same outfit overseas. Jacob was always good with his hands and clever with machinery. He worked in the motor pool that Mr. Tewes had charge of and they took quite a liking to each other. Well . . . Harold Tewes is not a man to forget his friends. He wrote to me after Jacob's death and suggested that I might like to come to work for him, as his last secretary had just gotten married and Jacob had always extolled me to him as a . . . a 'paragon of efficiency' was the phrase he used, as I remember. It sounded very like something Jacob would say. That's what I thought at the time and, I suppose, that's largely why I took the position. At any rate, it was one of the kindest letters I had ever received and it came at a time when I was sorely in need of kindness."

This last speech was delivered with such quiet dignity and total absence of self-pity that Gerrard was finding it increasingly difficult to come to the point of the interview.

"Was Mr. Tewes already married to Miss Weldon when you came to work for him?"

"Oh, yes. For nearly two years, I think . . . Why do you ask?"

"I was just wondering if you could tell me a little about what kind of marriage they had."

Instantly Gerrard knew that he had taken a wrong step. An invisible wall of reserve rose around Sybil Stearns, but it was too late for him to turn back now.

Coolly, she said, "I know all about Mr. Tewes's professional affairs but I'm certainly not privy to the nature of his home life."

"I appreciate that, of course. But surely you must have gathered some impressions during your long association. That's all I'm asking about."

"Impressions are all they are, Mr. Gerrard—and even that's an overstatement. But if you insist . . . I think they were quite devoted to each other. Mrs. Tewes was a wonderful hostess to Mr. Tewes's business acquaintances and he was very supportive of her career."

"Supportive enough to finance *Term of Trial,* obviously."

Sybil Stearns chose to ignore this remark and Gerrard decided to try another tack.

"What I really came here for, Mrs. Stearns, was to see if you could help me . . . firm up our facts about Mr. Tewes's movements on the day of the accident. He was, understandably, a bit incoherent when we first questioned him and I didn't want to trouble him again so soon."

"Of course. What would you like to know?"

"If you could just go over what happened after you spoke to Miss O'Roarke in front of the Ambassador."

"Ah, Jocelyn. She's a lovely actress, you know. Her part in the show is rather small but she's quite captivating in it from what I could judge from rehearsals. Have you ever seen her onstage?"

"No, I haven't," he said brusquely. "But, getting back to that day?"

"Oh yes. Mr. Tewes had a business conference at noon down on Wall Street, which I attended with him. After that we returned to the office—about one-thirty, I should say, and ordered out for lunch. We had a lot of dictation to get through. We finished at about three-thirty and I came out here to work on some letters while Mr. Tewes lay down for a nap in his office—he often does that if he has to work late and especially now, since rehearsals started for *Term of Trial*, and he has to be up late into the night."

"When did you next see him?"

"At five-thirty. That's when he asked me to wake him. His wife's appointment with Dr. Samuels was for six-fifteen. Mrs. Tewes didn't have to be back at rehearsal until seven-thirty as she doesn't . . . didn't come on until the second act."

"And where were you while Mr. Tewes was napping?"

"As I said, I was out here working on some correspondence."

"Did anyone come into this office while you were working, or did you leave at any time while Mr. Tewes was napping?"

"I don't believe so, no."

"Well, that's rather interesting, Mrs. Stearns, because we happen to have interviewed a messenger, sent from the Mann and Hilling Trust, who told us that he came over with an envelope around four-thirty. Your receptionist left early that day, if you recall, so he came in here with it and since no one was here, he left it downstairs with the security guard at the desk. How do you account for that?"

Levelly and without missing a beat, Sybil Stearns said, "I'm sorry if I misled you, Mr. Gerrard, but I'm sure that sometime between three-thirty and five-thirty I must've left my desk to visit the ladies' room. As our security staff is very good about intercepting packages for us, I have no qualms about stepping out of the office for a minute."

Demurring in the face of such eminent rationality, Gerrard asked if he might have a look around the offices, and Sybil Stearns gave him a Cook's tour of the world of high finance. So thorough was she that Gerrard found himself worrying that there might be a quiz later on. After her devastatingly precise summation, Gerrard thanked his tour guide and fled to the elevators. As the express elevator whisked him down to the lobby, he entertained a brief fantasy of how it might be possible, with someone like Sybil Stearns on your side, not only to catch up on your laundry, but also to put your income tax records in recognizable order. She was loyal, efficient . . . and Phillip Gerrard didn't believe for a moment that she had gone to the ladies' room.

CHAPTER 18

"I can't go through with this!"

"You have to."

"It's all too morbid."

"It's necessary."

Five o'clock on Tuesday afternoon, two days after Harriet's funeral, it was already getting dark and a strong wind whistled through the revolving doors of Gallagher's as Austin and Jocelyn sat at a corner table, both gripping sweaty margaritas.

There had been a company meeting that morning where a wan Charlie Martin had explained to them that, despite the recent tragedy, Harold Tewes still wanted to see his cousin's play on Broadway. Opening previews would be postponed a week while Jocelyn was put into the Lindsay Harding role and another actress found to take over her part. Jocelyn knew, via the grapevine, that her old role had already been assigned to Trish Hanley, a saucy redhead and Charlie's current bedmate.

And Jocelyn herself, after years of second-string roles, had now been handed a major part in a new Broadway play. Unfortunately, a one-way ticket to the gas chamber was attached to it: a high price to pay for the chance of a kind word from Walter Kerr. This was the source of her altercation with Austin.

"But Austin, didn't you feel how creepy it was at rehearsal?"

"That's only to be expected the first day back."

"But what about Gerrard? Will he let us go on?"

"I don't think Dick Tracy cares what we do, as long as we all stay in town."

"What about the papers?"

"What about them?"

"Oh, come on, Austin, don't be naive! They can't be more than twelve hours behind Gerrard. Do you want to open up *Variety* next week and read a headline that says: SLAIN ACTRESS IN FROST OPUS

REPLACED BY NUMBER ONE SUSPECT? What's going to happen then?"

"We'll sell a lot of tickets."

"My God, you're pretty cold-blooded about the whole damn thing, aren't you?"

Austin downed the last half of his margarita and slammed the glass down on the oak table.

"For chrissake, Jocelyn, if you weren't so bloody paranoid, maybe you could see our viewpoint! In the first place, the police still might decide that it was an accident. In the second place, we have a debt to our investors—not just Harold. Thirdly, you're the only one equipped to take on Lindsay at this point. Fourthly—and I hate to disabuse you of this notion—you are *not* the sole and primary suspect."

"Then who is, pray tell?"

"Any number of people, I should think."

"Care to narrow that down?"

"Oh Lord, you forcing me to make lists?! Well . . . first there's Kevin Kern."

Cautiously, she asked, "Why Kevin?"

"Jocelyn, you must know that gossip, like water, finds its own level. Despite all their precautions, anybody that cared to know found out that Harriet and Kevin had an affair at MST. John Baron told me years ago."

"Does Gerrard know about it?"

"If he's taken a stroll down Broadway lately, he probably does . . . Then there's John Baron . . ."

"John!"

"Sure. Harriet was furious about the little fling he's having with young Paul. Really, Jocelyn, I think you're slipping. If you hadn't been so busy playing Beatrice and Benedict with Kevin all these weeks, you would've noticed Harriet, in her ladylike way, telling John to back off—or else. I think something must have happened up in Boston; John was a wreck that week and I don't think he called Paul once."

Jocelyn had a vivid, unpleasant memory of John's tense and unhappy face as he entered the dressing room that morning to find Harriet on the stepladder. That recollection, coupled with the fact that Paul had been the one to fetch the light bulbs on the day of his mother's death, caused Jocelyn to light her fifth consecutive cigarette off the butt of her fourth and ask, "Austin, I thought you told me that Paul's been out of the closet for quite some time now?"

"From the cradle, I gather. But I'm sure Harriet looked upon it as one long adolescent 'phase.' And I don't think she was prepared to watch him go steady with someone from her own peer group, like John. It makes for a mess and Harriet hated anything messy."

"But John and Paul were with each other in the park for the whole dinner break!"

Austin quelled her protest with a tolerant look and took a calculated pause before replying.

"Exactly. And I'm sure the police figure it one of two ways; either they were together . . . or they weren't."

A pall fell over their conversation as Jocelyn finished the last of her margarita and felt dense—not just because of Austin's information, but because of a nagging sense that there was something very obvious right under her nose. She thought it vaguely had to do with Harvey Samuels and something he had said during their cab ride. Before her thoughts could coalesce, Austin's voice broke in on them.

"And finally . . . there's me."

"You? Austin, don't be daft! What possible motive could you have? You should excuse my bluntness—but playwrights don't murder their meal tickets. Gerrard must know that."

"Yes, but he also knows the contents of Harriet's will."

"Harriet left you money?" Jocelyn gagged on her drink.

"Good Lord, no. Harold might leave me a pittance from his estate—but Harriet, never. She didn't actually *give* me anything, but, you might say, she returned something. Harriet owned the rights—you know, the production rights. In the process of selling my soul to get this play mounted, I signed the rights to *Term of Trial* and about five of my other scripts over to Harriet . . . for life, only to revert back to me after her death. Well, they have . . . reverted. It was mentioned in the will and I'm sure our dashing detective knows all about it."

"But you were downstairs working on the script the whole time—in front of the tech crew!"

"Be real, Josh. The crew was going bananas getting those lights hung. I could have strangled Harriet in the orchestra pit and they wouldn't have noticed."

"But would you take such a crazy risk?"

"Whoever did it took a pretty crazy risk, don't you agree?"

"But what does Harold think? I don't see how he can bear to go on with the show, suspecting that one of us might have killed his wife."

"You must remember that Harold has a monopoly on the adjectives 'staunch' and 'loyal.' Once he commits to something, he stays committed. As to what he suspects—maybe nothing. Right now, as far as I can tell, he's clinging desperately to the fragile hope that the whole thing was a freak accident that the police are blowing all out of proportion. I don't think he can bring himself to think otherwise. Can't blame him really, the alternative's pretty awful."

"And Sybil—what does she think?"

"Sybil's a shrewd lady. She knows Harriet was done in. But I don't think she cares who did it. She simply views the whole incident as some sinister scheme to get at Harold. It's aroused her already acute protective instincts. I figure she plans to keep Harold cordoned off from the rest of the world till the entire thing blows over . . . or die trying."

"Before I forget, Austin, who did Harriet leave her money to? She must've had some money to leave."

"Oh, she had money alright—not nearly as much as Harold, but Harriet's estate was a little over a million dollars and, aside from a few small legacies, half of it went to Harold and the other half to Paul. So now he gets it all in one lump sum instead of the meager pittances Harriet used to dole out to him. He'll probably go out and buy black leather pants as part of his mourning garb."

"There's not much love lost between you two, is there?"

"Paul and I? No, I guess not. When I first started having dinner at Harold's, I received a lot of come hither looks from that Lolita of Christopher Street. Because I make it a rule never to seduce within family circles, I rebuffed him in no uncertain terms. Since then Paul has seized every available opportunity to be spiteful to me. He's a lovely boy but not particularly lovable."

"I wonder what John sees in him? John's such a sweet man."

"Oh, my dear, how you do cling to your innocence. John is indeed a sweet, intelligent, tasteful man—and a lonely one. Knowing all the nasty little facets of Paul's nature, I'd bet he'd still be willing to crawl over hot coals for the boy."

"You think so?"

"This is the voice of rude experience speaking. I *know* so. Just think back to when you were dating that twenty-two-year-old folk-singer with the raven locks."

"You have a hateful memory, Austin. I think we need another round."

Austin was in the process of ordering when Jocelyn heard herself paged to come to the phone. When she returned there were two frosty new margaritas on the table. She sat down heavily.

"I'm afraid we're going to have to chug these, Austin."

"How come?"

"That was your cousin, our producer, on the blower. He's working late at his office and he asked, quite nicely, if I could stop by on my way home for a little chat."

"Well, I'll be blowed. What could he want?"

"I don't know. Nothing . . . or maybe just my head on a platter."

"God, are you getting paranoid again, Josh?"

She answered rhetorically, "Is the dollar shrinking?"

Six o'clock found Jocelyn signing in at the security desk in the same black marble lobby that Phillip Gerrard had passed through three days earlier. She found Harold Tewes perched on his secretary's desk in the ante-office studying an appointment calendar, which he snapped shut upon Jocelyn's arrival.

"Ah, here you are. It was good of you to come, Jocelyn. Would you mind too much stepping into my office while I make a last call out here? I'll be with you in just a minute."

She gave a weak smile and made her way to the inner office. Once there she was struck by the complete disparity between the outer office and Harold's inner sanctum. Outside everything had been sleek and spare and very modernistic but Tewes's private domain was a return to the strictly traditional. With its mahogany desk and heavy curtains, it was the incarnation of Jocelyn's image of Judge Castle's chambers, save for the extra door on the left-hand side of the room. It was through this door that Harold Tewes made his entrance.

Tewes looked marginally better than he had the day of the funeral but, as he crossed to the teakwood cabinet to pour brandy into huge snifters, Jocelyn saw that his hands were unsteady. She took one of the crystal globes from his hand and waited for him to make the first move. It was a long wait.

He stood a few feet in front of her chair, with one large hand on his massive desk and the other holding the brandy snifter, staring deep into its depths as if gazing into a crystal ball, his face a study in pain and perplexity. Jocelyn didn't speak for fear of disrupting his train of thought. Finally Tewes broke the silence; he spoke quietly, and without taking his eyes from his glass.

"You must forgive me, Jocelyn, I'm having a little trouble absorbing facts lately. This whole horrible affair just has me . . . bewildered."

"That's more than understandable, Harold," she said kindly. "You'd hardly be human if you felt otherwise."

Tewes took a sip of brandy and began pacing the room.

"But the police—that Gerrard fellow—why is he so certain it wasn't an accident? It seems to me that they have precious little to go on."

"I don't know that they're all that certain," Jocelyn lied smoothly. "And yes, it's true they don't have much to build a case on. Still, it's their job to check out all possibilities . . . that's all they're doing."

Harold shook his head like a dog worrying a bone.

"But all these questions they ask! What's the point of them? They asked me about this delivery man of yours, Jocelyn. Why is that so important? It could've been anyone . . . one of the lighting crew that you just didn't recognize, perhaps?"

"I know the lighting crew pretty well, Harold . . . and the reason it's important for them to ask is because it establishes whether I have an alibi or not."

"But that's nonsense! Why should you need an alibi? Or anyone else connected with the show, for that matter. So you and Harriet had a little run-in. So what? Harriet was extremely nervous about the opening, she always got that way. But we would've talked it out and she would've come around. It wasn't that big a deal."

Dryly, she said, "I don't think the police have your degree of good faith in these matters."

"But that's just the problem, Jocelyn, don't you see? They don't have any understanding of the temperaments and personalities they're dealing with . . . artistic personalities. In the theatre, mountains usually resolve themselves into molehills after a day's cooling off period. I don't believe there's a single person in the company who ever meant Harriet any harm. Naturally, in any group of creative people, there will always be one or two slightly unstable or highstrung individuals, but that doesn't mean anything."

Alert and curious, she asked, "And who would that be?"

"What?"

"The 'unstable' element in *our* cast? Who were you thinking of, Harold?"

Tewes was embarrassed. "Oh, I didn't really mean . . . I was just talking off the top of my head."

Knowing that she was pressing her luck, but sensing that there was something vital to be learned, Jocelyn forged on boldly. "Were you, really? Somehow, I don't think so, Harold."

Reluctantly, he said, "Well, I don't know if Gerrard's aware of it—not that there's any reason he should be—but there *is* Charles Martin."

"Charlie? What about him?"

Tewes finally wrested his gaze from his brandy snifter and shot Jocelyn a quizzical glance.

"Don't you know about Charlie?"

Jocelyn merely raised her hands to indicate ignorance and waited while Harold seated himself in a leather armchair and lit a cigar. Very ill at ease, he said, "Well, you know Charles had a very big hit with *Twinks* two years ago?"

"Yes. I think 'blockbuster' would be the correct adjective."

"Exactly. They made a fortune off that show and still are. It's on tour all over the country right now and still running over on Forty-third Street. Anyway, it made Charles the golden boy of Broadway for a while there. He had carte blanche on his next production, *Songs of the Homeland*. But that didn't go so well."

"No, it didn't. The operative word there was 'bomb'—which teaches us all a lesson about casting dark Hungarian film actresses in light, musical comedy. But what of it?"

"Oh, nothing as far as the backers were concerned. Most of them had had money in *Twinks* and this gave them a nice juicy tax write-off. But, from what I gather, the whole rehearsal experience was a nightmare from beginning to end and Charles took it pretty hard."

"How hard?"

"Well, the reviews were fairly dreadful and most of them blamed the whole fiasco on Charlie. It was a pretty dramatic fall from grace after *Twinks*, you realize.

"After *Songs of the Homeland*, Charles had what I guess you'd term a minor nervous breakdown. He was shipped off to the Bahamas for three weeks and, when he came back, he went immediately into therapy. Turns out he's something of a manic-depressive. I think he takes lithium to help him even his keel."

Jocelyn asked bluntly, "Then why did you hire him?"

"He's a good director; they're not so easy to come by. As for his personal problems, he'd been in therapy for over a year and it seemed that a non-musical script would be just the ticket for him to make his comeback with. I've checked with his doctor and he's kept up his therapy all through rehearsals—even to the point of making long-distance calls when the show was on the road—and, it seems to me, he's been coping well all along."

In her mind's eye Jocelyn saw a montage of Charlie Martin over the past four weeks: Charlie perched on the balls of his feet at the edge of the stage; Charlie trying to reason with Harriet, hands jammed deep into his pockets; and Charlie endlessly running his fingers through his hair as each and every member of the company came to him with their problems. He'd been coping alright, but just barely. The pattern made sense now, and she had a strong hunch that Kevin had known about Charlie's problems from the beginning and had not seen fit to let her in on them. She was torn between admiring his powers of discretion and resenting his obvious lack of faith in hers. Eventually she gathered that Harold was waiting for her to say something reassuring, but unfortunately what she came up with was, "Where was Charlie during the dinner break that day?"

A fleeting look of surprise and pain crossed Tewes's face, but he recovered quickly.

"Why—he went over to Forty-third Street to watch the last act of *Twinks*—the matinee, you know. He'd heard rumors that the second act was getting a bit sloppy and wanted to check it out. Even after all this time, he's still very conscientious about 'noting' that show."

Conscientious to the tune of several thousand a week in royalties, Jocelyn thought, but instead she asked, "And did he go backstage and give notes to the cast after the matinee?"

"Oh, no, he *took* notes, of course. But he didn't want to get tied up backstage afterwards. Didn't want to have to soothe all those ruffled feathers, I suppose—afraid it would make him late for the evening rehearsal. So I gather he just phoned his directions in to Bill Seward, their stage manager, the next morning."

She was incredulous. "The next morning! The morning after the accident? He had the presence of mind to remember to call his stage manager and give notes on the matinee performance of a show that's been running *two years?!*"

"Oh, perhaps it sounds odd. But Charlie's a perfectionist . . . and

a professional, just as you and Austin are . . . and I do admire your
ability to . . . go on."

Jocelyn couldn't ignore the underlying despair in this last remark.
Harold Tewes finished the last of his brandy and sat slumped in his
leather armchair; he suddenly looked like a very old man. Though
she was still unsure of the whole point of this strange and sad interview, she realized that it had definitely come to its end. Murmuring
something lame about needing to look over her lines, she quietly
gathered up her things and made for the door. Just as she placed her
hand on the ornate brass doorknob, she heard Tewes's voice come
from behind the broad back of the armchair.

"Jocelyn . . . you're sure you saw that man come into the
theatre?"

"Yes, Harold, I'm sure."

"I see . . . I see. Then I hope they find him, Jocelyn, and soon
. . . for your sake. Thank you for coming."

Once back out on the street, she made her way to the nearest bar,
ordered another brandy and strolled over to the sole phone booth,
which was already occupied. Using her best Bette Davis eyes, she in-
timidated the little sandy-haired man inside the booth into abruptly
terminating his conversation and was soon dialing the number of
Midge Pierce, an old friend and scene partner from acting class days.

Midge was a thirty-five-year-old musical comedy ingenue who
yearned to conquer Ibsen and O'Neill while every pore on her radi-
ant blond body cried out for Neil Simon. Jocelyn had, in the past,
waded patiently through some very heavyweight discussions about
Norwegian sexuality and New England repressiveness to help Midge
achieve her artistic aims—all to no effect. Despite this the two women
had remained friends, owing largely to a mutual interest in the opposite sex. Midge was presently playing the second female lead in
Twinks.

The phone rang six times, and Jocelyn was on the point of hanging
up when the deafening sound of Cheap Trick came through the
receiver with Midge's happy and raucous voice somewhere behind it.

"Helloooo."

"Midge? . . . Hi, this is Jocelyn . . . Josh O'Roarke."

"Josh!"

"Listen, Midge, I called to ask you something."

"What's up, Josh? Hey, I'm real glad you copped that part in *Term of Trial*—but what a mess, eh?"

"Yeah, it's a mess, alright. In a way, that's why I'm calling. I . . . uh . . . need to check something out."

"Oh, I know what it is! And no, as far as I know, Kevin Kern isn't fooling around with anyone but you, you lucky stiff!"

"No, Midge, that's not it."

"Oh."

"I want to know if Smut-mouth Seward gave you guys notes from Charlie before the Thursday show."

"I'll say he did, the son of a bitch!"

"Who's the son of a bitch?"

"Charlie Martin, that's who! I swear that man is schizophrenic or something. I can't make up my mind if he's the best director on Broadway or a total moron."

"Why? What did he do?"

"He noted the Wednesday matinee, ya know? Well, sometimes Charlie's notes are great—he can really tell ya how to tighten up a scene. But this time—whew!"

"What do you mean?"

"Well, you know that duet I have with Roddy in the second act?"

"Uh-huh, your comic love song."

"That's the one. Well, both Roddy and I had had real swell dates the night before (of the same gender, of course). So we both sort of wafted into the theatre on Wednesday, really relaxed and loose for that number. We had a ball. It went better and smoother than it has in weeks. And the audience really picked up on it—they loved it! Then the next day, we get this note from Smut-mouth, via Charlie—who couldn't even come back to tell us to our faces—that *he* thought our number was, and I quote, 'stiff and labored'! Well, it wasn't! I do that turkey eight times a week, I know when we're off. And, I tell ya, Josh, we were on the money that time. It just made me so mad, I wanted to kick the guy's teeth in."

Deciding it was time to play devil's advocate, Jocelyn said, "But you know, Midge, it's always difficult to assess your own performance."

"Own performance, my ass! He pissed off half the cast with those notes. Seward didn't even want to give them; he looked like a sick dog the whole time."

"Seward always looks like a sick dog, Midge."

"Don't get cute, Josh. You know what I'm talking about. If Martin had given you notes like those you'd be chipping the paint off the dressing room walls with your teeth. I mean, those notes were the work of a sick imagination . . . has Charlie been drinking or snorting too much lately?"

"Not as far as I can tell. Though I'm starting to have very little faith in my own perceptions these days."

"Geez, it must be hell rehearsing that show right now . . . Is it true that the cops are hassling you about Harriet? 'Cause that's just ridiculous. Harriet pissed off everybody she ever worked with at one time or another, everyone knows that."

Silently damning to hell that theatrical grapevine which functions only seconds slower than the speed of light, Jocelyn forced herself to answer in bantering tones.

"Not quite everyone, Midge. But no, they're not hassling me. I'm simply 'aiding them in their inquiries'—I think that's the official phrase—and thank you for aiding me in mine. I gotta go, Midge."

"But, Josh, what's the dish about you and Kevin?"

"Bye."

Jocelyn left her empty glass inside the phone booth and walked out into a chill and windy night. It had been a long and confusing day, but as she made her way up Madison to catch the Seventy-ninth Street crosstown bus, one thing became exceedingly clear: not everyone had been where they said they were during that dinner break. But Phillip Gerrard was a man who demanded facts, not idle gossip; if she was going to convince him of her innocence, she would have to come up with the evidence herself.

She mounted the bus, slipped three quarters into the slot and sat down, pondering how she was going to open in a Broadway show and solve a murder at the same time.

CHAPTER 19

Tommy Zito was not a mean cop, and he didn't like to see people suffer, especially people he was fond of; like his superior officer Phil Gerrard. Tommy entered Gerrard's precinct office, a dim room with a metal desk, two straightback chairs and walls painted a sickly green, and laid his report on the desk. He hated doing it. Gerrard sat at his desk behind a small mountain of papers; he had obviously been there since early morning, judging from the three empty cartons of coffee, and was badly in need of a cigarette, judging from the stack of chewed toothpicks in his ashtray. Tommy knew that this report was going to make Phil want a smoke even more desperately and he hated being the bearer of bad news, let alone incipient lung cancer.

"Here, Phil. This is the compilation of all the interviews we did with the people who work in Tewes's office building."

Gerrard shot him a heavy-browed and brooding glance.

"And?"

"Uh . . . don't you wanna read it for yourself, Phil?"

"Tommy, I'm not in the mood. You know what's in the report. Now give."

"Well, I guess the gist of it is: not a soul saw Sybil Stearns leave the building after she and Tewes came back from their meeting until she went home at six-thirty that night. I don't know where she was when that delivery boy came into the office but it must've been someplace in the building."

"And Tewes?"

Reluctantly, Tommy said, "Ditto. Clean as a whistle. His alibi checks out all the way along the line. The security guards saw him leave the building when he said he did and the manager at the box office saw him getting out of the cab in front of the theatre when he said he did."

Gerrard cursed as he swept a fresh pile of toothpicks onto the floor. Ever since he had learned of Sybil Stearns' absence from her desk, he had constructed a honey of a theory hinging on a devoted and lovelorn secretary who had seized on violent means to eliminate her employer's wife and thus become the apple of his eye. He knew Stearns was cool on the surface, but it was often the cool ones who took the most drastic measures to gain their ends. He hated to see a good hypothesis die.

"Then where was she, Tommy?"

"Well, I hate to say it . . . but she could be telling the truth, you know. There's not that many female employees on that floor. She coulda gone to the can without anybody seeing her."

"But she didn't, Tommy! I just *know* she didn't!"

Tommy Zito, who admired his boss but had no faith in intuition, merely stared blankly.

"Alright, what've we come up with on this Kern character?"

"There's not much we could check on. Like he said, he didn't go to his agent's office. But he *did* call to tell them that he wouldn't be stopping by. As to his story about wandering around Central Park—well, he may be well-known in show biz circles but that don't mean that Joe Schmoe in the park is gonna spot him."

Sarcastically, Gerrard said, "Great. Terrific. Have you dug up anything about his affair with the deceased?"

"Geez, boss, that's an awful way a puttin' it. Makes it sound like . . ."

"Screw what it sounds like! What've you found out?"

"Nada. I mean, other than the fact that they did rub up against each other when he was at that drama school. There doesn't seem to be any connection between them since then."

"Then that pretty well puts him out of the picture as far as possible motive goes."

Phillip Gerrard was chewing thoughtfully on a fresh toothpick and Tommy Zito didn't want to upset him further, but he also believed in being thorough.

"Well, I wouldn't exactly say that, boss."

"What do you mean?"

"Well, he's been keeping pretty steady company with the O'Roarke dame ever since she filled in for Weldon in Boston that time. Seems he's pretty crazy about her. Now I know he didn't stand up for his girl when Weldon began chewing her tail off in rehearsal, but that doesn't mean he wasn't real burned about it. If he thought

O'Roarke was gonna be dumped from the show, it might've made him do something rash."

"I don't know, Tommy. Sounds pretty thin."

In his heart of hearts Phillip Gerrard knew that Zito's theory held at least as much water as his own about Sybil Stearns, but he found himself reluctant to acknowledge the possibility that Kevin Kern's attachment to Jocelyn O'Roarke was strong enough to prompt the man to murder. The simple fact was he didn't like to think of their attachment at all, but he wasn't about to let that fact be known to Tommy Zito or anyone else. "While we're at it, we might as well review the rest of our . . . cast. What about Max Bramling?"

"Went to his club to hit the steam room and take a shower—just like he said. He left around five-thirty to grab a bite at Wolfe's, though we don't have any confirmations from the restaurant. But the old guy woulda had to really move his ass to knock off Weldon between five-thirty and six."

"Any prior connection between Harriet Weldon and Bramling?"

"Not so far, Phil. They worked together some years ago, but that's it."

"Okay. How does Charles Martin check out?"

"Pretty solid. Said he went over to the Forty-third Street theatre when the rehearsal ended at four. One of the ushers saw him come in at the beginning of the second act—*Twinks* does a three o'clock matinee, ya know."

"Yeah, I know. Martin comes in a little after four. Anyone see him leave?"

Tommy continued with easy confidence.

"Nope. But I talked to the stage manager—guy named Seward. A real lame-o but he corroborated Martin's story. Said Martin called up first thing the next morning with a full set of notes for Act Two, plus detailed instructions on how to tighten up the curtain call. So I guess that puts the boy genius pretty well in the clear, huh?"

Gerrard wasn't so sure. "Well, it's better than nothing. I'd be a lot happier if we had somebody who saw him leaving the theatre, though . . . What time does the *Twinks* matinee come down?"

"A little after five-thirty. But, Phil, even if Martin left the Forty-third Street theatre at *five*, say, it *still* leaves too damn little time to stage a fake 'accident'!"

"There's something wrong about that. Unless someone went up to her dressing room as soon as the rehearsal ended at four, how could they be *sure* she would have fatally hemorrhaged by six?! And nobody could have done that because O'Roarke, Morrance and Kern were all up there until at least four-fifteen."

"Yeah, but O'Roarke and Kern were the last ones to leave. What if they hatched the plan between them up in her dressing room?"

More vehemently than he intended, Gerrard shot back, "No! The last thing I think this is is a spur-of-the-moment scheme! Everything about it points to smooth planning and adherence to a meticulous time schedule. That's why these alibis won't wash. *Nobody* had enough time to kill Harriet Weldon in the normal course of things. Whoever killed her *knew* that, once she was struck, she would die and die quickly."

"But . . . how could they be sure of that?"

"I don't know, Tommy. But once we figure it out, I think we'll have our killer."

CHAPTER 20

While Detective Gerrard was knocking toothpicks onto the floor of his office, Jocelyn O'Roarke was prowling backstage of the Ambassador Theatre in search of information and trying not to pay too much attention to what was taking place onstage: another flare-up between Kevin and Charlie. "That makes the third one this week," she thought, "and it's only Wednesday."

"Just tell me, Charles, *why* I have to cross *immediately* to the judge's desk when I make my entrance? Ferris would take a moment to check out the territory first."

"Oh, is that what you were doing while you were fondling that potted palm just now? For chrissake, Kevin, you're saying your first three lines in the friggin' *dark*. I'm just asking you to come in and find your *light!* I thought that was supposed to be your forte."

They weren't actually yelling at each other, and there was an attempt to keep the tone of their disagreement light and bantering, but they were fooling no one, least of all themselves. Kevin had been edgy and snappish all week and Charlie seemed to have no patience whatsoever with him. There was a definite estrangement but Jocelyn hadn't a clue as to the cause of it.

But then Kevin and Jocelyn weren't confiding in each other much these days. Although their working relationship remained sound and productive, Kevin had become a bit standoffish since that night at her apartment. This Jocelyn attributed to embarrassment, mainly; what made her uncomfortable was that she sensed an element of fear beneath it, and it is impossible to go to bed with a man who is afraid of you. Not that she had any desire to at the moment. Living in the shade of the hangman's tree can do terrible things to one's sex drive. Besides, she just didn't feel up to dealing with Kevin's anxieties along with her own. Turning onto the corridor that ran along the left side of the stage, she found what she was looking for: Ernie Bates, the backstage door man, propped up on his little stool by the back entrance reading his racing forms.

According to tradition, stage door men are supposed to be little white-haired, gnome-like gents with wire-rimmed glasses, whom you pat on the shoulder and call "Pops." Only those individuals with a death wish would ever contemplate addressing Ernie Bates as "Pops." With his full head of straight, jet-black hair, a face as red and meaty as the slabs of beef in Gallagher's front window, and a beer belly as round and as hard as a medicine ball, Ernie was a good example of casting against type. He was also a patsy for the ponies and an inveterate gossip; Jocelyn was depending on this last factor to help her out.

He didn't notice her approach until she was almost directly in front of him. He was mildly surprised to see her but not displeased, judging from his grin.

"Hi ya, O'Roarke! They send for the paddy wagon to pick you up yet?"

Outrageous a greeting as this was, Jocelyn found herself neither hurt nor angered by his words, but strangely relieved. At least it put things out in the open. The rest of the company had been treating her with the kind of polite solicitude usually reserved for terminal patients. She gathered that the consensus of opinion was that nobody blamed her for doing away with Harriet but neither did anybody want to be seen lunching with someone who was soon to be making a farewell appearance in the dock. But Ernie's friendly smile belied his words and she felt perfectly comfortable joking back.

"Nah, not yet, Ernie. I guess they're waiting to see if I'll crack. Anything look good at Aqueduct today?"

She offered him a cigarette, which he accepted with an appreciative grunt.

"Maybe the barmaids, but not much else. Though I think I got a good chance for the exacta in the sixth."

"Oh, what's that?" Jocelyn's interest was more than just politic. Having grown up near Saratoga, she had a lifelong interest in long shots.

"Nancy's Dan is running in the fourth position and Birthday Boy's running in the fifth. And . . . well . . . today's my wife's forty-fifth birthday."

"Don't tell me—her name's Nancy, right? Boy, Ernie, I never figured you to make book on sentiment!"

Bates growled good-naturedly. "Aw, what the hell, even if I blow a fin on it, I can tell the missus and she'll be all over me—now that's my idea of a birthday party!"

Ernie burst into a gale of laughter that eventually subsided into a coughing fit. While he was still hacking, Jocelyn slipped in her first question.

"Hey, Ernie, remember the call Harriet got that day?"

"Say what?"

"You came onstage during a rehearsal break in the afternoon and said there was a phone call for Miss Weldon and she took it, remember?"

"Oh yeah."

"Was it on the pay phone upstairs or this one down here?"

"It was this phone down here," he said, gesturing toward the black box on the wall, halfway between Ernie's stool and the door to the stage area.

"Right . . . Well, I was wondering if you might've been back here while Harriet was taking the call?"

Ernie took a self-conscious draw on his cigarette before replying.

"Well, I was around the general *vicinity*, ya know. I sweep out the corridors every afternoon, a course."

"Of course."

This was what Jocelyn had been banking on; everybody's business was Ernie's business.

"Do you remember who the call was from, Ernie?"

"Nah, they didn't give a name."

"Do you remember if it was a man or a woman?"

"Kinda hard to tell, Josh. It was a bad connection, I remember that—a lot of clicks and beeps on the line, see? But I *think* it was a woman. Though like I say, it was tough to tell, the voice was real low, ya know."

"Yeah. But did Harriet say anything when she got on the phone to give you an idea of who it might be?"

"Uh-uh. She didn't say no name or anything. I guess that's why I figured it musta been somebody she knew pretty well, or else she woulda put on that hoity-toity voice she had."

"But can you think of *anything* she said? I mean, I know you wouldn't eavesdrop, but sound carries pretty well down this hall, doesn't it?"

"Oh yeah, it's like a friggin' echo chamber down here. I did hear a word or two."

"Can you remember any of it, Ernie?"

Frowning hard to concentrate, he said, "Well, she wasn't in too good a mood when she came offstage, I remember that. Just grabbed the receiver right outa my hand without so much as a thank you, so I hightailed it down here to get my broom. I couldn't hear much of the first part, but at one point she said, 'Did you do what I asked?' then, 'Alright, alright, just see that you don't forget.' Then a little later whoever it was musta said something to tee her off 'cause she yelled into the phone, 'Yes, I took it! The way you harp on it, you'd think I was a moron. I don't forget these things!' It wasn't much after that that she hung up and stormed outa here. After that, I guess you know what happened better than I do."

"I do indeed, Ernie. But thanks a lot, you've been a big help."

Expansively, he said, "Hey, it's nothin'. You got any other problems, you just come to me. I don't like to see one of my ladies hassled. For two cents, I'd tell that joker Gerrard he's got the wrong dame pictured for this frame-up and no mistake."

"I appreciate it, Ernie. I may just take you up on that."

"Be my pleasure. You take care now, Irish."

In a daze, Jocelyn made her way back out to the stage. Ernie's kind words had moved her, and she was surprised to find herself close to tears. What surprised her even more was the overall effect of Ernie's use of the word "frame-up." For days now she had mentally been hearing the voices of Jimmy Cagney and George Raft chanting all those thirties gangster movie clichés. Phrases like "fall guy," "take the rap" and, indeed, "frame-up," had been reverberating in her head. Now, somehow, she felt that she hadn't just been inventing phantoms to terrify herself. Someone had murdered Harriet and planned it to look like an accident—but they had also arranged to have a patsy close at hand and she, Jocelyn, was that patsy. She didn't have an overly inflated opinion of herself, but she also didn't like to think of herself as anyone's dupe. The fact that someone else had obviously seen her so and placed her in this untenable position was beginning to make her very angry. And knowing that she was angry made her feel better and more sure of herself.

Filled with a new resolve, she was making her way across the back of the set when Peter Morrance intercepted her.

"Jocelyn, I've been looking for you. There's somebody at the front of the house waiting to see you. Look, if it's anything important, feel free to take off. We won't get to your scene till after lunch, the way Charlie and Kevin are going at it."

"That bad, is it?"

"I'll say. I mean, we're all working under a strain these days, but Charlie is unbelievable. He just keeps driving himself and he doesn't want to hear anyone so much as mention Harriet. He's acting like it was all just a bad dream and nothing more."

Jocelyn frowned. "That's an awful tough trick to pull off . . . I'll see you after lunch, Peter."

Jocelyn lit a cigarette as she abstractedly made her way out to the lobby. She drew the cigarette smoke up through her nostrils and immediately exhaled it. Granted, Harriet was already in an irritated state when she went to take the call, but when she came back she was in a positively murderous mood. What was it that Harriet didn't want the caller to forget? And why did Charlie note *Twinks* so badly that day? Had something upset him before he went to the matinee?

So absorbed was she by these musings that she gave little thought to the person awaiting her in the lobby. If anything, she figured it was probably her agent, Albert Carnelli, stopping by to buy her a drink and tell her that he'd like to drop her from his client list *before* her indictment. She was quite taken aback to find an agitated Harvey Samuels pacing back and forth in the lobby, his hands fiddling with the buttons of the same bedraggled raincoat that he had been wearing the night she had first met him. His head snapped up like an alert fox terrier's when she entered the foyer. He looked more composed than he had on the night of Harriet's death, but his entire body language bespoke a man who had recently received some kind of shaking up. He swiftly crossed the lobby and started pumping Jocelyn's hand.

"Miss O'Roarke! It's good of you to see me. I hope I'm not interrupting anything."

Gently extracting her mauled fingers, she said, "No, not at all, Dr. Samuels. We won't be working on my scenes till after lunch."

"Oh . . . splendid! Well, in that case . . . might we go somewhere for a bite? Somewhere we can talk?"

Jocelyn had planned to spend the lunch hour in her dressing room looking over her lines, but her curiosity was piqued by the urgency in Harvey Samuels' voice and before she knew it they were seated opposite each other in the U.S. Steak House, sipping cold beers and waiting for their orders. Jocelyn munched a potato crisp and waited for the good doctor to settle in. After an elaborate search through various jacket pockets, he extracted a crumpled cigar and lit it. This seemed to give him some measure of assurance, for he abruptly looked over at Jocelyn and asked, "You don't think Harriet's death was an accident, do you?"

"Why . . . uh . . . I don't think the police think it was—and they know more than I do about these things. I suppose they're right."

"Yes, I suppose so, too, though I can still hardly believe it. I guess I just wanted to hear someone else say it . . . I'm sorry to burden you this way, it's just that—well, I can't discuss it with Harold. It's all too fresh for him to deal with, poor man. And what Harold won't discuss, Sybil won't discuss. So I'm afraid you're my only other point of access to the whole affair. What do you make of this Gerrard fellow, Miss O'Roarke?"

Uneasily, she said, "Oh, I don't know. He strikes me as being one-third Lord Peter Wimsey and two-thirds Columbo, but that's just fancy. On the whole, I think he knows his job. Why do you ask?"

"Well, he came to see me this morning."

"Did he now? About what?"

"He asked a lot of questions. About Harriet's medical problems. He seemed particularly interested about that time in Boston when you had to fill in for Harriet and Harold brought her back to New York to see me."

"What did he want to know?"

"Technical things—about the nature of clotting disorders. He'd obviously done some homework on it, he seemed fairly well informed. And he asked all about Coumadin—its properties and side effects."

"What side effects?"

"Oh, it has almost none. It doesn't even show up in the bloodstream to any noticeable degree. That's what I told him. Then he wanted to know what the results of Harriet's blood tests were—the ones I did when she came back to the city. I told him that the tests showed that her condition was stable. I attributed her setback to stress and the fact that she'd probably forgotten to take her medication when she was in Boston."

"Did he ask about anything else?"

"Well, yes, he did. He wanted to know if I had changed Harriet's dosage of Coumadin after the Boston incident. I told him that it had taken several days to get the results of her blood tests back but that, when they came through, I saw no reason to adjust her medication."

"And that was it?"

"No, he asked me how I had passed that information on to Harriet."

"And how had you?"

"Well, Harriet and Harold were back in Boston by then. They were difficult to reach. So I just called Sybil at Harold's office and gave her my diagnosis. She always knows how to get in touch with Harold."

"And did she pass the information on?"

He was surprised. "Oh . . . well, I assume she did. Sybil's an extremely efficient woman, you know. She wouldn't forget something that important."

As Harvey Samuels finished the last of his beer, Jocelyn noticed that his hands were unsteady and a rheumy look was coming back into his eyes. She hoped that he wouldn't order another drink, for she had the uneasy feeling that he was apt to become maudlin with drink. Nevertheless she couldn't restrain herself from prodding him with another question, and she hit pay dirt with it.

"Dr. Samuels . . . Harvey, I don't mean to pry but I was just wondering—did Harold and Harriet have a sound marriage, do you think?"

Instantly his pale, freckled complexion flushed beet-red and he busied himself with extinguishing his cigar in the ashtray as a means of stalling for time.

"Well . . . yes, I'd say so . . . Of course, an outsider can never really be sure about these things. But they seemed quite content with one another."

At this point Harvey signaled the waitress and ordered a second beer, as Jocelyn had known he would. She lit another cigarette and played dumb until his drink came; she figured his own nerves would do the rest, and she was right.

"Of course, Harriet had a very . . . artistic nature, as I'm sure you understand. She was really quite—spiritual, in a way. And Harold is first, last and always a businessman. And a natural-born pragmatist—which was good for Harriet. She needed that balance. Still, I'm not sure that Harold always understood the more *ethereal* side of her. I think . . . perhaps . . . she sometimes found it difficult to unburden herself to Harold. He's such a busy man." Then quickly,

"But this is just speculation on my part, you realize. And what would an old bachelor like me know about these matters, eh?"

Jocelyn wasn't sure exactly what Harvey Samuels did know but she wasn't a bit deluded by his feeble attempt at levity. Harvey might not be anybody's idea of a dream date but he was clearly adoring of Harriet, and Harriet had had a huge craving for adoration in any shape or form. She had a pretty good hunch that at some point Harriet had "unburdened" herself to the good doctor, and in a none too "ethereal" fashion.

CHAPTER 21

At about the same time that Jocelyn O'Roarke and Harvey Samuels were tucking into their French dip at the U.S. Steak House, Detective Phillip Gerrard was back in his office speaking to an irate Harold Tewes over the phone.

"Yes, of course Mrs. Stearns phoned us in Boston with the results of the blood test! Really, Mr. Gerrard, I fail to see the point in this kind of nitpicking! What possible bearing could it have on my wife's death?"

"Probably none," said Gerrard, who was as disenchanted with this conversation as Tewes was. "But it's part of our job to doublecheck and verify all statements in a case like this. Now could you please tell me whom Mrs. Stearns spoke to when she phoned—you or your wife?"

Gerrard heard various snorts and huffs of exasperation over the line before Tewes finally answered.

"She spoke to me. Harriet was still at the theatre."

"I see. Thank you, Mr. Tewes. I'm sorry to be troubling you."

"Yes, well, I'm sorry, too. Good day."

There was a sharp click at the other end of the line and Phil Gerrard replaced the receiver, swearing softly to himself. The Sybil Stearns angle was quickly turning into a dead end. He buzzed Tommy Zito and asked him to come into the office. He hoped that his subordinate would have better news.

Tommy entered Gerrard's office more briskly and with far less trepidation than he had earlier in the day. He held a coffee cup in one hand, a half-eaten ham and cheese sandwich in the other and a slim folder under his left arm. But this time he also had some solid information and was, therefore, feeling much more confident.

"Got anything for me, Tommy?"

"Yeah, Phil, I think we do. I sent some men up to the Bushes, like you asked, to check out the story we got from Baron and the Radner kid. We got a couple of the boys to talk to us."

Gerrard knew the Bushes well from his days as a cop walking a beat. It's a well-known section of Central Park around the West Seventies where gentlemen go to engage in a little anonymous outdoor sex; sleazy but harmless enough.

"You didn't lean on them?"

"Nah, no rough stuff. We just asked them to 'assist' us. Anyways, we talked to a few of the regulars and showed 'em some pictures. They recognized Baron and the kid, alright. Seems they show up about once a week or so. He usually stands out on Central Park West and has a smoke with the boys while Radner goes into the park. But that Wednesday it seems Baron found something to his liking. He was seen with some young blond hunk. Nobody remembers what the Radner kid was up to that day, but they were both seen arriving together a little after four, just like they said."

"Did anyone notice what time they left?"

"Not exactly. But somebody remembered seeing Baron and the blond strolling out toward Central Park West right around six and he and Paul Radner showed up together back at the theatre at six-thirty so that seems to fit. And Harriet was long gone by then."

Gerrard just grunted and snapped a soggy toothpick in half.

"But we don't have any solid confirmation on Paul Radner's whereabouts."

"No, Phil. But that I can live with. If he *did* slip away to go boff his mom—and he strikes me as the kind of punk who wouldn't shed tears over trading in his old lady for a half a million bucks—but if he *did,* I think John Baron woulda got wind of it and I think he woulda tipped us off. The guy's a fairy but even I can see he's gotta lotta class. I just don't think he'd front for the kid."

Zito finished his speech rather lamely and started running his chubby fingers through his hair. Gerrard suppressed an amused smile as he regarded the younger man. For a hard-nosed Italian cop from Brooklyn, Zito was prone to the most unlikely partialities toward the most unlikely individuals. It made Phillip uncomfortably aware of his own predispositions in this affair, and he spoke more harshly than he intended.

"But Harriet Weldon was violently opposed to Baron's relationship with her son."

"Yeah, but . . ."

"Also . . . men will do strange things for love, Tom, and not just for the love of a woman."

As Tommy visibly shuddered in his seat, Gerrard choked back a laugh and spoke more gently. "I'm sorry to offend your middle-class sensibilities, Thomas, but that's the way of the world, you know."

Glumly, he said, "Yeah, I guess you're right. I guess it's just bein' around all these theatrical types. It gets to ya. Their whole life is built around *make-believe!* What's pretend is more real to them than what's *real!* Right now they're all over there at that theatre where a woman was offed just a few days ago. Talk about the show must go on!"

Gerrard inserted a fresh toothpick and began chewing on it broodingly. He leaned as far back as his tilt-back chair would allow, clasped both hands behind his head and stared intently at the peeling ceiling. Tommy Zito knew this pose well, knew that it meant that fresh ideas were clicking into place and forming patterns; he also knew enough to keep quiet until the brainchild was delivered. When Gerrard finally spoke, his eyes still fixed on the cracking plaster, his voice seem to come from far away.

"About that box . . ."

"Aw, jeez, we're not back to the guy with the box again, are we?!" Tommy was disappointed.

"Bear with me, Thomas. Assuming my timetable theory is correct —that our killer was someone on a tight schedule who tried to allow for all possible contingencies—and the killer, who must have been in disguise, is seen coming into the theatre by Miss O'Roarke—" Gerrard ignored Zito's skeptical grimace and continued. "Well, that must've been a nasty shock, a random factor that he hadn't counted on. Therefore, it seems to me, he would have wanted to ensure that his exit would be even more inconspicuous than his entrance— especially if O'Roarke remembered seeing him—so he would've ditched the box *in* the theatre."

Phillip Gerrard abruptly rose from his chair and began stuffing virgin toothpicks into his coat pocket.

"Get your coat, Tommy."

"Where are we goin'?"

"Back to the Ambassador."

"What for?"

"To look for something we haven't found yet—something that *has* to be there! Come on!"

Jocelyn returned to the Ambassador Theatre shortly after one only to find Peter Morrance, John Baron and a handful of overworked and frustrated stagehands milling about the set.

Peter was wearing one of his old Hawaiian print shirts, but its colors contrasted badly with the dark circles under his eyes and a pallid complexion that had probably not seen the sun in weeks.

"What gives, Peter? Are we up to my scene yet?"

"Yes and no, Josh. We finished with Act One before lunch but now the friggin' revolve is on the fritz. It's going to take us a while to get it working again. You might as well go upstairs and grab a nap. I'll call you when we get it rolling again."

"Okay, Peter. Try not to let it make you crazy, love . . . Oh, by the way, is Charlie around?"

"No, I think he's over at Gallagher's drinking his lunch. He nearly hit the roof when the revolve stalled, as you can imagine."

"Can't I just."

"Oh, and another thing—Kevin's upstairs in his dressing room. He told me that he'd like to see you when you come in."

"Oh . . . Thanks for telling me."

Jocelyn made her way up to the second floor, remembering that John Baron had withdrawn to the far side of the stage upon her arrival as if to remove himself from contagion. Well, that hurt, but she was too preoccupied with mulling over her conversation with Harvey Samuels to dwell on it. She had the vague but maddening feeling that she had been given a vital piece of information that was obstinately refusing to register itself in her conscious mind. She could only comfort herself with her mother's old bromide about evasive things on the tip of one's tongue: "If you try to force it, it won't come to you. You have to just relax and make a mental note to recall it later." Unfortunately, Jocelyn's mother was a dear but notoriously absent-minded lady.

She knocked softly and somewhat reluctantly on Kevin's door. If he was sleeping she didn't want to wake him. Jocelyn's knock was answered by Kevin's deep baritone voice calling, "Come in."

"Hi, Kevin. Pete said you wanted to see me?"

Before she could get another word out, Kevin crossed the room in two long strides, took her in his arms and began kissing her with a ferocious intensity. Unable to free herself, she meekly submitted while trite phrases from old Gothic romances like "He savaged her mouth with his" reeled through her brain. His hands too were insis-

tent, as if he were trying to pull her inside his own body. Yet somehow it did not excite her; she knew that it had little to do with his
desire for her as a woman and everything to do with some gaping
well of need within himself. When they finally came up for air, she
gazed at him blankly for a moment before asking, "What was that all
about?"

"What do you mean? I just wanted to kiss you, Josh. It's been so
long."

"That wasn't a kiss, Kevin. It was a statement! Now what gives?"

He took a short step away from her and stood rubbing his face
with his hands. Then it all came out in a jumble.

"God, Josh . . . it's just so awful. Everything's changed. You and
me . . . and Charlie! Charlie knew about my affair with Harriet. He
knew how uncomfortable she made me—how much I despised her
work in the show. And now I—I think that Charlie thinks I *did it!*
Thinks I killed her! Jesus, can you imagine such a thing? God knows
how long it will be before he goes and spills his guts to Gerrard. He's
already turned on me in rehearsals. You can see that, can't you?"

His voice had reached a high pitch, and as Jocelyn stood there
regarding him with stupefaction she was struck with the realization,
"My God, he's like a little boy who wants his mommy—me. I'm supposed to be Mommy." Suddenly she was filled with an enormous and
unreasoning anger. The egomania of the man was incredible! Then
she remembered him clearly, standing dully silent while Harriet had
vented her spleen on them during that awful rehearsal, and her rage
was replaced by a numbing depression and sense of loss. She forced
herself to speak in a normal tone.

"You're just torturing yourself, Kevin. You're paranoid about
Gerrard for no good reason. I don't think you're the one he's got in
his sights. As for Charlie . . . he's just overwrought. He'll settle
down in a day or two. Other than that, there's nothing to say. Just do
your job and try to be more concerned about the play than about
yourself. I have to go now."

"But Josh!"

"What?"

"Can I see you tonight after rehearsal?"

"No, Kevin. I'm tired and I've got things to think about. Lots of
things. I'll see you onstage."

She closed the door with a sense of finality and slowly made her
way along the U-shaped corridor toward her own dressing room. She

was gradually calming down and had almost made the right-angle turn that led to her dressing room when her eyes lighted on the metal ladder, affixed to the wall, that led up to the third floor storage area. A thought struck her like a bolt out of the blue and she stood transfixed, staring at the ladder: how thorough had New York's finest been in going over the theatre?

Having no inkling that her thoughts were running parallel to those of Phillip Gerrard, she quickly ran downstairs in search of Peter Morrance. He was still onstage conferring with the stagehands about the recalcitrant revolve. John Baron had seated himself in the front of the house and Jocelyn noticed that he'd been joined by Paul Radner, who sat one seat away from him gnawing on his thumbnail, looking for once like the schoolboy that he was.

"Peter, do you have a flashlight I can borrow for a few minutes?"

"Sure, Josh. I have a penlight here, if that'll do."

"That'll do fine. I'll get it back to you in no time. Thanks."

Peter silently unhooked the penlight from his belt and handed it to her. Whatever questions he might have had were stilled by the urgency of her voice and the determined look in her eyes. Once she had it, she clambered back up to the second floor and went directly to the ladder. Putting the penlight between her teeth, she began mounting the metal rungs and pushed open the trapdoor above it that led to the storage space.

Once through the trapdoor and on her feet, she was assailed by a dank, musty odor. She shone the thin strip of light over the seemingly endless expanse of ancient flats stacked against all four walls, silent testaments to all the turkeys and triumphs that the Ambassador had housed in years past. But she refused to be daunted by the enormous room. "It can't be far away, if it's here at all," she thought. "There wasn't enough time to hide it far away."

Methodically, she made her way over to the wall nearest the trapdoor and began poking the light between each of the individual flats. She struck gold when she reached the third flat from the back wall. There, wedged between the third and second to last flats, was a box! And there was something sticking out from underneath it; something that reflected the light from her flash.

Getting down on her knees, she put the penlight between her teeth once more and started wedging the box out from between the two flats. Then she saw what the box had been partially covering: a pair of glasses, aviator glasses, with one of the lenses shattered. Her hand shook perceptibly as she picked them up but she was still able to discern a gritty substance adhering to the broken glass—sand? The glasses and the box! She could have laughed out loud with relief. Just when she'd been beginning to feel like Ingrid Bergman in *Gaslight,* not certain if Charles Boyer was in the background, she'd found them!

Barely able to contain her excitement, she had pulled the box toward her and started tearing away at the tape on the top when her movements were arrested by a sixth sense. She hadn't heard anything, but she was suddenly aware of another presence. Not a sound but an odor, a scent permeating the dusty smell of the attic. She turned to look behind her, but before her head could come fully around there was a blinding explosion of red light that started in her left eye and swam across to her right, then muffled sounds that seemed to reverberate in her skull like some vengeful tuning fork. As the blackness slowly began to envelop her, she sank to the floor; and then, like one of the heroines in those Gothic novels, she "knew no more."

CHAPTER 22

She was having this lovely dream but someone or something was trying to intrude on it. There was a beautiful expanse of pearly gray sky, shot through with twinkling lights and the sound of chiming voices. She felt a little cold but was willing to bear that rather than face the pain which she knew would come with awakening. Yet there was still something nagging at her, something that she felt it was important to grasp, and it was right in front of her; she could see the vague outlines of it before her but they wouldn't come into focus. Someone was dangling something before her eyes; she thought it was Harvey Samuels but she couldn't make out the object that he was holding in his hands. Now her reverie was definitely being disturbed by a new element, some acrid smell invading her nostrils and making her eyes blink, and there was this insistent pressure on her arm. Reluctantly she gave herself up to consciousness.

When she first opened her eyes, she wasn't sure where she was, but she saw that there were about twenty other people in the room with her. Gradually the twenty came into sharper focus and narrowed themselves down to ten: Phillip Gerrard, his constant shadow Tommy Zito, Kevin, Charlie, Austin (where had he come from?), Peter Morrance, John Baron and Paul, Ernie Bates and a cop in uniform. The terrible smell, she soon realized, was coming from an ancient bottle of smelling salts beneath her nose that was usually stored in the backstage first-aid kit. The sensation of cold was due to the ice pack tucked behind her head and the pressure she was feeling in her lower arm was caused by—wonder of wonders—Phillip Gerrard's tight grasp on her left hand. She had no idea why she found this comforting. By degrees, Jocelyn became aware of the fact that she was lying on the cot in her dressing room and that all these people were looking at her anxiously. Once her eyes were fully opened, the loathsome bottle of smelling salts was withdrawn and she heard Detective Gerrard's voice speaking, as if from a distance.

"Miss O'Roarke . . . Jocelyn, can you hear me now?"

Groggily, she said, "Of course I can hear you . . . I'm not deaf."

"How do you feel?"

"I feel lousy, Mr. Gerrard, what the hell do you expect? . . . Did you get it?"

"Get what?"

In a fit of supreme irritation Jocelyn tried to sit upright, but the throbbing pain above her right temple convinced her to lie down again.

"The *box*, you ninny! The box that was between those flats—and the glasses underneath, those aviator glasses. I didn't make them up. And there was *sand* on them! I felt it on my hands! I touched them."

There was a long pause, and the room seemed to vibrate with the throbbing cadence in her head. When she heard Phillip Gerrard's voice again, it seemed filled with an infinite weariness.

"We didn't find anything, Miss O'Roarke. Just you lying against the left wall of the storage room. That's all."

Jocelyn shook her aching head from side to side and gave out a groan.

"But they were *there!* I saw them, I touched them! I swear they . . . oh, shit, shit, shit . . . never mind."

She gave herself up to a miasma of pain and despair and weakly let others do with her as they would. As if she were peering down a long, narrow tunnel, she saw Austin demanding that she be taken to Roosevelt Hospital for X rays and an examination. She felt herself being lifted and carried to the backstage exit. Everything came to her in fragments, but before she got into the squad car she felt Ernie Bates squeeze her hand and promise to bet Irish Pride in the next day's race and Paul Radner come up and give her a heartfelt and most uncharacteristic hug.

There were all these disturbing lights and colors before her eyes, and she permitted herself to remain unaware of all the prodding and X-raying that was being done to her at the Roosevelt Hospital Emergency Room. But she retained a vague sense that matters were being expedited at the behest of Detective Gerrard. Why else would she have received preferential treatment over all the knife wounds and possible ODs? Finally one of the white-coated interns gave her a little blue pill to swallow that diminished the pounding in her brain and gave her the pleasant sensation of being totally detached from her physical self. But with or without a sense of bodily awareness, her mind eventually began to regain its alertness somewhere on the Upper West Side, when she realized that she was once again riding in the patrol car with her head on Phillip Gerrard's shoulder and his arm around hers.

She had obviously been asleep for the past few minutes and, gazing up at his profile while he stared out through the misted windows, not knowing he was being observed, she realized for the first time that his eyes were not really steely-gray but rather a clear and opaque blue. There was also a certain softening around the lines of his mouth which she had never seen before. When she spoke, her voice seemed to startle him. "What did the doctors say?"

"What?"

"Well, am I long for this world or not? I think I'm entitled to know. I have an excellent bottle of Moët at home and I don't want my landlord to get his hands on it in case of my sudden demise."

"I don't think you need to worry about that, Joc—Miss O'Roarke," he said, chuckling. "The doctors said that you received a nasty blow to your right temple. But there are no indications of fracture or concussion. You're a very sturdy young woman, it seems."

"So I've been told. Well, that's a relief. Thank you for all your trouble, Mr. Gerrard."

The squad car had pulled up in front of Jocelyn's brownstone and she was preparing for a quick exit when she noticed that Phillip Gerrard was getting out of the car with her. Realizing that he intended to see her up to her apartment, she started to make a feeble protest.

"Really, Mr. Gerrard, there's no need . . ."

"Yes, there is. You're weaker than you realize. Don't worry, the car will wait."

So saying, he peremptorily took her arm and guided her up the stairs. Once inside, he led her to the sofa, went to her bar and poured out a double shot of brandy—half for her and half for himself—and began unlacing her shoes. Totally confused by these kind ministrations, she gazed down at his fine head of sleek black hair and blurted out, "You think I faked it, don't you?"

Without looking up, he said, "Faked what?"

"Oh, come on, Phillip." She was so exasperated by this point that she didn't even notice her use of his first name, but he did. "You think I faked this assault on myself to substantiate my claim about the delivery man with the box. Well, you found no box, no pair of glasses. And the blow was to my right temple and I'm left-handed—I could've done it to myself, I suppose."

Gerrard still did not lift his eyes to meet her gaze but continued to cradle her foot in his hand with seemingly disinterested speculation.

"Yes, I suppose that's possible."

Giddy with drugs and a righteous anger, she exploded, "Possible, probable—whatever it is, it's not true! That box and those glasses were there and someone boffed me and took them away. And I'm being framed. Now I know that sounds paranoid and crazy and there's no reason why you should believe me . . ."

"But I do."

Astounded, she asked, "Do what?"

"I do believe you," he said calmly. "I mean, logically, you *are* the perfect choice. But that's what's bothered me from the beginning. You're *too* perfect. I've tried to tell myself that it was my own ego— that I didn't like having anything handed to me on a plate. But it's just too obvious that someone's set you up. Now, the only way we're going to get to the bottom of this is for you and I to exchange a little information, Miss O'Roarke. I know you've had a rough day, but do you think you're up to it?"

Throughout this last speech, Jocelyn watched him, mesmerized, as he moved deftly around her apartment, lighting the log in the fireplace, pouring out dry food for her plump and ever ravenous black and white cat, Angus, and fixing another brandy, as if her home were already familiar to him and these were tasks he had performed dozens of times before. For his part, Phillip Gerrard was having much the same experience: an extraordinary and highly irrational sensation of déjà vu had him in its grip. Everything about her apartment, from the brightly woven Dutch rug to the modest but fine piece of stained glass hanging in the one large window, seemed to him instantly recognizable and . . . right. It was a highly eclectic potpourri of colors and textures that seemed to have simply been thrown together, but it worked; it all contrived to fit together and make a most pleasing impression of brightness and warmth and individuality. Then it came to him, the reason for this immediate familiarity: he had unconsciously imagined what her home would be like and he found himself absurdly pleased to have imagined correctly.

However, neither his voice nor his manner gave any hint of his internal self-congratulation as he pulled up a rocking chair opposite to the sofa and sat regarding her with his usual Icelandic gaze.

"Ready?"

Jocelyn lit a much needed cigarette and answered brightly, "Whenever you are, P.G." Her flippancy, she realized, was a feeble attempt to hide her nervousness at this unexpected turn of events. His apparent candidness might simply be a ruse to draw her out and get her to confide in him. Yet there was nothing remotely machiavellian in his manner as they sat before the now blazing fire, and Jocelyn felt inclined to trust him. "Though that might just be the effect of the drugs," her Gallic skepticism told her. What finally won her over was her own need to talk. For days now various ideas had been running around in her head and she had had no one to tell them to. At least Phillip Gerrard was prepared to listen.

"First off, what possessed you to go up to the third floor storage area?"

"Well, it was just a fluke, really. I was on my way to my dressing room and I passed the ladder and something clicked . . . You see, I felt all along that that box was *still* somewhere in the theatre. It seemed to me that whoever brought it in—assuming, of course, that it was the same person who killed Harriet, which I do—well he'd want to dump it somewhere inside the theatre, wouldn't he? I mean, he'd already been seen once by me and he'd be far less likely to be noticed if he left without it. So when I went past the ladder and remembered all the piles of stuff up there, it occurred to me that possibly your people had overlooked something. So I decided to go up and have a peek for myself . . . By the way, how did they find me so quickly? And how did you turn up on the scene so soon? I couldn't have been out all that long."

Silently wondering at her astuteness, Gerrard replied in a level tone, "You weren't. Not longer than fifteen minutes as close as we can figure. But to answer your second question first, I was already on my way over to the Ambassador . . ."

"You were? Why?" She was surprised.

"I . . . um . . . wanted to have another look around myself, as a matter of fact."

"A look around for what? The box?"

"Oddly enough, yes. I . . . wasn't satisfied with the initial reports of our search, you see."

Demurely but with an arched brow, she said, "Oh yes, I see. So you had a good idea where to look for me."

"Well, yes. But by the time we got there Mr. Morrance had al-

ready gone up to your dressing room to call you for the next scene
and found you weren't there. I asked when he'd last seen you and he
told me about your asking to borrow his flashlight. After that . . .
the storage area seemed the logical place to look."

"A sound deduction. My compliments," said Jocelyn with a gracious nod. She didn't know if it was the brandy, the drugs or just the
aftermath of shock, but she was beginning to enjoy herself in a perverse way. The reverse was true for Phillip Gerrard, who briskly
tried to regain control of the situation.

"Now tell me, Miss O'Roarke, what did you do once you got up
there? How did you come to find the box—and the glasses?"

"Well, I thought that if it was there at all, it couldn't be too far
away. Because he wouldn't have had much time to hide it, would he?
So I went toward the wall nearest to the trapdoor. I bent down and
shone the flashlight between each of the flats and, when I'd gotten
nearly to the end, I found it between the second and third to last
flats. I had to get down on my knees to wedge it out. That's when I
found the glasses underneath—one of the lenses was broken and
when I picked them up—I remembered to pick them up by the stems,
by the way, in case there were any prints on the other lens—anyway,
when I picked them up I felt something gritty on the surface which I
thought might be sand."

"Then what?"

"Then I started to tear open the box. I had no idea what would be
inside but I knew, once I saw what it was, that it would tell me something about the murder . . . But I stopped before I got it all the way
open."

"Why did you stop?"

Frowning, she said, "I thought . . . no, I *felt* that someone was in
the room with me . . . I can't remember why now," she finished with
a frustrated shake of her head.

"Did you hear something, perhaps?"

"No, that can't have been it. I would've turned around sooner if I
had. Besides, I'm pretty sure that I left the trapdoor open when I
went up there. I wanted the extra light."

"Well, that fits, at any rate. The trap was open when we went up
there to look for you. Morrance hadn't noticed it before because the
ladder is around the corner from your dressing room . . . which
reminds me, you said earlier that you went past the ladder on your

way to your dressing room. That means you were coming from the other side of the theatre. What were you doing over there?"

There was an awkward pause, as Jocelyn wondered for the hundredth time exactly how much Gerrard knew about Kevin and Harriet and wondered how much she could reasonably tell him without betraying Kevin's trust. Also, she felt ninety-nine point nine percent certain that he already knew *all* about Kevin and herself and this certainty only served to increase her sense of embarrassment.

Roughly guessing what was going through Jocelyn's mind, Phillip Gerrard decided to let her off the hook by gently prodding, "Were you coming from Mr. Kern's dressing room?"

"Well, yes I was. Peter told me when I came back from lunch that he'd asked to see me."

"Yes, I know."

She snapped, "Well if you knew why did you ask—"

"Never mind that. What did you talk about?"

Deeply irritated by his high-handed manner and wanting nothing more than to get his goat, she answered dryly, "First we spoke of sailing boats and sealing wax and then I think we moved on to cabbages and kings."

She got her desired effect, and for several moments they sipped their brandies and regarded each other in stony silence. Gerrard, who knew a thing or two about the Irish temperament, was the first to relent.

"Alright, Miss O'Roarke, if it will ease your mind, I might as well tell you that we know all about Mr. Kern's past relationship with the deceased when they were at the Manhattan School of Theatre—we also know that that relationship ended long ago . . . and we know that you and Mr. Kern have been keeping company of late. So, unless Mr. Kern made a full confession of guilt to you up in his dressing room, I don't think you need worry about divulging anything."

Unable to refute the logic of his statement, Jocelyn stubbed out her cigarette and immediately lit another, wishing fervently that it contained something other than mere tobacco. She took some small satisfaction from the look of envy on Phillip Gerrard's face as he inserted a fresh toothpick between his lips.

"Okay, you win . . . Kevin and I haven't seen much of each other, other than professionally, since Harriet's death . . . The strain has been too great, as you can imagine—and I just haven't felt up to it. Anyway . . . Kevin Kern is a very talented, very egocentric actor

—that's not so unusual. He's also fundamentally self-interested and not a little paranoid at this point." Jocelyn found herself amazed at her own blunt assessment, but felt compelled to continue. "He and Charlie Martin haven't been getting along too well of late—which again isn't so strange, all things considered. But Kevin's got this notion that Charlie thinks he had something to do with Harriet's death. That's what he wanted to talk to me about. He was afraid that Charlie might say something to you to get him in trouble—that's all."

"And what did you tell him?"

"I told him that he was being an idiot and to put a lid on it. Look, Charlie Martin is a good director. He knows everything that there is to know about what goes on inside a theatre—as for what goes on *outside,* he knows little and could care less. Homicide or no homicide, his sense of civic duty doesn't extend much beyond getting a production mounted."

"Okay, I get your drift. But what about Kern? Is it possible—now don't get upset—but is it conceivably possible that he's not being completely paranoid, that he does know something about Miss Weldon's death?"

With a deep sigh, she said, "Possible—but not probable. Kevin's a good actor but a lousy liar. If he were hiding something vital, I think I would've sensed it by now. And remember what I've just been saying: Kevin has a knockout part in a major Broadway play. Even if he hated Harriet's guts, he'd see his own mother in hell before he'd do anything to jeopardize this production—which is exactly what Harriet's murder has done. No, it just doesn't make sense."

"But what about Harriet herself? Did she know about you and Kern? If she did, she might've been jealous. Women often feel proprietary about old lovers, even if they have no further use for them."

It was Jocelyn's turn to be surprised by Gerrard's powers of discernment. She also thought that he probably had firsthand experience on this topic, judging from the fullness of his lower lip and the sensuous way he was caressing the fine wood arm of her rocking chair. However, she brought herself firmly back to the point.

"Yes, I think she did know. And it's possible that she was a bit jealous. But that was only potentially harmful to me, not to Kevin. Harriet had as much riding on this show as he did, you realize. I know she lit into both of us at that rehearsal, but I was the only one in danger of getting fired, really. They couldn't afford to lose Kevin."

"But if they had fired you, would Kern have quit the show?"

"Now that you mention it, he said something to that effect at the time. But I put it down mostly to remorse and bravado. Seeing as how pigs have not yet begun to fly, the likelihood was not great, if you catch my drift."

Gerrard did, and he found himself ridiculously gratified by the dryness of her tone. "She's not in love with him," he thought. Swiftly he moved on to safer topics, and they discussed other aspects of the case. Gerrard did so somewhat guardedly, keeping in mind the fact that Jocelyn was still a potential suspect, though he was fairly certain that that nasty blow to her head couldn't have been self-inflicted. Still, he would have to wait and read the hospital report in the morning. As they talked Jocelyn told him about her luncheon with Dr. Samuels and her hunch that he and Harriet Weldon had been involved in some way. Finally Gerrard noticed that the flames in the fireplace had been replaced by embers and that there were deep circles under Jocelyn's eyes. Feeling guilty for keeping her from her prescribed rest, he hastily took up his hat and made for the door. She roused herself to accompany him, moving with fatigued yet graceful strides across the room. They stood together at the doorway, suddenly overcome with awkwardness, until Jocelyn proffered her hand.

"Well, thank you for looking after me tonight, Mr. Gerrard. And I'm glad we talked—I know it doesn't change anything, but it's a relief to get some of it off my chest."

"Yes, of course." He pulled out a pen and wrote on a slip of paper. "And if you come up with anything else that you think is important, please let me know. You can reach me at this number anytime, day or night."

"Thank you. I'll remember that," she said softly. "Good night."

After Phillip Gerrard's departure, Jocelyn found herself so confused by their encounter and the day's happenings that, despite her exhaustion, she paced the floor for a good ten minutes, trying to sort out a myriad of impressions, and then decided there was nothing for it other than to wash off her makeup and go to bed. As she went into the bathroom she became aware of the pleasant scent her handshake with Gerrard had left on her fingertips; it was a pungent, woody odor, and very masculine.

Then it came to her in a flash: the thing that had alerted her senses up in the storage loft, another scent. And she had smelt it twice—once in the storage room and once just before she had gotten into the car on her way to the hospital—and she remembered from where, or rather from whom it had come. She walked numbly back into the living room and stood staring dumbly at the telephone. Should she call Phillip Gerrard? Suddenly she was filled with an overwhelming aching and weariness and her body screamed for sleep. Dispensing with her ablutions, she stripped and crawled up into her loft bed. Her next course of action she would think about to-morrow.

CHAPTER 23

She was trying desperately to hold onto the box but the man in the green cap was pulling it away from her. She shouted at him but he kept swatting at her with his free hand—he seemed to have three. As the blows buffeted her head she heard the voices of Kevin and Phillip Gerrard calling in the distance; they were warning her but their cries were unintelligible. She could feel the grit of sand on her palms making her grip all the more tenuous. She gave a final herculean tug that forced the man in the cap to look at her, but he was wearing the aviator glasses with the smashed lens. His eyes were crystal pinwheels but she thought that she could just make out his other features when a horrible ringing sound started in her ears, a sound that corresponded with the dull throbbing of her head, a throbbng which had continued unabated through most of the night. There was nothing for it other than to resume consciousness. Jocelyn reluctantly let her hand slip over the edge of her loft bed to the bellicose and offending phone beneath her.

"What is it?" she asked venomously.

"Jocelyn . . . are you there? It's me—Albert. Look, sweetie, can you make it to a commercial audition at eleven? It's for Dandy Diapers. They're looking for a young mother."

"Albert, I have to be at the theatre at eleven. You go to the Dandy Diapers call. You're more of a mother than I am—everyone knows that."

"Don't get cute with me, Josh. You should be grateful for this—all things considered. These days you're about as easy to book as an evangelist on the nightclub circuit, if you know what I mean."

"Yes, Albert my pet, I know exactly what you mean. But I still can't make this audition—which leaves you with one of two choices: You can either wash your hands of me like Pontius Pilate . . . or you can start negotiating for the TV movie rights to my trial. I know I can trust you to make the more lucrative choice."

"Now, Jocelyn, I know you're feeling testy but there are certain factors we have to consider . . ."

"Then you consider them, Albert. I still have a job to attend to—for the moment. Bye now."

Jocelyn slammed down the receiver and climbed out of bed knowing that she would have to find a new agent. The prospect did not fill her with joy, but she felt sure that she and Albert Carnelli had come to a final parting of the ways and it was probably all for the best. Now all she had to concentrate on was opening a Broadway show, solving a murder and finding a new agent.

Being above all else a pragmatist, and devoted to the notion of preserving her own skin, Jocelyn decided to deal with the murder first and worry about the show and her career later (she differed from most members of Actors' Equity in this respect). There was still a slight thrumming in her head, however, and in the hopes of vanquishing it she ambled over to the stove and brewed herself a brutally strong cup of coffee. She ate a cup of yogurt while the coffee dripped through the Chemex and tried to talk herself out of making the phone call that was the next item on her agenda. "After all," she rationalized, "what do I have to go on? A smell—a wispy little odor. How would that stack up in court? 'I *smelt* the identity of my assailant, your honor.' Terrific!" But Jocelyn's sense of smell was acute; it was one of the things that she used to make up her mind about people, and she knew, in her heart, that she was right about this one.

She lit a cigarette, which was uncharacteristic—she seldom smoked before lunch—but her hands were shaking slightly and she needed to steady them in order to make the call. After two rings, the phone at the other end was picked up and Jocelyn was startled to hear a soft, feminine voice on the line.

"Tewes's residence. Mrs. Stearns speaking."

"Oh . . . Sybil, is that you? This is Jocelyn O'Roarke calling."

"Jocelyn! How are you? I was so distressed to hear about your accident yesterday. Are you feeling alright?"

"Yes, thanks. Much better."

"Splendid. Did you want to speak to Mr. Tewes? He's on another line right now but I could buzz him . . ."

Quickly, she said, "Oh no, please, don't do that. Actually, I wanted to talk to Paul if he's around. He . . . um . . . promised to give me the name of the man who cuts his hair. I'm in the market for a new hairdresser."

Not only was this a lame excuse but a highly treasonable one to boot, and Jocelyn made a mental act of contrition to Ellery, her stalwart stylist for the past seven years. Sybil, with a secretary's keen ear for subterfuge, paused briefly before replying. "Oh yes, well, I think Paul is still here. I believe he's up in his room. Let me buzz him for you."

After a long series of beeps and clicks, which did nothing for Jocelyn's lingering headache, a thick and groggy voice came on the line. Paul sounded as if he had just been yanked out of dreamland into the nasty reality of a huge hangover. In a kindlier mood, she might have pitied him.

"Who is it? I said I didn't want to be disturbed before noon, for chrissake!"

"Paul . . . It's Jocelyn."

He was immediately contrite. "Oh, Josh . . . I'm sorry. I didn't . . . Hey, how are you feeling?"

"Alright—no thanks to you."

There was only the slightest of pauses but it was enough for Jocelyn.

"Why . . . what do you mean, Josh?"

"Why did you hit me, Paul?"

"I don't know what you're talking about."

"The hell you don't. It's pretty dark up on the third floor, so I couldn't see much, but right before all the lights went out I got a good strong whiff of your Royal Copenhagen. You really splash that stuff on, don't you? I used to date a guy who wore it. I bet you have a gallon of it on your dresser right now."

"Oh Jesus—I didn't mean to . . . Oh God, what you must think."

"What I think is that you've got your ass in a sling but that doesn't concern me at the moment. What I want to know is what was in that box?"

"Listen, I can explain." There was a strangled quality in his voice now and he was starting to sound very young . . . and frightened. "But you mustn't think . . . what I did yesterday, it doesn't have anything to do with my mother's death. I didn't have anything to do with that, I swear! I was just afraid."

"Afraid of what?"

"Afraid for someone else. Look, I can explain, but not now. It's too difficult over the phone."

"Then let me make it easier for you. Rehearsal's at eleven. I'll be at the theatre by ten. You be there too—with explanations coming out of your ears. Otherwise, I'm calling Gerrard."

"I'll be there. I promise."

"Just see that you are, Paulie my boy."

There was another series of clicks and then the line went dead. Jocelyn gingerly replaced the receiver and exhaled deeply, feeling thankful that she'd spent all those childhood Saturday afternoons watching Bogart movies; otherwise she would never have been able to pull it off.

She showered, dressed and did her makeup in record time. Once she was on the number ten bus downtown she contemplated calling Phillip Gerrard, but she decided to wait until she heard what Paul had to say. For some reason, she had believed him when he'd said that he had nothing to do with Harriet's death. And even if he had, he wouldn't be fool enough to try anything drastic in the lobby of the Ambassador . . . or would he? Harriet had been done in at the Ambassador, in more or less broad daylight. But that had been planned and most carefully at that, which was another reason why she tended to believe the boy's protestations of innocence. Paul Radner might be venal enough to wish his mother out of the way for any of a number of reasons, but Jocelyn found it impossible to envision him as the guiding intellect behind this particular crime. He lacked finesse. An accomplice he might be—that remained to be seen—but the brains of the operation he certainly wasn't. Of that she felt sure. Finally all thought of Paul's possible culpability was driven out by her own overriding desire to find out what exactly was in that infernal box.

When she got off the bus at Forty-eighth Street it was just a little past nine-thirty. Surprised to find herself with this much time to spare, she stopped at a deli and got coffee and a buttered bagel to take to the theatre. The box office staff was understandably surprised to see her at this early hour but merely smiled and nodded as she made her way to the inner lobby. Once there she unwrapped her bagel, took the lid off her already tepid coffee and prepared to settle down with her script for the next thirty minutes. Murder or no, she owed it to Austin and to Lindsay Harding to devote some time and attention to the second act. For the first five minutes the words on the page simply refused to come into focus, as her mind invented various scenarios for her confrontation with Paul, but after a stern admonition to "Cross that bridge when you come to it" (another one of her mother's old favorites), she marshaled her not inconsiderable powers of concentration and in no time she was totally engrossed in Lindsay's relationship to Judge Castle and the manipulative Ferris. At one point, and for no reason, she was struck by the image of Phillip Gerrard sitting in her rocking chair, his jet-black hair and chiseled features highlighted by the glow from the firelight, and it occurred to her what a striking figure he would make on a stage. Then she chuckled to herself, remembering an old acting teacher who had once said that being a good actor was like being a good detective, you had to ask yourself every possible question. Well, maybe the same held true in reverse. This fanciful notion immediately turned sour on her: maybe he was a good actor . . . and maybe he had been giving the performance of his life last night when he told her that he believed her. This possibility instantly filled her with a hurt and angry resentment that startled her. After all he was a cop; he had to do his job using whatever means possible. But she didn't like to think of herself as a "means," and her pride was stunned by the idea of being taken in by an "amateur."

She lit a cigarette and downed the last dregs of her coffee while she gazed around the lobby, mentally pursuing this unpleasant train of thought. The lobby was as quiet as a library reading room; the only sound that filtered through the heavy metal doors was the dim wail of a siren in the distance. Glancing down at her watch, she was amazed to see that it was nearly ten-thirty and Paul hadn't arrived yet. She debated whether or not to call him a second time and was just about to make her way over to the pay phone when Max Bramling staggered into the lobby.

His face was ashen and he was breathing heavily; he seemed to have aged a good fifteen years overnight. "My God," Jocelyn thought, "he looks like he's about to have a heart attack." She hurried over to him and guided him to the red plush settee where Harold and Sybil had sat on the night of Harriet's death.

"Max, you look awful. What is it? Are you alright?"

"I don't know . . . I can't believe it."

"Believe what? What's happened?"

"I had a voice-over call this morning. I was walking over here from Madison. I was nearing the corner of Fiftieth and Seventh and I heard all this noise . . . sirens and flashing lights. There was a car—a little green MG. It had shot onto the curb and plowed into a street-lamp. The front end was all smashed in and the door had come open. The driver's body was on the pavement and there was blood everywhere."

"Oh Max, how awful for you. It's a terrible thing to see."

He seemed not to have heard her at all and continued his narration in a stunned monotone. "There was a big crowd around already and I was trying to get through . . . to get here. And then I saw—I saw."

Gently, she asked, "Was he dead, Max?" Her voice penetrated this time and he slowly nodded his head.

"Yes . . . yes he was . . . my son is dead."

"Your son! Max, I didn't even know you had . . ."

Finally the old actor looked up at her; there were red lines in the whites of his eyes and it was the deadest gaze she had ever encountered.

"Oh yes, he was my son . . . Paul. He didn't know, of course. I was going to tell him sometime . . . later. Paul Radner was my son . . . and now he's dead."

Jocelyn stood frozen with shock in the middle of the lobby as Max Bramling lowered his head, took a handkerchief from his breast pocket and silently began to weep.

CHAPTER 24

Forty-five minutes later Jocelyn was on the phone to Phillip Gerrard. The company had all arrived and numbly absorbed the news of Paul's death. In order to spare Max, Jocelyn had taken it upon herself to inform them of the facts, taking care to refrain from mentioning Max's personal bereavement and attributing his distress to the shock of witnessing the accident. Charlie Martin and Peter Morrance were quietly conferring in a corner, trying to decide upon the best tack to take and whether or not to postpone this much needed rehearsal. Jocelyn had seized the first opportunity to slip away and call Gerrard.

"Did *you* know that Max was Harriet's ex-husband?"

"Well no, not at first. We knew that her first marriage had taken place some twenty years ago in Europe and that she was divorced soon after. She was performing at the Edinburgh Festival at the time. Everyone assumed that she'd had some brief liaison with a foreigner that didn't work out. It took us a while to tumble to the fact that Max Bramling had been part of the festival and that his real name was Radner. He'd had to change it because there was already a Max Radner in Actors' Equity when he joined the union."

"When did you find out?"

"We didn't get final confirmation until this morning. I was planning to come over to the theatre and talk to him about it this afternoon. Where is he now?"

"Upstairs in his dressing room . . . asleep, I think. After he told me what happened and about Paul being his son I broke into the lobby bar and got him a walloping brandy. He took his medicine like a good fellow—in one stiff swallow. Then I took him up to his dressing room. He rambled on for a bit then seemed ready to doze off, so I slipped out."

"What did he say?" Gerrard demanded. There was the tiniest of pauses before Jocelyn's innocent question, "Say when?" but it was enough to let Gerrard know that she was holding back on him. He forced his voice to remain in a quiet register despite an intense desire to shake her by her stubborn shoulders.

"You know damn well what I'm talking about. What did Bramling say when he was rambling on?"

"Well, he didn't confess to any murders, if that's what you're driving at!" Jocelyn snapped. She heard the note of defensiveness in her voice and felt her cheeks flush like a child caught hoarding chocolates. *Why* did she have such a short fuse when dealing with this man? She entertained a brief fantasy of standing in the center of his office and breaking every one of his fresh toothpicks in half. Feeling better, she went on in a more reasonable tone, "After all, he was probably already in shock by the time he got here. He was barely coherent telling me about the accident. After that it was all downhill as far as lucidity goes."

"Come on, Jocelyn, give . . . it might be important to the case . . ."

"No, *Phillip*," she fairly spat out both syllables—if he wanted things on a first-name basis, by God he'd get it!—"It had *no* bearing on the case. Good lord, if Max had said something vital, don't you think I'd tell you in a second? I'm not a complete fool. And it wasn't important, it was just . . . sad." Jocelyn was rendered suddenly speechless by a lump in her throat as the old actor's face, a landscape of devastation and loss, rose before her eyes. Phillip Gerrard kept perfectly quiet until she was ready to go on. "He was talking out loud . . . to Paul most of the time. I don't know why they never told the kid before who his father was but Max said something about planning to tell him someday. I bet you—I just *bet* you!—this was a scene that Max had rehearsed a thousand times in his head with a hundred different variations . . . over and over, until he had it distilled and perfected. Looking at him, I had this feeling that half of the shock came from realizing they'd never get to play the parts—he and Paul. Can you imagine what that would *do* to an old warhorse like Max—that kind of termination?"

Jocelyn detected a certain strain of Lindsay Harding creeping into her voice and wondered what impulse had led her to plead Max's case to this maddening man. She endeavored to delete all the melodrama from her speech as she went on. "Anyway, what it boils down to is that he started playing the scene on his own—just had to get it out of his system, I guess. He probably didn't even know he was talking out loud."

Gently prodding, Gerrard asked, "And he said . . . ?"

"Oh, all the old cliché stuff like 'hope you can find it in your heart to understand,' 'thought it would be for the best,' 'certain advantages I couldn't give you,' that sort of thing. Max played the soaps for a couple of years and you have to allow for that. All the same it was pretty damn moving and more than a little sad. He obviously had a lot of affection for the boy. You know something? I bet if you asked a competent psychiatrist about it, they'd say what Max did was a fairly healthy way of dealing with his grief, all things considered."

"All things considered, I'm sure you're right," Gerrard said, caught somewhere between ire and amusement, "but it doesn't tell me the real reason for hushing the whole thing up . . . and it doesn't tell me where Paul Radner was headed this morning. Nobody seems to know."

"Oh, he was—" Jocelyn literally bit her tongue but the damning words were out already and Gerrard pounced on them like a bobcat.

"He was *what*? What do you know, Jocelyn?"

"Just that he was . . . on his way here, to the theatre."

"What for?"

"To . . . uh . . . see me."

"What! *Why?*"

"Because I called him this morning, that's why!" She deeply regretted not having had the foresight to work up to this particular topic more gracefully, but the situation now seemed irretrievable. She felt as ditzy as Lucy Ricardo making lame excuses to Ricky. There was nothing for it but to brazen things out. "Look, I remembered something last night after you left, something I'd been trying to put my finger on . . ."

"So why didn't you call and tell me? You said you would if anything came up."

"I know I did!" she said guiltily. "And I was going to—really. I just wanted a chance to talk to Paul myself, first. That's all."

"Talk to him about what exactly?"

"If you'd kindly stuff a sock in it for five minutes, I'll tell you. Geez, Gerrard, have a little patience and let me start from the beginning . . ." Jocelyn briefly described identifying the scent of Paul's cologne in the storage room and the gist of her conversation with him that morning. By the time she had finished, Phillip Gerrard was thankful that he was alone in his office because he was visibly trembling with rage; if he had had Jocelyn O'Roarke in front of him at that moment, he would have done a good deal more than just shake her.

"So you were going to make this little rendezvous with a man who had recently assaulted you . . ."

"What man? A boy, just a kid really."

With infinite sarcasm, he said, "Of course, you're right—I fell victim to hyperbole. Just a boy . . . who happens to be half a foot taller than you and a good seventy-five pounds heavier . . ."

"I appreciate the thought, but I'd say fifty pounds tops . . . really."

"And I say you're friggin' insane!" Gerrard exploded. "Where's your sense of self-preservation, woman? If he'd go so far as to knock you out with dozens of people in the building, what might he do in a deserted theatre?"

"It wasn't deserted. The box office people were there. They saw me come in. Besides Paul said he had nothing to do with his mother's death . . ."

"Oh, well, of course, that makes it all alright."

"Just hush and listen. I believed him and I can spot a con as well as you can. He wasn't lying—I'd bet my life on it. He'd just woken up and he was too shook up and scared to even attempt a good bluff. But he knew something—he knew something about what was in that box—and I was just crazy to find out what it was."

Grudgingly, he said, "Well, it was totally irresponsible, you realize . . . but I suppose your sense of . . . urgency was understandable at the time."

"Your empathy underwhelms me, sir."

"Listen, O'Roarke, you're damn lucky I didn't haul you down here to give a formal statement. I have a good mind to—"

There was a dead silence. Jocelyn hit the pay phone thinking that they had been cut off, but there was no dial tone so she shouted into the receiver, "A good mind to what? I hate it when people stop in mid-threat."

"Never mind that now." It was Gerrard's voice but the tone was entirely different; he sounded strangely calm and entirely focused in on something. "Paul said something about that box over the phone?"

"Yes, I asked him what was in it and he said he couldn't talk about it then."

"On the phone, you mean?"

"Well, yes, I suppose that's what he meant."

"Who else was in the house at the time?"

"How the hell should I know? Sybil answered the phone. She thought I was calling to talk to Harold. He was on another line. Maybe Austin was around—he's been spending most nights there for the last week or so. I have no idea who else. Austin tells me that Harold's home is not unlike Grand Central. But I don't see what that . . ."

"I'll talk to you later."

Stunned, she asked, "You'll what?"

"I have to go now. I'll speak with you later."

"Go where, for Pete's sake?"

"I have to go look at a car, right now! A little crumpled-up MG. If Paul didn't kill Harriet—I'm just saying IF mind you—and if Paul knew what was in the box, and if what's in the box is important, then . . ."

"Sounds like an iffy proposition to me."

"Well, it's the best one you got, sister," he shot back mercilessly, "and if I were you, I'd keep my fingers and anything else you have handy crossed while I go check out that car. If somebody didn't want Paul to tell you what was in that box, they might have arranged a little accident—a *second* little accident, *tu comprends?* Bye now."

Jocelyn spluttered indignantly into a receiver that actually had the temerity to emit a dial tone. She hung up the phone silently cursing all men and especially smart-alecky detectives who thought they knew it all. What drove her really crazy was that she was unaccountably pleased at Gerrard's use of the *tu* form. Amid all this Sturm und Drang, what could be sillier? She ran upstairs to check on Max, who was sleeping soundly, and then ambled back out onstage, just in time to catch Peter Morrance in mid-oratory, speaking with the authority of Moses newly arrived with his tablet, ". . . So until we hear different, our job is to keep on keeping on, folks. We'll start with Act One, scene three and go to the act break with full tech—except for costumes and makeup, of course. The people only involved in Act Two can break for lunch now and come back at two-thirty, okay?"

"Terrific," she thought, "a two-hour lunch break. Too long to just eat and too short to do anything really useful—like trail Phillip Gerrard down to that garage and find out what's with that little sports car." Her internal grousings were cut short by the sight of John Baron, pale, shrunken and huddled in the last row of the orchestra. He had obviously heard the news about Paul, and, at first, she couldn't understand how he could bear to be there among them while his loss was so fresh and so excruciating. But it didn't take her long to comprehend.

John Baron lived, as she well knew, in a tastefully appointed one-bedroom apartment a few blocks away from hers on the Upper West Side. He had no roommate and kept no pets. If he were to go there now with his grief, it would be like consigning himself to one of the rings of Dante's inferno. At least here, at the theatre, he had an illusory sense of family, people willing to witness his sorrow and accept it for what it was.

Jocelyn settled into the seat next to Baron.

"John, I'm so sorry."

Baron kept his eyes fixed on the stage in front of him and answered mechanically, "He never did know how to control that car. I warned him a hundred times not to buy an MG. He just got it this week—bought it off a fellow student at Fordham—with a small down payment and on the prospects of his inheritance, you know. I even went out with him the other day to test-drive it and I *hate* the things! They look like mutant cockroaches. And I told him not to buy it. We had it out on the West Side Highway in the early afternoon. We were up past the Cloisters and the traffic was light, so Paul let it out full throttle—I was terrified. He was ecstatic. That was Paul's lifestyle, you see—he was a speed demon. Things just couldn't happen fast enough for him. Waiting was intolerable. I found that quality exciting at times . . . and, at other times, draining. But when he was driving that car it wasn't either, it was pure fear. There was a terrible affinity between Paul and that machine. And so middle-aged conservatism triumphs again over the folly of youth! There's nothing like hindsight, is there . . . ? And you know what the worst thing is, Jocelyn? The money. Paul had all these fantastically glorious dreams of how he was going to blow his inheritance. I kept telling him to hold on to it and let Harold build a good portfolio of investments and he listened to me . . . Now I wish I'd told him to blow the whole wad—that would've made him happy."

After this unexpected outpouring, John and Jocelyn sat side by side, both breathing deeply and saying nothing. From the age of eight

Jocelyn had harbored a deep distaste for the Catholic ritual of confession; she had never understood the need for a go-between to talk to God, which probably accounted for her ingrained distrust of agents and casting directors. Nevertheless, her adult experience had taught her that there was a certain universal impulse toward the confessional especially among theatre people. And what Baron was patently asking for was some kind of absolution. Jocelyn briefly toyed wth the idea of simply saying, "Recite five Hail Marys and resolve to do good works," but discarded it in the interest of obtaining solid information.

As gently as she could, she asked, "So, is that how you think it happened, John?" His gaze was as blank and uncomprehending as a French maître d' when a patron asks where the ketchup is. But Jocelyn, who was past caring if people held a low opinion of her tact and good taste, pressed doggedly on. "The accident, I mean. Do you think Paul was driving too fast and just lost control of the car?"

"For chrissake, Jocelyn, why the hell ask me?" Baron cried in anger, as he leapt out of his seat and started pacing the aisles with both hands clenched rigidly by his sides. Somewhat abashed, she scurried out of her seat and followed him as he began to rant.

"What possible goddam difference does it make *how* it happened? It just *did,* that's all. He's dead—that's all there is to it." He stopped to take an unsteady breath and then spat out, "But if you want the *facts*—the plain, gruesome details—to press in your memory book, allow me to oblige you: Paul was driving west on Central Park South. He swung onto Seventh Avenue—a wide turn it seems . . . there were witnesses, you see. Just as he got to Fifty-fifth Street the light turned red. He was going a bit fast—faster then the speed limit, certainly, but then he always did . . . Anyway, he seemed to be about to hit the brakes—something he liked to do at the last possible second—when the car just lurched forward and went up onto the curb and into the lamppost. Paul's head went through the windshield and made contact with the pole. He was dead before the police even got there . . . He wouldn't have been wearing his seat belt, you see. Hated the things because they were too constricting. He hated anything that was . . . binding."

By the end of this recitation, John had reached the inner lobby and was standing at the center of it, hands limply hanging at his sides. Standing a few feet behind him, Jocelyn looked on dumbly as thirty-five years of well-bred Southern gentility struggled to master overwhelming grief. It was an awesome sight. When he spoke again, without turning to face her, his voice had regained a semblance of its usually dulcet tone.

"I'm sorry, Josh, I didn't mean to . . ."

Brightly, she said, "Sure you did. And why not? I had it coming to me."

"But there's no reason for me to—"

"To what? 'Rage against the dying of the light'? Hell, John, there's every reason. It's a very fine way of mourning someone . . . and I know another."

So saying, Jocelyn took John Baron firmly by the elbow and drew him over to the lobby bar, which she was about to raid for the second time in one day.

CHAPTER 25

"Players' Club. May I help you?"

"Yes, I'd like to speak to Frederick Revere, please . . . If he's not in his room, you might try the pool room."

"Whom should I say is calling?"

"Jocelyn O'Roarke."

Jocelyn waited while the phone hissed and spat with static; when the line was reconnected she could hear the gentle click of billiard balls in the background as a sonorous and beautifully modulated voice spoke on the other end.

"Jocelyn! Delighted to hear from you, old girl. But why aren't you in rehearsal?"

"You don't know?"

"No, should I?"

"No . . . no, I guess not. Look, Freddie, weren't you at the Edinburgh Festival back in fifty-nine?"

"Indeed, I was. We did that dreadful modern dress production of *As You Like It* and I had to play Jacques in white chinos. An unforgettable experience."

"I'm sure it was. Listen, if you're not tied up tonight, could we get together for a drink?"

"Best proposition I've had all week . . . all month actually. Tell you what, why don't you come down here and join me for dinner. That veal marsala you like so much is on the menu, and it's Ladies' Night tonight."

"Lovely. I'll jump in a cab and be there in twenty minutes. Bye."

Jocelyn grabbed her purse, flew out of the Ambassador and headed toward Broadway. After the inevitable revelation of Max's connection to Paul, the day's rehearsal had been a waste. Bramling's understudy kept blowing his lines, Kevin Kern was walking around in a fog, John Baron got royally pissed on bourbon and even Charlie Martin seemed unable to concentrate. After several painful hours of plodding work, Peter Morrance had tactfully suggested that Martin let the cast go so they could do a dry tech of the show with the crew.

Jocelyn had been champing at the bit all afternoon waiting for news from Phillip Gerrard. When she had called her service and found that there was no message from him, she decided, in a fine fury of frustration, to do a little digging on her own; hence the call to Frederick Revere. In his heyday back in the forties, he had been dubbed "Rex" Revere, the king of Broadway and the darling of matinee ladies everywhere. Having emigrated from England in the early 1930s, he picked up where John Barrymore had left off when he deserted Broadway for Hollywood. When his matinee idol days were numbered, he managed the transition to character actor with grace and aplomb and also became a truly fine Shakespearean actor after years of doing light romantic fluff. During her first year in New York, Jocelyn had seen him do Prospero in *The Tempest,* and she left the theatre tear-drenched and shaking. She wrote her first and most heartfelt fan letter to Frederick Revere and was bountifully rewarded by his invitation to tea at the Players' Club. A firm friendship was established, and Jocelyn sincerely doubted that she would have survived that first grim year in New York without his kind encouragement.

Jocelyn got out of the taxi a few blocks from the Players' Club in order to stroll through Gramercy Park and savor the effect of early twilight on the old and gracious houses surrounding the square.

Revere was waiting for her in the foyer, elegant in a velvet smoking jacket and silk cravat, a style of dress that would have looked silly and pretentious on a lesser actor. Somewhere in his seventies (no one was sure exactly where, as his proud carriage and full head of silver-white hair belied his years), Revere had taken up residence in the club five years before, shortly after the death of his adored wife Lydia, a well-known costume designer. Revere strode up to Jocelyn, grasped both her hands in his, and planted a resounding kiss on her cheek.

"Dear child, you look all in! I'm itching to hear all about your show, but I'll restrain myself until we've gotten some sherry and a good meal into you. I know how badly actors eat during rehearsals. Personally, I could never even taste what I was eating until after opening night. Now come along."

Jocelyn was more than glad to let him lead her into the long oak-paneled dining room on the first floor and order dinner for both of them. True to his word, Revere chatted gaily as they ate, of mutual acquaintances and the London theatre season, leaving Jocelyn ample time to collect her thoughts. It wasn't until the plates were cleared and they had their coffee and brandy before them that she began to tell him of the day's events. Revere was an old drinking buddy of Bramling's, and when Jocelyn's narrative reached the point where Max told her of his relationship to Paul Radner, his face showed deep concern. When she had finished her story, there was a long silence as they both stared into the depths of their brandy snifters; Revere was the first to speak.

"I was afraid of this."

"What? Afraid Paul might be killed?" She was shocked.

"Oh no, no, nothing that drastic, my dear. I only meant that I worried about Max not telling Paul that he was his father. I felt that the longer he waited, the greater the repercussions would be when he finally spoke up. And now . . ."

"So you *did* know about Max and Harriet, then. I thought you might."

"Oh yes, I knew. I'm one of the very few who did. After all, I was there at Edinburgh when it all . . . happened."

"How did it happen, Freddie? I don't mean to pry but . . . well, it just seems so fantastic!"

"Does it? I suppose, in retrospect, it would seem unlikely, but not if you'd been there at the time. Harriet was quite young then and very impressionable. But then, she always was as far as the theatre was concerned; she felt far too great a sense of awe. Most unhealthy. I used to tell her that a good actor was on a par with a fine carpenter. You keep your tools in good repair in order to build something sound and functional that is also a pleasure to the eye. But she never was well disposed to analogy. Anyway, she had been studying at RADA that year. I gathered, at the time, that Cyrus had pulled a few strings or, more likely, written a few bountiful checks, to get her accepted. So she came to Edinburgh with her fellow students, all starry-eyed, to play a small part in their production of *Lady Windermere's Fan*. It was rather dreadful, if I remember correctly, but then I don't much care for the piece."

"But what was Max doing there? He's never been a great one for the classics."

"No, that's true enough. It was . . . oh, a form of therapy in a way. Max had lost his first wife the year before, a lovely young woman—leukemia, you know. He was cut up pretty bad, as you can imagine, and he needed something to take his mind off his misery. So I suggested that he work up a one-man show. One of his favorite writers is Henry James, so he put together an evening based on James's correspondence and I convinced him to bring it to Edinburgh. It was truly first-rate. Max had really thrown himself into the project with a passion. Not only do I think that it saved Max's sanity at the time, I also believe it was the finest piece of work he's ever done."

"How was it received at the Festival?"

"Wonderfully! The audiences just ate it up. Max honestly brought James to life in that show. Got the best notices of any actor that year."

"And got Harriet into the bargain?"

"That's right. They had the common bond of being among the few Americans there that year and she worshipped him. Went to see him every night that she wasn't performing. It's a rare man that can withstand that kind of adoration, Jocelyn. By the end of the summer, they were married. Harriet became pregnant almost immediately but they were already separated by the time Paul was born."

"What broke them up?"

"Reality, I imagine. They'd eloped, you see, and that didn't go down at all well with Father Weldon—that plus the fact that Max was nearly fifteen years older than Harriet. But I don't lay all the blame on Cyrus. I think a good deal of it had to do with Harriet herself. Once they got back to the States, I think she realized that she'd only hooked a relatively small fish in a very big pond. Max was neither willing nor able to play Alfred Lunt to her Lynn Fontanne. He's a modest man with a modest opinion of himself. Harriet had grander designs."

"I still don't understand how so few people even knew of the marriage, Freddie."

"Oh, we have Cyrus to thank for that. He wielded his considerable influence with the press to keep things as low-key as possible. Max had entered his real name on the marriage certificate and that's how Cyrus had it recorded in the papers. Only a handful of people knew that Max Radner was Max Bramling, and most of them are dead now."

"But how did they persuade Max to stay away from his own son?"

"Ah, that was the cruelest thing of all. The hardest thing Max has had to live with in his life. Cyrus bought him off. Max rented a fabulous new apartment when they came back from England. He wanted Harriet to live as she had always lived—in luxury. But there wasn't much work for Max back in '59. Plus the fact that he had some heavy debts left over from his first wife's long hospitalization. It crushed him financially and emotionally. And since Harriet seemed eager to see the last of him, he took the money Weldon offered him and slunk off to lick his wounds. He drank heavily for the next five years or so and his career suffered for it. But, gradually, he began to pull himself together. The last ten years, he's been paying back the money to Weldon in dribs and drabs. His idea was that when he had the debt paid off, he'd have the right to tell Paul who he was."

"But if Harriet wanted nothing to do with him, how did Max end up in *Term of Trial?*"

"I'm not sure. I think guilt might have had something to do with it. Harriet liked to picture herself as Lady Bountiful. Or maybe it was just another bribe to keep him away from Paul . . . but it wouldn't have worked. Max would rather have lost that role, much as it meant to him, than give up his claim to Paul. I know that for a fact. But now, dear child, we must go."

Blankly, she said, "Go where, Freddie?"

"Uptown, of course. I should be with Max. This will be a bad night for him and no one should have to drown their sorrows alone."

In dumb admiration, Jocelyn followed Frederick Revere out of the Players' Club and into a cab like a page following a king. They rode most of the way in silence until Revere turned to her and said, "Do you know what the saddest thing is, Jocelyn? Right now, I know exactly what is going through Max's mind. Henry James wrote a letter to Hugh Walpole which said, 'I only regret, in my chilled age, certain occasions and possibilities I didn't embrace.'"

As their cab was traveling up Central Park West, a grimy and grease-stained Phillip Gerrard was sitting hunched in a garage, smoking his first cigarette in three months.

"Looks like you were right, Arnie."

Arnie Weiner, the station mechanic, put down his beer can and wiped his mouth with a dirty sleeve.

"Well, you tipped me to it, Phil. Otherwise, I wouldn't have known what to look for. It's such a minor thing. I mean, once you check out the motor and the brakeline and you see nothing's been tampered with, you figure it's all kosher. But then you come in here and tell me the kid has a reputation for driving like a demon, so we take a closer look. But who'd have figured it, huh?"

"That's the million dollar question, Arnie. Who'd have figured it?"

"I mean, a simple little thing like unbolting the bucket seat from the floor runners. The kid hits the brakes hard, the seat pitches forward, he loses control of the car and BAM! It's all over. What does it leave you with?"

"I'll tell you what it leaves me with, Arnie. A murderer who's killed twice and won't hesitate to kill again. That's what it leaves me with, goddammit."

CHAPTER 26

After dropping Frederick Revere off at the Ansonia, where Max
Bramling lived in a small, drab, one-bedroom apartment, Jocelyn decided to walk the rest of the way home in hopes that the brisk night
air would prove a tonic to her troubled mind. The scene in Max's
apartment had been both touching and upsetting. She and Revere
had discovered Max, dressed in a moth-eaten bathrobe and slippers,
staring blindly at an old newspaper photo of Harriet Weldon holding
a three-year-old Paul on her lap. The caption read, "Busy Actress
Combines Career with Motherhood," and in the photo Harriet sat,
madonna-like in a velvet dress, beaming fondly at her son, whose
tousled curls and Little Lord Fauntleroy outfit were overshadowed by
his bright gaze; he stared avidly at the camera as if he couldn't wait to
jump down and get his hands on the mysterious contraption. The shot
captured Paul's essence perfectly.

Max seemed almost unaware of their presence until Frederick Revere strode over to him and gently removed the clipping from his
hands. He looked up at his old friend with bloodshot eyes and whispered hoarsely, "He's gone, Freddie . . . I've lost my boy."

Revere eased himself down onto the arm of the overstuffed chair
and, slipping one arm around his friend's shoulder, said, "I know,
Max, I know. That's why I'm here."

Without a word, Jocelyn tactfully stepped back out into the hallway and softly closed the door. Not wishing to ride in an elevator full
of people with tears streaming down her face, she took the stairs
down to the lobby and made her way out onto Broadway. Frederick
Revere's small but eloquent gesture had all but undone her.

The walk home helped, but as she mounted the stairs to her apartment she realized how bone-weary she was, despite the fact that it
was only a little past ten. However, all signs of fatigue evaporated as
she slipped her key into the lock and heard the phone ringing inside
her apartment. Hoping that it would be Gerrard, she sped across the

room, leaving the keys in the door, and pounced on the receiver. It was a man's voice on the other end, but not the one she wanted to hear.

"Josh, it's Kevin. Look, I'm in the neighborhood and I wondered if we could go for a drink?"

"Oh, Kevin, hi. Listen, I just got in and I'm really beat . . ."

"I know, Josh. It's been a hell of a day. That's why I need to see you. I just don't know what's going down."

"Well, if you think I *do,* you're—"

"No, it's not just that, believe me. Jocelyn, if you don't want anything to do with me after this whole mess is over, I'll understand. Guess I really can't blame you. I should have told you everything from the start. But Paul's dead! They say it's an accident, but I don't know what to make of it. I just need to talk to you, Josh. Please."

They haggled a few minutes longer until, partly from fatigue and partly from irritation that Gerrard hadn't called her, Jocelyn agreed to meet Kevin at Dobson's, a local West Side bar. After all, she had no reason to believe that Kevin was directly involved in either Harriet's or Paul's death. His affair with Harriet was ten years old and he had hardly known Paul. But he might possibly have information that would shed light in other directions—so what the hell.

When she walked into Dobson's the first familiar face she saw was not Kevin Kern's but Charlie Martin's, seated at a table where he'd obviously been for some time as he was, quite clearly, three sheets to the wind.

"Lo, Josh. What a party! Kev's here, too, ya know. At the bar, gettin' drinks. Have a seat, why don't ya. It's been a long day."

Jocelyn circumspectly picked her way over to Charlie's table, having spotted Kevin at the bar. He was being waylaid by a buxom blond chorine, a circumstance that might have aroused Jocelyn's jealous ire four weeks ago. But right now she was more interested in having discovered her semi-detached director with his hair down; a rare occurrence.

"Hello, Charlie. How did the dry tech go? Alright I trust?"

Winking, he said, "Dry tech was fine. Everything's gonna work. Script's fine. Actors fine—we're gonna have a hit. So what if a few people die? That's show biz, right?"

"No, Charlie," she said gently. "That's not just show biz."

"Damn right, it's not," he muttered lugubriously. "I tell ya, Jocelyn, your buddy, Austin . . . that flit's written a goddam gem.

Could win the Pulitzer. At least a friggin' Tony. I mean, *Twinks* made me a fortune but it's not what the critics call a 'work of art,' is it? No sir, it was strictly a take-the-money-and-run proposition. And, hell, I was damn lucky to get the chance. But I've been in this rotten business a long time and I would like . . . I would really *appreciate* just a little goddam recognition!"

Charlie concluded this heartfelt speech by draining the last of his drink and slapping the empty glass smartly down on the table top. He waved one arm in a wide, wobbling arc to attract the waitress' attention. While he was ordering their drinks, Jocelyn glanced over toward the bar to make sure that Kevin was still preoccupied with his chorine. Their heads were bent low, leaning toward each other over their drinks, the forelock of Kevin's auburn hair almost touching the girl's forehead. She was giggling and Kevin was smiling and chatting easily, obviously at his most charming and, even more obviously, completely unaware of Jocelyn's arrival. This suited her purpose admirably. She'd never heard Martin speak in so garrulous and unguarded a fashion and, as long as he felt like talking, she was prepared to listen. If she could just keep him talking long enough, she felt sure that she could learn something.

The waitress brought their drinks and Jocelyn waited until Charles had taken a ruminative sip of his Wild Turkey before picking up the thread of their conversation.

"Listen, Charlie, I know things have been awful but you shouldn't worry. Like you said, the show's solid and your work has been superior. I think you'll be a shoo-in for Best Director this year."

"Oh, hell yes! Best Director of the finest goddam play that was *never* seen on Broadway, toots. They'll have to invent a new category for me, won't they?"

Jocelyn blinked her eyes in feigned shock and disbelief. Playing dumb wasn't her strong suit but at this point she didn't think that Martin would notice.

"Is it really that bad, Charlie? Is it Max? I mean because of . . . Paul and everything. Do you think he won't be able to pull it together?"

"Max?" Charlie paused with his glass halfway to his lips, as if this possibility hadn't yet occurred to him. "He *better* pull it together, the old sod, or I'll bust his ass. They made me hire him in the first place."

"They being who?"

"Harriet and Harold, of course. It was their idea. Hell, the compromises I had to make to get this friggin' job! First I had to swallow Harriet as part of the package. Then ol' Harold takes me aside and says they want Bramling as the judge and mutters something about paying an old debt—which I didn't understand until today. Thank God I was able to sell them on Kevin, at least. I knew Harriet would balk at that—which she did—but Harold was all for it. And then—"

Martin broke off in mid-sentence with a perplexed look on his face, then quickly bent his shaggy head over his drink to cover the moment. But Jocelyn, who had a swift suspicion of what he had been about to say, wasn't having any.

"And then who else, Charlie?"

Martin lit a cigar and took several short, angry puffs before allowing his gaze to meet hers. "And then you. Look, I'm sorry, O'Roarke, but I thought you were just too young to understudy Lindsay. What can I say? But Harold was hot to have you in the show. I figured your friend the author was behind the whole thing and I don't like to antagonize my playwright if I can help it. So I hired you—luckily, I was dead wrong."

It was far from heady praise but, coming from a man who seldom admitted to errors in judgment, it meant something. Anyway, Jocelyn had no time to nurse a wounded ego.

"Thanks, Charlie, nice of you to say so. But what about John Baron? Whose idea was it to hire him?"

"Baron? Oh, I wanted John, alright. He may be a piss-elegant faggot but he's the best there is. His sets are classy—John has that antebellum flair," he said somewhat begrudgingly. "Course, I had to fight like hell with Harriet to get him. Fortunately, Harold backed me up in the crunch. I must say . . . as far as producers go, Harold is a prince among schmucks. I mean he protected his wife's best interests all the way down the line, but I expected that. But I tell ya, after some of the major scumbags I've had to deal with, ol' Harry was a joy! Even stood by the show after Harriet popped off. I mean, he coulda pulled the plug on us then, but he didn't . . . But now, after this thing with Paul . . . I just don't know how much he can take. He's a smart enough businessman to know that the play will sell tickets. Of course, whether they'll be coming to see *Term of Trial* or to view the scene of the crime is another matter. But I tell ya, at this point I don't give a damn *why* they come as long as they come.

What they think when they leave the theatre is up to us and how well we do our job, right?"

Jocelyn grew increasingly uncomfortable as Martin loomed perilously near to giving another one of his infamous and interminable pep talks, which would only be rendered the worse for drink. Out of the corner of her eye, she could see that Kevin had finished his drink and was growing tired of his bar-mate, judging from his glazed expression and the near dementia of her laughter. If she was going to play her cards, now was the time to play them. Abruptly dropping the pose of an enthralled listener, she asked flat out, "Charlie, where were you when Harriet was killed?"

Martin choked on his whiskey. "What do ya mean where was I?"

Evenly, she said, "You didn't watch the whole second act of *Twinks* that day. Where did you go between then and rehearsal call?"

"What the hell are you talking about, O'Roarke? Course I saw the damn second act! Gave notes, didn't I?"

"Yeah . . . and they were bullshit."

"What?" This time Martin's consternation caused him to spill a few drops of Wild Turkey down the front of his flannel shirt.

"The hell you say!"

"Oh, come off it, Charlie." Jocelyn spoke with far more assurance than she actually felt, but every poker player knows that you can't back down in the middle of a bluff. "Those notes were garbage. Even Seward thought so and he's a moron. You came to the theatre, watched a few minutes of the performance and then mocked up notes for the rest of the act."

For a long moment Martin said nothing, just stared at her, wild-eyed, as if she were some gypsy hag making foul predictions. Finally, in the softest of whispers, he said, "That's crazy . . ."

Jocelyn picked up her cue with a vengeance. "No, *that's* not crazy. But I'll tell you what is. Calling Seward to give notes on a show that's been running two years the morning *after* your leading lady's been killed . . . that's pretty damn crazy, even for someone as meticulous as you . . . You see, it should've slipped your mind completely, but it didn't. And that makes me wonder."

"But you can't think that I—"

"You hated Harriet in the part. That was obvious. She might have ruined the whole production . . . or she might have gotten you canned. Maybe you figured that Tewes'd keep his money in the show

even if Harriet were no longer . . . around. That way you could still
have a shot at your Tony."

Now Martin was the one who had an anxious eye on Kevin Kern
as he picked his way through the crowded room toward their table.

"Have you said anything to Gerrard?"

"No, I wanted to talk to you first. Where did you go, Charlie?"

She almost pitied him then. His stricken brown eyes, framed by his
unkempt hair and beard, gave Martin the look of a trapped animal.
Then something within that aggressively masculine exterior seemed
to cave in; she almost fancied that she could hear the faint sigh of an
escaping spirit rising above the table.

"I went to the park."

She was incredulous. "To the park? For what—a stroll?"

"No, I went to the Bushes . . . to meet Paul. For chrissake, don't
tell Kevin. I couldn't . . . stand that. It's not something—I mean, I
don't often." Then simply, "Paul was a very hard boy to say no to.
There didn't seem any harm in it. No one knew, no one at all."

Kevin now stood by their table, gazing down at both of them
serenely, his usual bonhomie heightened by alcohol and flattery.

"Well, well, well, you two must have been having quite a tête-à-
tête. Has Charles been trying to lure you into his bed, Josh? He usually does . . . and usually succeeds, don't you, Charlie ol' boy?"

Martin looked up at Kevin with a sickly smile, a death mask's
grin. Jocelyn, who only wanted to curl up in a ball beneath the table,
braced herself for a very bad half hour.

CHAPTER 27

"What in God's name did you say to Charlie, Josh? He looked like a sick dog looking for a ditch to die in by the time we left."

"I didn't say anything. He's just worried about the show," she snapped back irritably. They were walking uptown on Columbus Avenue. The cool night breeze was a relief after the claustrophobic atmosphere of the smoky bar but Jocelyn, ineffably tired and still dazed by the shock of Charlie Martin's revelation, found the effort of putting up a pretense almost more than she could bear. If she didn't watch herself, she would start taking things out on Kevin who, despite his anxiousness on the phone earlier that evening, seemed to be in a maddeningly congenial mood. It was just as well, seeing as how he had had to bear the brunt of keeping up the conversation for the last half hour, before they left Dobson's. But it still seemed slightly unfair to her that he should appear so carefree while her stomach was tied in knots. However, she was quite willing to let him chatter on aimlessly as they strolled along; it left her mind free to try to absorb this latest piece of information.

What amazed her most was that, in a profession where everybody knew everybody else's business, there should still be so much going on beneath the surface; a seemingly endless myriad of intrigues and involvements that never saw the light of day. The past twenty-four hours alone had presented her with more eye-opening disclosures than are usually found in the last scene of a Molière farce. First Max, and now Charlie. Who would have dreamed that Charlie Martin, one of the most infamous womanizers on Broadway, would swing both ways . . . and with Paul Radner of all people! A very imprudent and potentially dangerous liaison that had obviously been managed with the utmost discretion—a quality that she would not normally have attributed to either man.

She was still meditating on nature's infinite book of secrecy when

Kevin's voice finally permeated her consciousness. "Charlie was there when it happened, you know."

"Charlie was where when what happened? What are you talking about?"

Reprovingly, he said, "Jocelyn, you really are lost in space tonight. It must be that knock you got on the head. I just said that Charlie was with Harold when they got the news about Paul. He went over there early this morning, to talk over some production changes with Tewes, and he was there when the police called. I figure that's why he's so out of it tonight. Though it's not like Charlie."

"Well, we can't all be as resilient as you, Kevin." She was unable to keep the bitchiness out of her voice but went on quickly. "What time did you say he got there?"

"I didn't say . . . but I guess it was around nine, nine-thirty. He told me yesterday that he was going over there to have a breakfast business meeting with Harold. Why do you want to know?"

"No reason. I just wondered," she said evasively.

"Tell me, Josh," a little of his earlier anxiety creeping back into Kevin's voice, "what do you think happened to Paul today? Was it really just an accident?"

"Kevin, I have no idea," she said wearily. "I just wish you'd get over this notion that I have clairvoyant powers—I don't. Or maybe it's just that you think I'm in a position to *know*—is that it?"

"Lord no, no, of course not." The degree of his evident embarrassment told Jocelyn that there was some grain of truth in her last observation. But if he did think that she was in some way involved in the two fatalities, why was he so eager to be in her company? Was he hoping to learn something, or was it possible that he just didn't much care if it were true or not? She found both alternatives equally disturbing.

"Jocelyn, these past few weeks have been awful for all of us—you especially. And I'm sorry. I'd like to make it up to you."

"Kevin, I appreciate the thought. But whatever I've been through, it's not your job to make amends for it."

"I know that . . . but I'd like to try, anyway." They were almost at her building by this point. "Let me come up, Josh. For a few minutes, at least. Okay?"

He placed one hand caressingly along the side of her neck and turned her to face him. She was tired and confused and her body yearned for the consolation of a strong pair of arms. More than anything she wanted peace. But although the dancing green eyes and knowing smile promised pleasure and, yes, passion, there was no real warmth there.

Kevin was leaning over her, his mouth coming closer to hers as she ransacked her brain for a graceful "out," when a steely voice broke the silence.

"I'm sorry to disturb you . . ." The tone belied the words; Phillip Gerrard was patently uncontrite as he stepped out of a blue sedan, arrogantly parked alongside the fire hydrant in front of Jocelyn's building. Jocelyn, initially relieved by the appearance of this deus ex machina, immediately checked her enthusiasm when she saw the grim set of Gerrard's mouth and the glint in his eyes. If looks could kill, it appeared that Kevin and she would be well on their way to a better life.

"Phil—Mr. Gerrard, what are you doing here?"

"I'd like a few words with you, Miss O'Roarke," he said coldly.

"Look, Gerrard," said Kevin, in his best highhanded manner, "aren't you working overtime? Or can't you confine your harassment to the hours from nine to five? Jocelyn's had quite enough . . ."

"Kevin, easy now, it's alright," she said placatingly. But as she took a tentative step in Gerrard's direction, Kevin's hand shot out to grab her elbow. Unfortunately he miscalculated and grabbed the strap of her shoulder bag instead. The strap broke, scattering the contents of her purse onto the sidewalk. The next instant, Kevin, Gerrard and Jocelyn were on their knees gathering up pens, notebooks and cosmetics from the sidewalk. Jocelyn hadn't felt this exposed since the time her suitcase had burst open at LaGuardia. Mercifully, by the time they had everything stuffed back inside the bag, the moment of tension had passed. Kevin bid Jocelyn a sulky good night and Philip Gerrard accompanied her up to her apartment. Neither of them spoke until they were inside her door. Once there, they both had plenty to say. Jocelyn, having a more acute sense of timing, got in the first word.

"You make quite an entrance, Gerrard, I must say. I think you missed your true calling."

"Could be. Though I think I lack your boyfriend's flair for melodrama."

"He's not my boyfriend!"

"Could've fooled me. But then appearances are deceiving. And theatre people are so indiscriminately affectionate."

"Oh, that's cute. And all policemen are pigs on the take! I'll swap clichés with you all night, if you like. We met for a drink—that's all. He wanted to know about Paul. I didn't tell him anything. But then, I had nothing to tell, did I? Seeing as how I've been left in the dark all day . . . You could've called, damn it."

They faced each other across Jocelyn's bar, both of them breathing heavily. It occurred to Phillip Gerrard that he was behaving in a most un-policeman-like manner and had been for some minutes now. After the long hours in the garage with Arnie, he'd stopped briefly to wolf down a quick meal in a coffee shop and then driven straight over to Jocelyn's apartment, anxious to tell her what he'd learned. The sight of her coming home with Kern had given him a nasty jolt and all his years of police training had gone up in a cloud of pea-green smoke. Now it was time to get back down to business—if only there wasn't such a golden flame in those strange hazel eyes and if only that damp black curl wasn't clinging to her cheek.

Jocelyn, for her part, felt dangerously close to tears. She exhaled deeply, lowered her eyes and asked Gerrard if he'd like a drink. She poured out two glasses of Remy Martin and watched Phillip Gerrard as he paced the floor, rolling the brandy snifter between his hands.

"First of all, I'd like you to tell me what else happened at the theatre today. Anything at all that might be of value—might shed some light on all this. I need as much background as you can give me."

She sat down in the rocking chair, took a deep sip, shut her eyes and gave him a nearly verbatim report of her encounter with John Baron, her dinner with Frederick Revere, and her conversation with Charlie Martin, including Kevin's bit of information about Charlie having been at Tewes's apartment that morning. She was lucid and concise and, once again, he was struck by her ability to grasp the most salient pieces of information. But when she raised her head and he saw the deep shadows under her eyes something tugged at his heart and he knew that he must tell her what he'd learned, and quickly—she deserved to be let off the hook.

"I went over Paul Radner's car with a fine-tooth comb."

"And?"

"It wasn't an accident."

"Oh my God! The brakes?"

"No, it wasn't the brakes or the motor. Something much more subtle . . . and it'll be hell to prove; the seat runners."

"The *what?!*"

"The bucket seat had been unbolted from the runners on the floor. A very minor piece of tampering. But anyone who knew Radner and how he drove that MG—always waiting to brake until the last moment—could figure on creating a fairly nasty accident. Not necessarily fatal, perhaps, but serious enough to keep him from getting to the theatre and talking to you. That was the point."

Jocelyn turned a deathly white. "You mean, if I hadn't called him this morning . . . he'd still be alive?"

Gerrard abruptly set down his drink and turned to kneel in front of Jocelyn, placing two strong hands over hers, which were tightly clutching the arms of the rocking chair. "Don't think that! Not now or ever. What happened to Paul was inevitable. Once the murderer realized that Paul was the one who attacked you in the theatre and taken what you'd uncovered—he would have to be eliminated . . . unless Paul came to us, which I doubt that he would have."

"But how"—she fought to keep her voice from breaking—"how do you know that?"

"I found it—what Paul took from the attic. Right before I left the garage, I checked the trunk of the car and it was there. He was bringing it to show you . . . it was the cardboard box."

"The box? It was there? But how can you be sure . . . what was in it?"

"Light bulbs. GE soft pink light bulbs . . . and a few grains of sand."

Caught between relief and horror, Jocelyn silently rocked back and forth in the chair until a huge wave of sobs engulfed her and she slid forward into the waiting arms of Phillip Gerrard.

CHAPTER 28

"He's so fine. Wish he were mine. That handsome boy over there. The one with the wavy hair . . ."

For the first time in weeks Jocelyn found herself singing during her morning shower. The bathroom tiles created a pleasing echo chamber effect as Jocelyn soaped herself. As Phillip Gerrard had said the night before while she was drying her eyes and sponging the mascara stains from his lapel, "It makes perfect sense really. If the murderer wanted Harriet's death to look like an accident, those light bulbs *had* to be there! His initial plan was to make everyone think that Harriet had fallen off a chair and hit her head while installing her precious pink lights. And we almost fell for it, too. Those light bulbs were a vital prop in the killer's scenario. Now, only you and John Baron were present when Harriet asked Paul to pick up those bulbs. Nobody else knew about that. So rehearsal breaks up, everybody leaves and Harriet goes up to her dressing room to wait for Harold. The killer comes back into the theatre from the backstage entrance, disguised as a delivery man, carrying his 'prop.' He must have had a nasty shock when he saw the other box of light bulbs sitting on the dressing table. And he's on a tight schedule because he knows that Harold is going to turn up and discover the body fairly soon so he stashes the box behind the flats on the third floor."

"But it was days before I went up there to look for the box. Why didn't he just go back earlier and get the box out of there?"

"Too risky, Josh. Once you'd spotted him and made that whole stink about a mysterious man carrying a package, he couldn't trust to luck that he'd be able to get it out of there unobserved. When we didn't come across it in our initial search, it was safer for him to just let it sit there. And let everyone think you were lying to save your skin."

"Which is exactly what everyone *did* think, damn it."

"Well . . . not everyone."

"But Phillip, you just said something about the killer coming *back* into the theatre after rehearsal. Does that mean you think the murderer is definitely someone in the company?"

"Not necessarily . . . although, on the surface, it's the most logical deduction. It had to be someone who had a sound knowledge of the theatre's layout and of the production schedule . . . where people would be at certain given times . . . but there are other possibilities."

"Such as?"

"Well, for one thing . . . I know it's a wild notion . . . but are you *sure*, Josh, that the delivery man you saw actually was a man?"

"It *had* to be! Well, of course, those overalls were awfully baggy. But still, he was so . . . tall," she ended feebly.

"Lots of women are tall too."

"I know that but—"

"Sybil Stearns is tall."

"Sybil! But why . . . Phillip, what are you getting at?"

Gerrard told an incredulous Jocelyn about Sybil's absence from her desk on the day of Harriet's death. Jocelyn lit a cigarette and tried to let this new piece of information sink in. Her concentration was disturbed by the sight of Gerrard sliding a cigarette out of her pack and lighting it.

"Phillip! What are you doing? Listen, I've got toothpicks in the cupboard . . ."

"Jocelyn, give me a break, okay? I'm tired of picking slivers out of my gums."

"Well . . . okay. But it's a terrible habit."

"She says, puffing on her tenth cigarette."

"I only French inhale, though."

"Great. So by the time my lungs go, your nose will be sliding off your face."

"Have it your way," she sniffed. "But look, about Sybil . . . I just can't buy it. I admit I only got a glimpse of the guy with the box, but I'd swear that it *was* a guy . . . And I'm fairly acute about these things," she said with a smile. "After all, I did Viola in *Twelfth Night* once. Besides, what did Sybil have to gain from killing Harriet?"

"Maybe a new husband. Come on, Josh, you've seen how she is around Tewes. She devotes her whole life to that man. In many ways she's a hell of a lot more wifely than Harriet ever was, from what I've heard."

"Okay, I'll grant you that—Sybil's a possibility. A mighty slim one, if you ask me, but a possibility nonetheless. But what doesn't make sense to me is—why *then?*"

"Why then what?"

"Why was Harriet killed at that particular time on that particular day? It was so . . . well, so inconvenient, wasn't it? There was so little time! Why not stage the accident in the morning? Harriet always got to the theatre early for rehearsal and stayed up in her dressing room until she was called for her scenes in Act Two, and Act One takes forever to run through. That would allow much more time for a fatal hemorrhage."

"But, as it was, she died right after having a huge row with you. Making you the immediate suspect if the accident plan fell through."

"No, that's no good. You said yourself that this was all carefully preplanned. No one could have *known* that a big flare-up was going to take place between Harriet and me that afternoon. God knows, the warning signals had been there ever since I took over for her in Boston, but you'd have to be clairvoyant to predict the exact hour and day of combustion!"

Gerrard ground out his cigarette vigorously. "You know, I think you're on to something! The time element for this crime has been driving me buggy from the beginning. Like you said, no matter who did it, it had to have been damnably difficult in such a short space of time. But if there's a reason why Harriet had to die that particular day and no earlier or later, then the whole thing makes more sense. Unfortunately, I haven't an inkling what the reason could be. How about you?"

"Uh . . . I don't think so. Do you think it could tie in with why Paul clouted me up in the attic?"

Gerrard gave a quick negative shake of his head. "Doubt it. Looks like you were right about Paul. I think the only crime he was involved in was having a somewhat exaggerated opinion of himself."

"Meaning what?"

"Meaning that he didn't have any more of a notion of what was in that box than you did. Probably didn't even know it was there until he saw you kneeling over it. I think he was afraid that John Baron might've done mommy in and was trying to shield him. When he got the box home and saw what was in it, he must have realized that it put Baron in the clear. That's why he was so willing to meet with you this morning. He just wanted to straighten the whole mess out."

"But the box! How could the murderer know Paul had it unless he overheard our conversation on the phone?"

"There are quite a few people who could've listened in on your little talk, for one thing. We checked with the doorman—Charlie Martin, Sybil Stearns, Austin Frost and even Harvey Samuels were all at Tewes's apartment this morning and the place is chock full of extensions. Also, there's a good chance that someone might've seen Paul take the box out to his car from the theatre the other night. Needless to say, it would have been child's play to sneak into the garage and fix the MG. So it doesn't really help us narrow the field. We still have to figure out why Harriet had to be killed before we'll know who killed her."

They spent another thirty minutes rehashing the case, trying to approach it from every conceivable angle, but nothing concrete emerged; no brilliant hypothesis that would pull all the various threads of evidence into a whole fabric of proof occurred to either one of them. Completely talked out, they sat in companionable silence sipping the last of their brandies. It was close to 2 A.M. when Jocelyn, for the second night running, walked Phillip Gerrard to the door. The awkwardness of the previous evening had vanished, but in its place was a crosscurrent of kinetic energy that obliterated their mutual fatigue and left them both, momentarily, at a loss for words. With her hand in Gerrard's firm, warm grasp Jocelyn noticed, for the first time, the tiny dimple in his chin and could think of nothing else save how delicious it would be to place the tip of one's tongue into that cleft. Restraint not being a trait native to her personality, she was thankful for the stringent Police Academy training that prompted Gerrard to break the prolonged silence.

"Look, I hate to be redundant, but if you think of something—anything at all—call me. I mean it, now. No more solo Nancy Drew stuff. Okay?"

"Nancy Drew, my ass. I've always fancied myself more the Harriet Vane type."

Smiling softly, he said, "Well, your neck does have an arum lilly quality to it, but I don't think romantic stoicism is quite your style. G'night now."

Jocelyn accompanied the Doobie Brothers singing "You Keep Me

Runnin'" on the radio, as she made her morning coffee and mentally replayed Phillip Gerrard's parting comment. More pleasing to her than the compliment was the fact that he read the right *books!* In her view *Antony and Cleopatra* was just a story about sexual infatuation compared to what Harriet and Peter Wimsey had going for them. Her fond literary reverie was broken by the ringing of the phone.

"Josh, my sweet, it's Austin. I'm calling for two vital reasons: business and dirt. Which do you want first?"

"Well, I don't know," she answered weakly, surprised by the blitheness of his tone until she remembered that, for the world in general, Paul's accident was just that and nothing more. "Tell me the business part first, I guess."

"Okay, we'll save the best for last then . . . Anyway, rehearsal has been postponed till one o'clock. Charlie, Peter and Harold have been in a powwow all morning and Harold's coming in at one to give a reassuring despite-our-bereavement-all-systems-are-go type speech to the company . . . Look, I don't mean to sound callous, but there hasn't been a day in the past six months when I haven't expected to pick up a paper and read of Paul's early demise. That boy lent new meaning to the term 'life in the fast lane.' I knew he was going to burn himself out one way or the other and, once he got Harriet's money, I figured it would only be a matter of days, frankly. Not to be cruel, I figure the only true mourner at his funeral will be John, the poor sod."

"Don't be an ass, Austin," she snapped, truly perplexed by her friend's lack of feeling. "Remember Max, for chrissake. The man is totally bereft."

"Oh Lord, you're right. I'd forgotten all about that—it's so perfectly Dickens, it's hard to credit as real. I mean Harold never gave me the slightest clue—ever! But you're right. Listen, Josh, I don't mean to sound like a prick but the gloom and doom around that theatre yesterday really got to me. I didn't know if the show was going on or not and I couldn't face another night of silent sorrow with Harold and Sybil . . . so I found myself a little *divertissement*, don't ya know."

Acerbically, she said, "Don't I just. Who with . . . anyone I know?"

"No, only because you're too highfalutin to take any notice of the boys on the crew. And let me tell you, not all those hunks screwing lekos onto the grid have the same idea of what a Miller's High Life is. His name's Ronnie."

"Ronnie, huh. How quaint, how dear—and stars fell on Alabama. Is that your dirt?"

He was testy. "Don't be daft. I know you're not interested in the carnal details. I just thought you might like to know that not all techies are as unobservant as we sometimes think."

"How so?" she asked sharply.

"Ronnie was in the wings gelling a light after we broke rehearsal that fateful Wednesday. Harriet was going up to her dressing room as Kevin Kern was coming downstairs on his way out. Ronnie overheard their passing remarks."

"Which were? Don't tease, Austin, I haven't had my coffee yet and I could turn ugly any second."

"Oh, hush! I'm not teasing. You just have no sense of dramatic narration. Anyway, Ronnie heard Kevin diplomatically suggest to Harriet that she quietly forget about everything that had happened at rehearsal, in the best interests of the show . . . a sentiment I quite applaud. Harriet, who, I gather, was worked up to quite a hysterical state by this point, had several suggestions for Kevin—the least rude of which was that if he didn't button his lip, she was going to tell Harold all about their past involvement and have him fired because the 'pressures of working together were too great.' She then went on to name several hotshot actors who were available to take on the part at a moment's notice."

"What did Kevin say?"

"Ronnie couldn't catch everything Kevin said. He wasn't playing to the balcony the way Harriet was. But he did mumble something about taking the whole mess before the Equity Council and, basically, lambasting Harriet from one end of the Great White Way to the other if she 'got in his way'—quote, unquote. But he ended on a more or less conciliatory note and suggested they both give themselves twenty-four hours to cool off before doing anything they might regret later. After that they both went sotto voce and Ron went back to repairing the light."

"He didn't catch anything else?"

"Well, he did hear one odd thing. He thought he heard Kevin walk down the corridor toward the backstage exit and Harriet start up the stairs to the dressing rooms until her footsteps stopped about midway and he heard her *moan*."

"Moan how? There are all sorts of moans, Austin!"

"Well, she wasn't having a *petit frisson,* that's for damn sure. Ronnie said it sounded like she was in pain, maybe. She seemed to hold onto the stairs for a few moments and he heard a faint rustling sound but couldn't figure out what it was. Then she went the rest of the way up the stairs. *Fini.*"

"And he hasn't told this to anyone—Gerrard or Zito?"

"Nope, not a soul. I wouldn't even know about if it weren't for the joys of pillow talk. Ronnie's an attractive boy but a bit naive. Seems he has a schoolboy crush on Kev and thinks you the luckiest girl alive for having been among the chosen."

"Yes, well, everyone can master a lust except he that hasn't had it."

"Exactly. But anyway, Ronnie would never breathe a word to Gerrard about it. That would be like Scarlett snitching on Ashley Wilkes to the carpetbaggers, you see."

"'All for love and nothing for reward,' eh? It is sort of touching in its own sick way."

"You will excuse me if I don't choke up over it. It didn't make for the most ego-gratifying postcoital chitchat, as you can imagine."

"I'd rather not." She paused, pondering the best way to shift the conversation toward her more immediate areas of interest, and finally opted for a semi-direct approach. "Listen, Austin, were you by any chance at Harold's apartment when they got the news of Paul's accident?"

"God, yes, worse luck," he groaned. "Harold wanted me there for his breakfast conference with Charles. It was *awful,* truly the pits. As bad as the shock was—coming on the heels of Harriet and all—what was even worse was that everyone felt they *should* feel something but didn't! Paul, for all his charm, was one of the most totally self-centered people I've ever known. And in this business that's saying something. *We* didn't mean anything to him when he was alive, so his death wasn't a great personal loss to any of us—except John, of course."

"John?" Jocelyn spluttered coffee on her best cotton shirt. "John Baron was at Harold's yesterday morning?"

"Oh, sure. John's there all the time, now that Harriet's not around. He 'dropped by for coffee'—I think that's the proper euphemism."

"Meaning what?"

"Meaning he never dropped *out*. That's a big apartment with a front *and* a back entrance. The back entrance is right by Paul's room. So when John appeared at the breakfast table in a fresh shirt but wearing yesterday's socks, it wasn't hard for me to put two and two together—one and one together, I should say."

"No wonder the doorman didn't tell Phillip," she thought. "He didn't know!" Out loud she asked, "And Harold had no idea?"

"Not a clue, as far as I could see."

"Did Paul have breakfast with you?"

"No, but then it was never his favorite meal. He just peeled out of there like a bat outa hell. Sybil told us he'd gotten a call, but I don't know who from. I figured it was either a new beau or his coke connection—another one of his little predilections that the folks had no inkling of. He didn't usually galvanize like that in the morning hours. Hell, he never took a course that met before noon if he could possibly help it."

Jocelyn had a brief impulse to tell Austin who Paul's mystery caller was but thought better of it. Instead she asked, "What was the whole breakfast conference about?"

"Nothing much. It was Charlie's idea. He wanted to talk about publicity—which isn't really his job. We've got the best publicists in the business and they're doing a great job, all things considered. But you know Martin, he's got to have a hand in everything. As it turned out, nothing much got accomplished. Harold had to leave the room every two seconds to take one pressing call after another. It's ridiculous that they don't have a phone in the dining room but Harriet felt that it interfered with 'civilized dining.' We were just starting to get down to business when the police called and then that was that."

"But what was . . . I mean . . ." she paused mendaciously, "was anyone else there?"

"Just Harvey. He's Harold's doctor too, you know. Harold has that chronic complaint of the big investor—high blood pressure. He stops by now and again to take Harold's blood pressure. Actually, I think he's just hooked on Sybil's coffee—which is great. He spent most of his time with her in the kitchen. They're thick as thieves, those two, seeing as how they both serve the Lord with gladness, so to speak."

"Why, Austin, I didn't know you were so well versed in your psalms!"

"Of course I'm not, silly girl. We don't all have twelve years of parochial schooling behind us. However, like all writers, I'm extremely well versed in Bartlett's Quotations.

"Anyway, that's all my news. I'll see you at the theatre at one, and let's hope to God that we can get through this day without any more nasty surprises."

Jocelyn put down the receiver and polished off the last of her coffee. She felt like having another cup but decided against it, as it would make her want to smoke, and it was too early in the day for that. But she had several hours to kill before she needed to leave for the theatre so, in true Virgoan fashion, she cast her eye about the apartment looking for something to put in order. She immediately ze-roed in on her leather handbag with the broken strap. Well, she couldn't change to her winter bag because that one matched her mauve wool coat, so there was nothing for it but to pull out her sum-mer canvas bag from storage. Taking it down from the top shelf of her closet, she had an uncomfortable sensation of déjà vu, remember-ing that the last time she had used this purse had been the day of Harriet's death. She unzipped the bag and was starting to transfer the paraphernalia from her leather bag when she spied something at the bottom: a small plastic vial with a pharmacist's label on it. She opened it, looked at the one capsule left inside the container and read the label again. Having reread it, she placed the vial gingerly on the table in front of her, knowing that Austin's hopes for an unevent-ful afternoon had been shot to hell.

CHAPTER 29

Jocelyn barely heard a word Charlie Martin was saying. Sitting in the last row of the orchestra she was, without realizing it, following Kafka's advice: "Do not even listen, simply wait." Though simple waiting, in itself, was no mean feat. Outside the weather was brisk and autumnal but inside the theatre the air was warm and fetid, which only served to increase her sensation of being on a storm watch.

John Baron and Max Bramling sat at opposite ends of the front row, creating the distressing image of chief mourners at a funeral. They both looked as if they had been to hell and back, though John wore his misery with an air of romantic Southern decadence while Max merely looked sodden with grief and last night's whiskey. Kevin Kern, still smarting from his run-in with Gerrard, had asked Jocelyn, somewhat snidely, if she had had a trying time with "that mini-Mickey Spillane" and then taken a seat as far away from her as possible without waiting for her reply. Observing him now as he sat slumped down, fingertips pressed together in a steeple, with pursed lips and deeply furrowed brow, she recognized all the earmarks of one of his dark, Byronic moods. He would have to look elsewhere for sympathy today; Jocelyn had absolutely none to spare.

Even Sybil Stearns seemed off her stride. For one thing, she had come to the theatre with Harold wearing tinted glasses, which she hadn't bothered to remove once she entered the darkened house. Jocelyn wondered if she had been crying or if she simply hadn't had time to do her normally subtle but effective eye makeup. What surprised Jocelyn even more was the other woman's carriage: Sybil, devoid of her usual grace, moved with the extreme caution of the elderly as she took her place beside Tewes, a few rows in front of Jocelyn. Once she was seated, Jocelyn saw that several strands of hair had fallen loose from Sybil's always impeccable chignon. With any other woman such a minor slip would indicate mere inattention to detail, but on Sybil it seemed to signal some sort of ultimate resignation.

Charlie Martin, still droning on, had resumed the role of the unflappable director, though he had not once been able to bring himself to meet Jocelyn's gaze and probably wouldn't for a long time. Even Peter Morrance was far from his usual soothing self, as he stood at the back of the stage tersely snapping orders at various technicians. On the whole, only Austin seemed relatively normal: thanks, Jocelyn supposed, to the rejuvenating effects of Ronnie. He slid into the seat next to hers a good ten minutes after the start of Martin's oration and asked cheerily, "Where's the house dick?"

"Talking about Ronnie?"

"Don't be vulgar, Jocelyn. I meant where's Gerrard? I thought, after the accident and all, he'd be bound to be sniffing around, trying to make two and two equal five."

"I'm sure he has more important things to attend to, Austin." Really, she was getting quite annoyed with people making derogatory remarks about Phillip Gerrard and she didn't enjoy having to resort to subterfuge with a friend. Detective work sorely taxed her capacity for discretion.

"Well, don't get all huffy, girl. I was just asking . . . How's everyone holding up?"

"Well, Charlie, as you can see, is going to start quoting *Uncle Vanya* any minute now. Kevin's sulking and John and Max are just barely holding in there."

"Yes, I can see that. Poor old Max . . . Well, at least John's got some consolation coming his way."

Jocelyn shot Austin a puzzled glance. "What could possibly be of any comfort to John now, pray tell?"

"Money, of course."

"What do you mean 'of course'? What money?"

It was Austin's turn to look surprised. "Didn't I tell you? Guess not—everything's happened so fast . . . John is one of the principal beneficiaries in Paul's will. Paul told me so himself."

"You're kidding!"

"I never kid about money. Listen, Paul might've been a cold-hearted little ass. I doubt if he ever cared for John the way John cared for him. But he did have his own strange kind of loyalty. John gave that boy a better background in the workings of professional theatre than he would've gotten in eighteen years at Juilliard—or anywhere else, for that matter. Paul knew it, and if he couldn't return John's affection in kind he at least made sure that John would get some kind of return on his investment."

"Well, I'll be damned! Did John know this?"

Austin shrugged. "He might've. Paul didn't say."

"Did he say who else would inherit?"

Austin's blithe spirits dulled somewhat under Jocelyn's interrogation. "Oh, some of it will revert back to Harold, I'm sure . . . and I guess some of it will come to me."

"You didn't even *like* Paul!"

"Yeah, I know. I think that was part of it. I think it was more or less a political move on his part. I mean, he wasn't planning to die, you know. And he was a very ambitious boy. Believe it or not, he had great faith in me as an up-and-coming playwright. I'm sure he let me know about the inheritance as a way of getting some kind of hook into me as far as any of my future works were concerned. He really did fancy himself a budding David Merrick . . . and wills can always be changed later on. Paul was no fool."

"No, I can see that."

She was debating whether or not to make another call to Phillip Gerrard when an agitated Harvey Samuels scurried into the back of the theatre and took a seat directly behind Harold and Sybil. He tapped Tewes's shoulder with a tentative, birdlike gesture.

"Harvey! What on earth are you doing here?"

"I was . . . asked to come. By Detective Gerrard."

Sybil Stearns's head snapped over her shoulder and Jocelyn heard a hushed but intense, "Why?"

"He . . . I don't know. He called me this morning and asked me some questions. They didn't seem to make much sense. Then he asked me if I could come here straightaway. It was very peculiar but he was quite insistent."

Harold uttered a sound that was halfway between a "huh" and a grunt and Sybil Stearns turned silently and bowed her head. Before Samuels could say anything more, Charlie Martin wound up his pep talk with, "And now because, as Chekhov says, 'an artist must pass judgment only on what he understands,' I'd like to hand things over to our remarkable producer, Harold Tewes, who's in charge of all those practical matters that I *don't* understand."

It was a feeble joke at an uncomfortable time but it did allow Charles a Chekhovian out, which was probably all he wanted at that

moment. Harold rose slowly and went to take his place in front of
the proscenium. All eyes were riveted on the somber, dignified figure
before them except Jocelyn's, which were intently focused on the
box-office manager, who had just entered and tapped Sybil Stearns
on the shoulder. She jerked upright at his touch but quickly regained
her composure and rose to accompany him out of the auditorium.

Tewes was taking his time gathering his thoughts. All in all, it
wasn't a bad ploy, Jocelyn thought. After Martin's forced prolixity,
Harold's quiet presence made an impressive contrast. Finally, after
Sybil had come back to resume her seat, he began speaking in slowly
measured tones as he looked down at his hands and gently twisted
his wedding band round and round his finger. When he spoke it did
not seem that he was addressing a large gathering but, rather, as if he
were engaged in a very private soliloquy.

"I know that some of you must think me some kind of . . . mon-
ster. To be up here discussing business amidst all the sorrow and loss
that we have . . . all experienced. We say 'The show must go on'—
but at what price? That's what's crossing your minds, as well it
should. It's certainly crossed mine. All I can say is that there's an investment involved here. There's the investment of your time, talent,
effort and . . . expectations. And there's the investment of my
money. Well, let me tell you, I can well afford to lose that money
. . . I have very good tax lawyers. What I can't afford to lose is *your*
investment—your commitment to make this show work. Because that
is what my wife and my stepson wanted: to see this play produced
and performed. I can bear the loss of their presence, as we all must,
but I cannot bear the loss of their dream—their last desire. I hope
that you feel the same way I do. There will, of course, be detractors
in the press who will accuse us of sensationalism and 'cashing in.' We
have to expect that but we can't let it stop us. I think Austin has
written a very fine and important play which has been given—thanks
to all of you—the production it deserves. I feel very strongly—as I
hope you do—that there is no finer memorial we could make to Harriet and Paul than to do our best to ensure the success of *Term of
Trial*."

There was a long silence in the house after Tewes's speech, broken
only by the rustle of Kleenex and the snuffling of noses. Actors tend
to view producers as a breed apart; a not quite human breed at that.
But Harold's simple yet eloquent plea had made its impact on even
the most cynical members of the company. Jocelyn, who thought that

Tewes's whole tone and delivery was a masterly piece of understatement, was the only member of the audience to observe the entrance of a new character into the drama. For the past five minutes Phillip Gerrard had been standing at a side entrance, under the shadow of an unlit exit sign. Now he soundlessly glided toward the pool of light that encompassed Harold Tewes. Putting a deferential hand on the older man's arm, he said, "Excuse me, Mr. Tewes, but there's something I'd like to say to the company."

CHAPTER 30

For the first time in his life, Phillip Gerrard was experiencing stage fright. He'd never actually been in the spotlight before, but now all eyes were upon him. His visceral reaction was one of pure panic and he wondered, briefly, how people could do this sort of thing for a living. For he was, in a way, playing a part—one that he didn't relish— and he wasn't at all sure that he knew his lines. He had voiced these doubts earlier in the day to Jocelyn O'Roarke when she had convinced him that this was the only way to resolve the case. Her instant reply had been, "Improvise. Isn't that what most of detective work is —improvisation? You take the facts of a case and imagine what could have happened to bring about certain results that led to a crime."

"Yes, in a way . . . But there's so little *proof!*"

"Exactly! And there's precious little hope that we're going to come up with anything more in the way of hard evidence. So this is the only way."

"It's completely unorthodox. And if it doesn't work . . ."

"If it doesn't work we'll be no worse off than before. And if I know anything about psychological motivations—which, God knows, I should—it *will* work. Besides . . . it's the only chance we've got."

But more than the irrefutable logic of this last argument, his own sure instincts had finally convinced him, and now it was too late to go back. Many things weighed on his mind, not the least of which was the question of whether or not Jocelyn O'Roarke could ever come to care for an ex-police detective, ignobly drummed out of the ranks. Well, what the hell, he thought, it *was* the only way and she'd asked for it.

Phillip Gerrard was a better actor than he gave himself credit for, however. As he turned his implacable gaze toward the house, there wasn't a person among them, Jocelyn included, who perceived his anxiety. On the contrary, his dry, clipped tones instilled attentiveness and disquietude in equal measures.

"I think it's only fair—as most of you have been involved in this case in one way or another—that you should be given the facts of our investigation up to this point. The newest development has to do with Paul Radner's death."

Jocelyn saw John Baron's back go ramrod straight and heard Austin's hissing intake of breath.

"We have good reason to believe that Mr. Radner's death was no accident," Gerrard continued in his most professional manner. "For one thing, we've found evidence that the bucket seat in his car had been unbolted from the floor-runners. Anyone who knew his driving habits could count on this to create a serious—if not fatal—accident. Secondly, we found something in the trunk of the MG: a box of pink light bulbs, the kind that Harriet Weldon used in her dressing room . . . which leads us to think that Paul Radner was the one who attacked Miss O'Roarke in the attic the other night—not because he knew what she had discovered but because he was worried that what she had uncovered might incriminate someone. Presumably, that someone was you, Mr. Baron."

John Baron gave an infinitesimal nod as he lit a cigarette. Phillip Gerrard regarded him closely before going on. "He knew that his mother vehemently objected to your relationship and had strongly insinuated that, if it didn't cease, your position in this company—your whole career—might be in jeopardy. Isn't that so?"

"Righter than rain, as they say where I come from," was Baron's response.

"And he showed you the contents of the box, didn't he?"

"How did you—oh, never mind. One shouldn't underestimate the long arm of the law, I suppose." Baron maintained his composure but there was a faint tremor in the languid hand that held his cigarette. "Yes, he showed me the light bulbs. I was with him the night before he died. I had asked to see him. He had disappeared from the theatre shortly after Jocelyn came down to borrow Peter's flashlight, so I had my suspicions. When I got to the apartment, he let me in the back door. We have . . . had an arrangement with the doorman, so no one else knew I was there. He admitted what he'd done and why and showed me the box."

"What did you say to him?"

"I . . . we had words. I was very angry with him, not because he had suspected me of . . . eliminating Harriet. In a way, I guess I should've been flattered that he'd gone to such lengths to protect me. But I was appalled by what he'd done to Jocelyn."

Gerrard asked, "For the benefit of the others present, could you tell us why Mr. Radner's suspicions were immediately allayed once he saw what was in the box?"

"Oh, yes, that. Jocelyn and I were there when Harriet asked Paul to go pick up the lights, you see. So I would've known that a box of lights would already be in her dressing room later that day . . . and so would Jocelyn."

Austin gave Jocelyn's hand a squeeze and whispered, "Score one for our side." He was puzzled by the total absence of relief or gratification on her face as she sat tensed, leaning forward on the very edge of her seat.

"When did you leave the apartment that night?"

"I . . . uh, didn't. I stayed the night. We had a lot to talk over."

Gerrard, who wasn't hearing anything that he didn't already know, had time to wonder how it was possible for a man to be as uncomfortable as Baron obviously was and still speak with a drawl.

"What did you talk about, then?"

"We discussed what he should do next. I was very worried about Paul withholding evidence. Isn't that the term? Plus, I felt that it might be a danger to him to have it in his possession. He, on the other hand, was worried about assault charges being brought against him if he went to the police. His notion was to go to Max and ask him to act as a sort of go-between."

For the first time that afternoon, Max Bramling gave signs of being present in more than a solely physical sense. John turned to him with a weak but sincere smile. "It's true. I don't think Paul had any notion of your real connection but, for what it's worth, he always was fond of you in his own undemonstrative way. He thought of you as someone he could trust."

Max said nothing, merely nodded, but there was fresh moisture in his eyes.

Gerrard broke the spell. "So presumably you were there, Mr. Baron, when Miss O'Roarke called Paul Radner that morning?"

"Yes, I was. And it threw Paul for a loop when he found out that she knew he was the one who'd hit her. I told him that the best thing to do was to go over to the theatre and make a clean breast of everything to Jocelyn. I figured once she learned what was in the box, she'd overlook what Paul had done and bring the whole matter to you. I told him Jocelyn wasn't vindictive and wouldn't be likely to press charges—though, Lord knows, he deserved it. And I told him to try not to make too big an ass of himself . . . That was the last thing I ever said to him."

John Baron dropped his head, evidently incapable of further speech. Gerrard proceeded to address the company in general.

"There have been certain factors in this case that have troubled me from the beginning. First, we have a murder that was obviously planned to look like an accident and would've been accepted as such if it hadn't been for the small detail of the broken sandbag. But once accident was ruled out, we found ourselves confronted with a plethora of possible suspects with adequate motives: Miss O'Roarke, who had been vilified by Miss Weldon and stood to inherit an important role; Mr. Baron, who had been threatened by the deceased; Mr. Kern, who had once been romantically involved with Miss Weldon and also had words with her shortly before she went up to her dressing room . . ." It was Kevin's turn to come to attention, and the look of shocked surprise on his face was something to behold. He made a few strangled sounds of protest but Gerrard's voice overrode him. "Austin Frost, who knew that Miss Weldon's passing would allow him to regain control over his own plays . . ." Out of the corner of her eye Jocelyn saw Austin shoot her a questioning glance but she dared not return it. "Max Bramling, who might have resented his ex-wife for keeping him away from and unknown to his own son. And Mr. Martin, who was afraid that her performance might destroy a play whose success was vitally important to him." There was a stunned silence in the theatre. Before any voices could be raised in self-defense, he went briskly on. "The second thing we came up against was the time factor: who had sufficient time to kill Harriet Weldon between four and six o'clock? The answer to that, as far as I can see, is everyone. Any one of you had ample time to re-enter the theatre and stage the 'accident,' due to the veritable un-checkability of your alibis. But the action of the crime was not what concerned me most—the risk involved in assuming that Mrs. Tewes would fatally hemorrhage by six o'clock did. It was a huge chance to take and it didn't fit in with the careful and precise style of the crime. Which brings me to my third point: the basic inconvenience of this particular time span—a brief few hours while she was alone between rehearsal and her doctor's appointment. Why not before or later, during the many hours Miss Weldon spent in her dressing room during

rehearsals? This led me to the inevitable conclusion that Harriet
Weldon had to die *then*, no earlier, no later. One thing was obvious—
she never made it to her appointment. I've asked Miss Weldon's physician, Dr. Samuels, to come here to tell us what the nature of that
visit was to have been. Dr. Samuels?"

Harvey Samuels rose from his seat with the greatest of reluctance
and addressed the house with the air of a timid schoolboy.

"Well, it was quite usual, really. She was coming to have another
Protime reading, that's all."

"Yes, doctor. But could you explain to us what a Protime reading
is and why Miss Weldon required one?"

"Oh, yes, I see. Harriet . . . Mrs. Tewes was troubled by blood
clots in her legs—an affliction that can be quite painful and sometimes dangerous. But you know that, don't you? Because of that time
in Boston. Anyway, the usual remedy is Coumadin—a drug which
permits the blood to flow more freely and guards against overcoagulation. Mrs. Tewes was on the standard maintenance dose of
five milligrams a day. But, like diabetics with insulin, the individual's
need for the drug can sometimes fluctuate, so we do periodic read-
ings to determine how quickly or slowly the blood is coagulating
. . . just as a safeguard."

"Yes. Now, Dr. Samuels, are you aware of the autopsy findings
regarding Mrs. Tewes?"

"Ah, yes, I am." A violent blush rose to the doctor's scalp. "I
. . . uh . . . asked to be informed of them."

"And was Coumadin found in the bloodstream?"

"Well, of course it was!"

"Of course. But can you tell us how *much* Coumadin was found?"

"What? Oh, no, I couldn't. You see, it's not an easy substance to
measure, especially after . . . death. You can detect its presence,
certainly, but not the exact amount. That's quite . . . impossible, really."

"Yes, I see. Then perhaps you could tell us this: what if a person
with Mrs. Tewes's condition was taking twice or even three times her
normal dose of Coumadin a day—ten to fifteen milligrams, say. What
would be the physiological effect on that person?"

The florid color abruptly left Harvey Samuels' face and he turned
quite pale as he sensed what Phillip Gerrard was driving at.

"That . . . it would greatly liquefy the blood . . . cause it to flow
at a highly . . . accelerated rate."

"Indeed? Then, in that case, a person who normally had a problem with overcoagulation might develop quite opposite symptoms and, for all intents and purposes, have the same problems as . . ."

"As a hemophiliac, yes." Samuels finished Gerrard's sentence for him. "Even for a person with a clotting disorder, it would be too much of a good thing. And just as for a hemophiliac—or bleeder, as people say—the danger would be great. So much as a small cut would be serious."

"Not to mention a blow that would create hemorrhaging," Gerrard said sharply. "Now, doctor, I'd like you to go back to your last examination of Harriet Weldon, after her trouble in Boston. What was the result of that last Protime reading?"

"It was . . . more or less, the same as before. The clotting had gotten no worse, so I assumed that Harriet had been remiss about taking her medication. It was just one tablet a day, like a vitamin, and she sometimes forgot."

"So you had no call to increase her dosage, then?"

"No, of course not! And I *didn't*. It stayed the same—five milligrams a day."

"And after her visit to New York to see you, you called a pharmacy in Boston so that she could refill her prescription up there?"

"Yes, Alpert Pharmacy. I've had dealings with them before and they've always been most obliging."

"How long should that refill have lasted her?"

"Oh, now, let me see . . . Thirty tablets, I think . . . well past her next visit to my office. Almost another two weeks, I'd say."

"Dr. Samuels, would you please look at this vial I have here." Gerrard held up the plastic container that Jocelyn had found in her purse earlier that day. Moving with a hesitant, almost shuffling gait, Samuels slowly approached the bright circle of light where Gerrard and Harold Tewes stood. Glistening beads of sweat stood out on his forehead and upper lip as he warily took the vial.

"Would you read to us what's on the label, please?"

In a barely audible voice Harvey Samuels read aloud the name of the pharmacy, the date the prescription was filled, the name of the drug, the administering directions and Harriet Weldon's name at the bottom.

"Dr. Samuels, can you estimate for us, figuring from the date indicated on that label, how many tablets of Coumadin would've been left in that container on the day of Harriet Weldon's death?"

There was a long pause as Harvey Samuels, brows deeply knit in concentration, made his calculations. In the darkened auditorium there was, as the poet said, a "silence deep as death, and the boldest held his breath." When the anxious physician finally spoke, his voice held an edge of deep foreboding.

"There . . . uh . . . as well as I can figure . . . there *should* be eighteen Coumadin tablets left."

"Thank you, Doctor. Your calculation tallies with mine. Now would you kindly open the vial?"

He did as he was asked, with hands made clumsy from tension. When he looked inside, the plastic cap fell from his hand onto the floor with a dull click. "But it's not poss— There's only one tablet here!"

"Precisely. The other seventeen, presumably, were in Harriet Weldon's bloodstream when she was struck from behind. Whoever knew that knew that she would bleed to death in a very short time. And whoever it was also knew that a Protime reading would show that her blood had thinned to a dangerous degree . . . which is why she had to die that afternoon, before she reached your office. It's obvious that whoever planned Miss Weldon's death was not in possession of a private cache of Coumadin. In that case there would still be eighteen tablets in that container. The killer was far cleverer than that, and arranged for Harriet to overdose herself . . . When you got the results of Mrs. Tewes's last Protime reading, doctor, did you give them to her yourself?"

"Why . . . no. They were back in Boston by then. It was easier for me to call Mrs. Stearns and tell her."

"I see. And you took that call from Mrs. Stearns didn't you, Mr. Tewes?" Gerrard asked, turning to the older man. Harold, whose face now matched the gray of his flannel suit, spoke softly, with his eyes fixed on Sybil. "Yes, I did . . . but she told me exactly what Harvey said . . . that the Protime reading was fine and Harriet should just go on with the same dosage . . . nothing else."

"So you've said. However, I have here a record, from the hotel where you stayed in Boston, of all incoming calls. It shows that there was another call later that day from your office in New York. It came in at one o'clock. Did you take *that* call also, Mr. Tewes?"

"No . . . I didn't. I was at a business luncheon with some investors."

"So it would seem that your wife received that call, wouldn't it? I assume Sybil Stearns made this second call also . . . I also assume that it would've been very easy for her to invent some story about mixed-up records and tests at the lab and tell your wife that the initial information was wrong and that she needed to increase her dosage of Coumadin."

"But I would've known!"

Gerrard shook his head. "I seriously doubt that. Your wife loathed any reference to her physical ailment. And if she thought her condition was deteriorating, she'd be all the more likely not to mention it for fear you'd cancel the production—or, worse yet, allow a younger actress to take over her role. That's why there was never so much as an allusion to her problem after she missed that performance in Boston. Sybil Stearns could count on that. She could also count on you taking a nap that afternoon, as had become your habit once you'd started attending the evening rehearsals. We know that she wasn't at her desk that whole time . . ." Tewes shot Sybil Stearns an incredulous glance and Jocelyn thought she saw the older woman give an almost imperceptible shake of her head as if in weak denial. Gerrard went on unrelentingly. "We also know that in the hallway outside your office is a storage closet where the maintenance man keeps, among other things, an extra pair of overalls. Sergeant Zito, would you come up here?"

Tommy Zito approached the front of the theatre carrying a paper sack, which he handed to his chief. Reaching inside the bag, Gerrard withdrew a green lump of khaki material, which he shook out and said, "Miss O'Roarke, would you just stand up where you are and tell me if this looks familiar to you."

He held up a pair of workman's overalls. Jocelyn felt her legs shake as they never had before, not even on opening nights, but her voice was calm and clear. "Yes, I think so. The delivery man—well . . . whoever it was I saw carrying that box wore a pair exactly like those."

Silently Phillip Gerrard folded up the material and handed it back to Tommy Zito. He then walked down the center aisle of the theatre, stopping just in front of the woman with the unkempt coiffure. "Mrs. Stearns, I'm afraid you'll have to come along with me."

Sybil Stearns gathered up her things and rose soundlessly from her seat, looking ten years older than the woman who had entered that theatre an hour ago; her bowed shoulders spoke of meek acceptance and despair.

A hushed gasp went up in the auditorium, but behind it there was a dull, low, rumbling sound, like a subway passing below, which quickly accelerated and grew into the roar of a human animal.

"You goddam, bloody bastard! Leave that woman *alone!*"

In a split second Harold Tewes was hurtling down the aisle. He flung himself at Phillip Gerrard and both men fell to the floor, Tewes with both hands on Gerrard's throat. A moment later Tommy Zito and two uniformed policemen were pulling a furious, cursing man, now completely unrecognizable as that bastion of New York finance, off Gerrard. He continued to struggle against their hold for some minutes until hysteria overtook him.

"She never . . . never did," he wept. "She never hurt anyone. The dearest woman in the world—so good. I did it! *I* did it! To be free . . . to be with her. But she never knew a thing—not a thing."

Phillip Gerrard knelt down to face the other man and said, quietly and with great gentleness, "But she did know one thing. She knew that you weren't in your office napping that afternoon. Though she never told us—ever. She probably also knew that you overheard Jocelyn O'Roarke's conversation with Paul, but she was still willing to protect you . . . if that's any consolation."

Phillip Gerrard rose to his feet and resumed his official manner. "Now I must ask you to come with us to the station, Mr. Tewes. You can call your lawyer from there."

Everyone stood watching in stunned silence as a subdued Harold Tewes left the theatre with his police escort. They heard the heavy thud of the lobby doors shutting and still they did not move or speak. They might have stood that way indefinitely, like figures frozen in a landscape, had not Sybil Stearns given a low moan and crumpled to the floor in a dead faint. Everyone sprang into motion at once and, for the third and last time, Jocelyn found herself running toward the foyer to raid the lobby bar.

CHAPTER 31

"Can I get you another drink?" a seductive voice cooed in Phillip Gerrard's ear.

"Ah, no, thank you. I'll wait till my friends get here."

The young redheaded waitress sauntered back to the long mahogany bar, slightly miffed by the lack of response. For his part, Gerrard didn't even watch her back as she retreated. He was the only male in Lady Astor's of which this could be said.

Sitting in a front booth by a window, his attention was focused on the doors to the Public Theatre across the street. The Sunday matinee audience would be coming out soon and he wanted to spot Jocelyn O'Roarke as soon as possible. Like most good detectives (and all good actors) he keenly enjoyed watching people unobserved, especially people who interested him and about whom he was curious. Right now he was very curious about Jocelyn. He hadn't seen her since the day of Harold Tewes's arrest, though they had spoken on the phone several times, and he was curious, to put it mildly, to see how they would react to each other now that they didn't have a murder case looming over their heads. Of course, it wasn't to be the intimate tête-à-tête he had initially hoped for. Jocelyn had called him the day before to ask if she could bring Austin Frost with her, saying something vague about it being her last chance to see him for a while. Gerrard recalled his twinge of disappointment and how he had covered it with some asinine remark about the more the merrier. "It's going to be merry as hell having a nice, friendly chat with someone whose cousin you just put away and whose show you helped put on ice," he thought.

But all his forebodings vanished the minute he caught sight of them. He spotted Austin Frost first, his tall frame towering above the heads of all the little matinee ladies—and then he saw Jocelyn and a slow smile of recognition spread across his face. She was so familiar to him, like someone he'd known all his life, and at the same time so unknown. There were so many things he wanted to find out about her and he intended to take a long time satisfying his curiosity, his maxim being: never rush something good. And she looked very good indeed at that moment, wearing a black and mauve jacket of soft wool and a black skirt with an intriguing slit in the front. The wind gently tossed her dark curls and her eyes danced with laughter, as Frost read notes from the program with a mock-serious expression on his face. At the same time, he thought he detected a certain nervousness in the way she kept glancing at her wristwatch and running her hand through her hair.

Then they were coming through the heavy oak doors of the restaurant, Frost still reading in a high, adenoidal voice. "Mr. Clifton's last appearance was in the Hang 'em Highlites revival of *Juno and the Paycock* as the Paycock. For which he received the Frank Perdue Golden Feather Award and which led to his signing a contract with Paramount . . ."

"Oh, Austin, stop! I can't breathe . . . ah, there he is! Hello, Phillip. Hope you haven't been waiting too long. They took the curtain up late. Sorry about that."

"I'm sorry they took the curtain up, period," Austin said, easing himself into the booth and flapping a long hand to gain the attention of the waitress. "How are you, Phillip?"

"Fine thanks. How was the show?"

"In the words of one of our old drama professors: it was monumentally adequate—which is to say, it was two points above lousy."

"Austin, be fair. Three points. I thought Angie Louis was lovely."

"Wasn't she in *A Doll's House* last spring?" said Gerrard. Gerrard saw Austin's left eyebrow rise in surprise and was gratified by Jocelyn's delighted smile.

"Yes, that was Angie. Did you like her Nora?"

"Very much. Though I didn't think her leading man was up to her level. Of course, the husband is a rough role."

Jocelyn concurred enthusiastically and the three of them launched into a lively discussion of how an actor approaches the part of Torvald in a feminist age. By the time their second round of drinks had arrived, Phillip felt comfortable enough to ask Austin if any new plans had been made for *Term of Trial.*

" 'Fraid not," he said with a rueful shake of the head. "My agent thinks that the best thing, for the time being, is to put it in mothballs and wait for all the notoriety to die down. And I have to agree with him. But while we're on the subject, there's a few things I'd like to say . . ." "Uh-oh, here it comes," thought Phillip. "First of all, I want you to know that I harbor no grudges about any of this. Harold's my cousin but our relationship was more professional than anything else. And if he did what you say he did—and it looks that way . . . well, you were just doing your job, weren't you? Course, with Josh, it's another matter. She was just plain meddling."

"Austin!"

"Well, you were. Not that you didn't have good reason. But face it, Jocelyn, you *are* a born meddler—always have been. You took to this whole detecting game like a duck to water. Just see that you don't take it up full time, please. I have plans for you."

"Well, in this instance," Phillip interjected, "she was a very effective meddler and we were damn lucky to have her."

"So it seems . . . which brings me to my second point: How the *hell* did you two figure out it was Harold, anyway?"

Jocelyn stubbed out a cigarette and some of the gaiety left her eyes. "Well, we didn't for the longest time because I was so miserably dense. I mean, I had Harriet's prescription bottle in my apartment all that time and completely forgot about it! All I could think about was saving my own skin. But once I did find it, everything fell into place with a deafening thud. We knew we were dealing with a master planner and the game plan was right under our noses but we didn't see it. Harold was the moving force behind everything right from the beginning. The whole production was designed—not to launch you on Broadway or to give Harriet's career a boost—but as a backdrop for her death. Harold set out to assemble a company of ideal suspects just in *case* the 'accident' plan didn't come off. He knew about John and Paul, so John got hired; he knew about Kevin's affair with Harriet, so Kevin was cast. He knew about Charlie's breakdown, so Charlie was in. He knew about Max being Paul's father and he of course knew that Harriet held the rights to some of your best scripts."

"But what about you? You didn't have any prior connection with Harriet. And you were the prime suspect for a while."

"But I was her understudy and a formidable one, in that I was your friend. After I went on for Harriet that time in Boston there was bound to be friction."

"But that was just a fluke."

"No, I doubt it was," Gerrard said. "Harold probably arranged that, too. All he had to do was restrict her intake of Coumadin for a few days—the inverse of what he later did. Harriet didn't pay much attention to her medication, so it wouldn't have been too difficult to substitute placebos for a few days until her leg kicked up. It served two purposes: it made Jocelyn a dangerous rival in Harriet's eyes and, more importantly, it set the stage for the lie about the increase of her dosage."

"Good God, Josh," Austin said with horror, "he *planned* to frame you!"

Jocelyn shook her head vigorously. "No, I don't think he did—at least, not me specifically. The only reason I became the obvious choice was because of Harriet's attack on me during that last rehearsal. Harold couldn't *know* that that would happen. If anything was a fluke that was. It's a funny thing to say but Harold's not a vicious person, really. What I think he was trying to do was arrange to have so *many* suspects on hand, with so many viable motives, that the police would never be able to sort them out. That way the whole investigation would just exhaust itself chasing down blind alleys."

"I still don't see how finding the Coumadin bottle led you to Harold."

Phillip picked up the story as Jocelyn paused for a sip of wine. "There were only three people who could have given Harriet the wrong information about her dosage: Harvey Samuels, Sybil Stearns, and Harold. Harvey, however, had no motive that we could see—far from it. And there was no record of his calling Harriet when she was in Boston and the overdosing had to have started *then*. Sybil I had my doubts about because of her absence from her desk that afternoon and the fact that she lied about it. Also I could see how attached she was to Tewes. But Jocelyn was convinced that the man she had seen *was* a man and I figured she knew enough about makeup and disguise to spot a phony."

"But, despite Harold's denials, couldn't they have cooked it up together?"

"We weren't sure about that, so we had to test it. For one thing, if Sybil had been in on it, she would *never* have left her desk. Not for a second. She'd need a cast-iron alibi. Secondly, Tewes knew nothing about that second call Sybil made to Boston. It shook him badly when he found out and it showed."

"What was that call about anyway?"

"Nothing much. Harriet had asked Sybil to make arrangements for a dinner party and Sybil was calling to check the guest list. That was why Sybil left the auditorium for a few minutes the other day. I was out in the lobby and I asked her about it. She was a little puzzled but in no way distressed. It was important to our scenario, you see, to make sure Harold wasn't there when she talked to Harriet."

Austin let out a low whistle. "So that was quite a bluff you pulled off at the theatre . . . and a risky one, too."

Phillip smiled wryly. "Yes, it was Jocelyn's idea and it scared the shit out of me, to tell you the truth. But, as the lady said, it was the only game in town. There just wasn't enough proof."

"How'd you find the overalls?"

"I figured they had to be there," Jocelyn said. "If they had been found missing from the maintenance closet, the janitor might have said something. You see, that closet is right outside Harold's office. After I found the vial in my bag, I remembered going to see Harold at his office and how he came into the room from an outside door, not the anteroom. So I called Phillip and told him to go over there and look for a closet in the hallway. By that time I was remembering a lot of other things, too. Like how Harold and Harvey had taken advanced chemistry together and how Sybil had told Phillip that Harold was in charge of a car pool in the army. It all clicked into place and Phillip had a very busy morning, tracking down the overalls, questioning Harvey and getting the records of those calls, all by one o'clock. Then he had to show up at the theatre and make his acting debut!"

Austin shook his head in slow bewilderment. "Talk about amateur actors—Harold was certainly no slouch at it. I mean, I was with him when we 'discovered' the body and the man seemed stunned. It's incredible to think that he'd just walked out of his office, put on workman's clothes, walked or rode to the theatre, killed his wife, hidden a box, got back to his office and then left it again to return and find the body! Picking me up on the way to provide a witness. It's so cool and calculating and still . . . my God, he seemed so *genuinely* distraught!"

For the second time that day Phillip Gerrard surprised his companions as he quoted, "'All his visage wanned, tears in his eyes, distraction in his aspect, a broken voice, and his whole function suiting with forms to his conceit? And all for nothing, for Hecuba!'"

They sat for a moment saying nothing, lost in their reflections, until Jocelyn raised her head and asked, "Speaking of Hecuba . . . what do you suppose is going to become of poor Sybil?"

Austin patted her hand fondly. "Not to worry. I was talking to Charlie Martin yesterday. He's starting his own production company, you know, and thinks that Sybil is just the gal to run it for him. He's going to wait a bit before he approaches her with the offer but I intend to do my best to see that she takes it. She'll probably help ol' Charlie make a fortune and vice versa."

"Ah, Austin, you old meddler, you," Jocelyn said with great affection.

"By the by, did I tell you Charlie's getting married."

"*Married?* To whom?"

"To your old understudy, Trish Hanley. I don't know how or why but Charley's finally decided to settle down. Haven't you noticed all the chorines wearing black this week?" Austin tossed back the last of his drink and rose with alacrity. "Look, I'm glad we had a chance to talk all this out but I have to run now. I'm meeting Ronnie for dinner."

"Still seeing young Ronald, eh?" Jocelyn chuckled.

"Yes, thank God, at least one good thing came out of this sad business. Now, Josh, you promised to write me, remember. Don't forget."

"Where is it you're off to, Austin?" Gerrard asked, trying to mask his delight at the playwright's departure.

Austin regarded him blankly. "I'm not off anywhere. Josh is. Off to conquer the land of film and fun. Don't forget to pack your sunscreen, Jocelyn. You know how you burn."

Austin bussed Jocelyn on the forehead and was gone, leaving Phillip Gerrard and Jocelyn O'Roarke locked in silent confrontation. Gerrard was the first to find his voice.

"You're going . . . away? Where? For how long?"

"I . . . uh . . . have to go the West Coast. Not for very long—a month, maybe six weeks."

"Six weeks! Why didn't you tell me?"

"It all happened so fast, Phillip. I had an audition Thursday morning and a callback the same afternoon. They called my agent yesterday and said they wanted me. It's a small but what they call 'pivotal' role in a TV movie about disturbed teenagers. I get to play a lady shrink, wear suits and say a lot of wise things." She was trying to be flippant but it wasn't coming off.

"When do you leave?"

"See, that's the thing. They start shooting Tuesday and I have to go in for costume fittings and what not . . . so I'm flying out tonight."

"*Tonight?!* Damn it to hell, Jocelyn O'Roarke, you are the most maddening—well, all I can say is that, for an actress, you sure as hell have a lousy sense of timing."

"Phillip, be fair! I didn't expect this to happen but, now that it has, I can't turn it down. It's good exposure and very good money—and, frankly, it will do me good to get out of town for a while, after all this . . . it will do us *both* good."

"How do you figure that?"

"Listen, I know about this kind of thing. In the theatre, every time you do a new play, you're thrown together with an entirely new set of people, and you come to depend on one another for your own welfare and the welfare of the show. You become 'family' for a time. But when the show ends, so does the family. You all say you'll keep in touch and make plans to get together afterward, but you never do. Maybe once in a hundred times you make a single connection strong enough and real enough to last. Well, we've been in that kind of situation, you and I, and now our contracts are up. So we've got a one in a hundred chance . . . and I'm willing to take it, eternal optimist that I am. But I'd like to be sure . . . and I'd like you to be sure. I think this will give us time to find out how certain we are about things. What do you think?"

"I think I'm going to get the check."

"Then what?" she asked doubtfully.

"Then I'm going . . . to take you to the airport."

They drove uptown to collect Jocelyn's luggage. They spoke little in the car and even less at her apartment, as the telephone kept ringing every two seconds with friends calling to say goodbye, good luck and don't forget your sunscreen. Again he was aware, as he watched her talk warmly with half a dozen different people, none of whom he knew anything about, of how much of her life was beyond the ken of his experience. Much of what she had said at Lady Astor's made sense. What was he letting himself in for with this quirky, intelligent, excitingly difficult woman, and how could it possibly jibe with the life of a hardworking, underpaid cop?

"Ladies and gentlemen, Flight 936 to Los Angeles will be boarding in just a few minutes."

Phillip and Jocelyn were sitting in the boarding lounge at Gate 22 in Kennedy Airport. Their conversation had been more or less desultory, as Phillip Gerrard disliked crowds almost as much as he disliked public scenes.

"Tell me something, Miss O'Roarke."

"What's that, Inspector?"

"How devoted are you to this acting business?"

Jocelyn's smile was a mixture of knowing amusement tinged with sadness; it was a question she'd been asked several times before. "Oh, I guess about as devoted as you are to this detective business. Why do you ask?"

"Just trying to get my facts straight, that's all."

"I see," she said softly.

"Ladies and gentlemen, you may now start boarding. Please have your boarding pass ready as you enter the plane. Thank you and have a pleasant flight."

"Well, I guess they mean me. Phillip, thank you for driving me here . . . and for everything."

She slung her bag over her shoulder and was starting for the door when Phillip Gerrard caught her wrist.

"Just one more thing."

"Yes?"

"When you finish shooting your movie and hop a plane back here . . . I'll be waiting to take you home."

"Oh, damn you, Phillip. I think I'm going to cry."

"No you're not."

So saying, Detective-Sergeant Phillip Gerrard set aside one of the cardinal rules of police deportment and gathered her into his arms for a long and lingering kiss. When Jocelyn O'Roarke finally boarded Flight 936 her eyes were very bright indeed, but not with tears.

FOR THE BEST IN PAPERBACKS, LOOK FOR THE 🐧

In every corner of the world, on every subject under the sun, Penguin represents quality and variety—the very best in publishing today.

For complete information about books available from Penguin—including Pelicans, Puffins, Peregrines, and Penguin Classics—and how to order them, write to us at the appropriate address below. Please note that for copyright reasons the selection of books varies from country to country.

In the United Kingdom: For a complete list of books available from Penguin in the U.K., please write to *Dept E.P., Penguin Books Ltd, Harmondsworth, Middlesex, UB7 0DA.*

In the United States: For a complete list of books available from Penguin in the U.S., please write to *Dept BA, Penguin*, Box 120, Bergenfield, New Jersey 07621-0120.

In Canada: For a complete list of books available from Penguin in Canada, please write to *Penguin Books Canada Ltd, 10 Alcorn Avenue, Suite 300, Toronto, Ontario, Canada M4V 3B2.*

In Australia: For a complete list of books available from Penguin in Australia, please write to the *Marketing Department, Penguin Books Ltd, P.O. Box 257, Ringwood, Victoria 3134.*

In New Zealand: For a complete list of books available from Penguin in New Zealand, please write to the *Marketing Department, Penguin Books (NZ) Ltd, Private Bag, Takapuna, Auckland 9.*

In India: For a complete list of books available from Penguin, please write to *Penguin Overseas Ltd, 706 Eros Apartments, 56 Nehru Place, New Delhi, 110019*

In Holland: For a complete list of books available from Penguin in Holland, please write to *Penguin Books Nederland B.V., Postbus 195, NL-1380AD Weesp, Netherlands.*

In Germany: For a complete list of books available from Penguin, please write to *Penguin Books Ltd, Friedrichstrasse 10-12, D-6000 Frankfurt Main 1, Federal Republic of Germany.*

In Spain: For a complete list of books available from Penguin in Spain, please write to *Longman, Penguin España, Calle San Nicolas 15, E-28013 Madrid, Spain.*

In Japan: For a complete list of books available from Penguin in Japan, please write to *Longman Penguin Japan Co Ltd, Yamaguchi Building, 2-12-9 Kanda Jimbocho, Chiyoda-Ku, Tokyo 101, Japan.*

FOR THE BEST IN MYSTERY, LOOK FOR THE 🐧

☐ A CRIMINAL COMEDY
Julian Symons

From Julian Symons, the master of crime fiction, this is "the best of his best" (*The New Yorker*). What starts as a nasty little scandal centering on two partners in a British travel agency escalates into smuggling and murder in Italy.

220 pages   ISBN: 0-14-009621-3

☐ GOOD AND DEAD
Jane Langton

Something sinister is emptying the pews at the Old West Church, and parishioner Homer Kelly knows it isn't a loss of faith. When he investigates, Homer discovers that the ways of a small New England town can be just as mysterious as the ways of God.   256 pages   ISBN: 0-14-012687-2

☐ THE SHORTEST WAY TO HADES
Sarah Caudwell

Five young barristers and a wealthy family with a five-million-pound estate find the stakes are raised when one member of the family meets a suspicious death.

208 pages   ISBN: 0-14-012874-3

☐ RUMPOLE OF THE BAILEY
John Mortimer

The hero of John Mortimer's mysteries is Horace Rumpole, barrister at law, sixty-eight next birthday, with an unsurpassed knowledge of blood and typewriters, a penchant for quoting poetry, and a habit of referring to his judge as "the old darling."   208 pages   ISBN: 0-14-004670-4

You can find all these books at your local bookstore, or use this handy coupon for ordering:

Penguin Books By Mail
Dept. BA Box 999
Bergenfield, NJ 07621-0999

Please send me the above title(s). I am enclosing _____
(please add sales tax if appropriate and $1.50 to cover postage and handling). Send check or money order—no CODs. Please allow four weeks for shipping. We cannot ship to post office boxes or addresses outside the USA. *Prices subject to change without notice.*

Ms./Mrs./Mr. _____

Address _____

City/State _____ Zip _____

☐ **THE PENGUIN COMPLETE FATHER BROWN**
G.K. Chesterton

Here, in one volume, are forty-nine sensational cases investigated by the high priest of detective fiction, Father Brown, whose cherubic face and unworldly simplicity disguise an uncanny understanding of the criminal mind.
718 pages   ISBN: 0-14-009766-X

☐ **BRIARPATCH**
Ross Thomas

This Edgar Award-winning thriller is the story of Benjamin Dill, who returns to the Sunbelt city of his youth to attend his sister's funeral—and find her killer.
384 pages   ISBN: 0-14-010581-6

☐ **APPLEBY AND THE OSPREYS**
Michael Innes

When Lord Osprey is murdered in Clusters, his ancestral home, with an Oriental dagger, it falls to Sir John Appleby and Lord Osprey's faithful butler, Bagot, to pick out the clever killer from an assortment of the lord's eccentric house guests.   184 pages   ISBN: 0-14-011092-5

☐ **GOLD BY GEMINI**
Jonathan Gash

Lovejoy, the antiques dealer whom the *Chicago Sun-Times* calls "one of the most likable rogues in mystery history," searches for Roman gold coins and greedy bird-killers on the Isle of Man.
224 pages   ISBN: 0-451-82185-8

☐ **REILLY: ACE OF SPIES**
Robin Bruce Lockhart

This is the incredible true story of superspy Sidney Reilly, said to be the inspiration for James Bond. Robin Bruce Lockhart's book tells the thrilling story of the British Secret Service agent's shadowy Russian past and near-legendary exploits in espionage and in love.
192 pages   ISBN: 0-14-006895-3

☐ **STRANGERS ON A TRAIN**
Patricia Highsmith

Almost against his will, Guy Haines is trapped in a nightmare of shared guilt when he agrees to kill the father of the man who will kill Guy's wife. The basis for the unforgettable Hitchcock thriller.
256 pages   ISBN: 0-14-003796-9

☐ **THE THIN WOMAN**
Dorothy Cannell

An interior designer who is also a passionate eater, her rented companion who writes trashy novels, and a rich dead uncle with a conditional will are the principals in this delicious thriller.   242 pages   ISBN: 0-14-007947-5